Subway to
Samarkand

BOOKS BY J. R. HUMPHREYS

Subway to Samarkand
Vandameer's Road
The Dirty Shame
The Lost Towns and Roads of America
The Last of the Middle West

Subway to Samarkand

J. R. Humphreys

1977
DOUBLEDAY & COMPANY, INC.
GARDEN CITY, NEW YORK

*All of the characters in this
book are fictitious, and any
resemblance to actual persons,
living or dead, is purely
coincidental.*

From *The Silk Road* by Sven Hedin, translated by F. H. Lyon. Copy-
right 1938, renewal © 1966 by E. P. Dutton & Co., and reprinted with
their permission.

Library of Congress Cataloging in Publication Data
Humphreys, John R   1918–
    Subway to Samarkand.
    I. Title.
PZ3.H8888Su   [PS3515.U474] 813'.5'4
ISBN 0-385-11079-0
Library of Congress Catalog Card Number 75-36595

To S.S.V.

I

The Safe Adventure

June 20th—

My daughter, Perse, called us the other evening from Boston. She lives there now. When I answered the phone, she said, "What's the matter with your voice?"

"I'm a little hoarse."

"Have you got a cold, or are you getting another polyp?"

"It's a cold, I think."

"At this time of year?"

"I like to beat the season in."

She didn't laugh. "Is Mother there?"

"Just a minute, I'll get her."

Janice got on the phone and they talked for almost an hour. I considered going out for a walk, but I thought Perse might want to talk to me again, and I stuck around. She didn't.

A poet's death—

They went up to one of the castle's turrets and looked out over the land, and MacLeroy said, "What gets me is the softness of all the colors out there. I feel as if I could fall into them." Whereupon he promptly fell. He fell into the colors and the two men in the turret stood and watched him.

"Are they soft?" the tall man in the Panama hat called down.

But MacLeroy didn't answer. It looked as if he'd tried to do the splits as he fell. He had hit the ground seventy feet below, his legs spread, and he'd bounced.

The man in the Panama hat, Ferresen, said somberly, gazing downward, "MacLeroy is too much of a poet at heart and being a poet, he is always trying to prove his poetry, and of course it can't be done."

Below them MacLeroy lay on the ground, his arms and legs outstretched, his face to the sky.

"MacLeroy!"

MacLeroy didn't answer.

The other man in the turret, a man in a tweed jacket with leather elbow patches and cuffs, was trying to light a cigarette in the wind.

"Mac doesn't answer," Ferresen said.

"I shouldn't wonder."

"Why?"

"You know how he hates his name. He always refuses to answer to it. Try him by some other name."

The man in the Panama hat leaned out and called, "Leitz . . . Leitz, can you hear us?"

"Not some damned Teutonic name," Hale, the man in tweed, said.

"Jabenowsky . . . Jabenowsky," Ferresen bawled down.

But there was no response.

Hale had managed to light his cigarette and he flipped his paper match out over the turret, and they watched it fall. It fell on the grass between MacLeroy and the castle.

"Do you suppose he's dead?" Hale said, frowning.

"It's possible."

"Poor bastard."

Ferresen sighed, "It was a poet's death."

"Yes." Hale nodded. "It was every bit of that."

"Well . . . let's go inside."

"I think we'd better," Hale said. "The wind is getting cold."

July 1st—

Attention is limited, it's finite. It's like money in a savings account. There's just so much to spend and no more and a nearly infinite number of choices on how it can be spent.

And so—we can think about the devastation of a hydrogen bomb for just so long, about the plight of the poor, about women's lib, about Israel, about spray cans and our ozone shield, about Con Ed, about our miserable jails, about our impossible marriages. A lot of people are waving for our attention: television advertisers, book and magazine editors, newspapers, stockbrokers, Ford Motor Company, Nader, politicians, actors, poets, painters, musicians, the Secretary of State, our friends, our wives and husbands. And then some.

How does anyone have enough attention left over to read a novel any more? Is that why the short story is invisible and the novel is dying?

I can ramble on and on in class, discursively, as long as I relate whatever I'm saying to writing—and that's not hard, because writing is all of life, the inner and the outer reality, the reality and the truth—but the door of the classroom is closed. There are no interruptions and I have their attention captive.

In the classroom, the audience is part of my reality; at this moment, as I write, the audience is imaginary. Except for me.

*   *   *

The actor as a whore who pleasures his audience; the writer as—a what—who pleasures himself?

*   *   *

I keep these pages more or less within the limits of a man whose attention is more or less on going to Samarkand—or on that part of the man heading there. It's a journey that—like the subject of writing—is as large as life. Why not?

July 4th—

A subway train goes by over on Broadway: a steady low rumbling in deference to all of us who live around here. The trains pull slowly into the station weekends and evenings. Weekdays are another matter, maybe because the IRT figures everyone is off at work. The rumbling is fast and loud and the sound rockets off all the twenty-one-story buildings rising to the east of the station like card decks on end.

New York, otherwise, is quiet. It's possible to drive almost anywhere and find a parking place. On Christmas and at Easter, everyone out of town jams into New York. On the Fourth of July, everyone seems to clear out. Everyone who can.

There'll be folk dancing today down in the Wall Street area at the tip of Manhattan, where the town began—and Indian dancing.

Yesterday's rain cooled the town off. The sky is clear. I can even see clouds—rather misty apparitions floating there. A breeze is moving in the leaves of the trees below on our lawns.

Janice and I have breakfast on our balcony, reading the *Times*.

There's a piece on the front page about the Appalachian Trail. I read it with surprise because I'd nurtured the notion the trail went through a last strip of unspoiled American wilderness and that along the shaded length of it from Maine to Georgia things look about as they did when the Indians kept it open. There are now, I read, so many picnickers swarming along the trail from nearby highways and so many squatters living in the shelters built for hikers that the use of the thing is being restricted to preserve it.

"I've decided," Janice says, looking over her section of the paper, "we ought to try a tiny bit harder to make what we have work. We can't get along together, but then neither of us can get along with anybody."

I feel instant relief. I hate her stereotyped thinking and the way she calls everything she doesn't like "icky." I think I have her figured out *ad infinitum* and she says something like this. I look at her with a kind of wonder and say, "We can't even get along with Tucker."

Our cat, Tucker, is walking by. I reach out one hand to stroke him and as usual he shies away. Janice and I laugh together. It's the first time we've laughed together in a couple of weeks. What's this we have here on Independence Day, togetherness? With old adversaries like Janice and me? With the old incompatibles?

Her hair is still up in the curlers she's slept in all night; her skinny legs and big feet stick out of the awful floral housecoat she wears. Once something of a beauty, she's still a good-looking woman, though not even the stretch girdle she wears—has always worn, even in college when I met her—helps her much any more. And she frowns all the time. She is frowning now; but she's really a good sort. Most of the time.

Over on the lawn by a city housing building, at the top of a flagpole almost as high as our balcony, hangs the American flag, in sunlight.

Yesterday she told me bitterly I had my head in such a cloud I couldn't do the simplest thing she asked. "I have to harp and harp at you." She was getting nothing, she said, from our marriage. I had answered that I got nothing from it either, that I was more or less hanging around putting in my required time before I died my natural death. She had then offered me our second divorce. I turned the offer down. I'd felt wretched. She had too.

Today is better. I might even tell her, one of these days, about Samarkand.

I don't know where the kids get the firecrackers, but night after night we hear them going off and all day Saturday and Sunday. Tucker is used to them, but from time to time a super bang will make him raise his head. Year 'round the town sounds as if it were under siege, people firing from windows and from street to window, and from window to window—a spasmodic fire from handguns, Saturday night specials, all the way up to shotguns, along with an occasional grenade and a mortar shell. Everyone taking deliberate aim. And along with the firing: the sound of sirens. As if the cops were . . . what? Trying to keep the town in their control? Serving as referees? Or are those only ambulances we hear?

Summer session and classes have started—

My specialist, Dr. Baker, took a look down my throat in his shade-drawn examination room. I did indeed have another polyp on my vocal cords. When, he asked, would be a good time to check into his hospital?

I said I'd have to think about it. I didn't want to raise hell with my classroom performance and voice rest in the past had meant as much as two weeks of total silence. Could the operation be postponed for six weeks? He was the fifth doctor I'd had, and when I mumbled something about two weeks of silence, he said he'd have me using my voice after only a couple of days' rest. I could have the operation on Friday and be talking by Monday, if that was what was bothering me. But too many doctors had told me too many different things, and I said I'd have to think about it. Anyway—what was the rush?

The next morning I called his office early and set the operation for the end of August, a couple of weeks before fall registration. Janice is a registered nurse. She called a doctor and a couple of nurses to get a line on Baker. Baker was conservative, she said, and a highly respected surgeon.

I gave in. Then I sat around the apartment reading about Mayas and Spaniards, my project of the hour. I didn't know yet if I'd turn what I read into fiction or nonfiction.

It was hard to keep attention on the page. About ten-thirty I quit and walked up to school. The problem with writing about a bygone period is that the people are bygone, all portraits are imaginary, a mere tracing of action, of mannerism, of words and deeds. What's vanished can still be imagined, but it's not there to touch, and that's what most of us think of as reality: tactile solidity; everything else is sensual and therefore secondary, however pleasurable or beneficial or necessary to an orderly, even a disorderly life.

I live in both worlds. Who doesn't? Whose world is totally touchable? I have never been able to swallow words like Truth and Reality. I have come to uneasy terms with them. I've learned to trust them, live with them. Truth and Reality get my attention. I take them seriously. Truth is a voice, Reality a substance. Reality doesn't talk back. No, only Truth counsels us. Reality just stands around. We can photograph and describe him.

I stopped in front of the grid of mailboxes attached to the wall outside our offices, little oblong cliff dwellings wide enough and high enough for the mail and packages that come to the faculty. The few envelopes that lay in the cave under my name did not look particularly interesting. I looked over at Kate's box. She had a letter from the English department of another college. I thought: She's looking for another job.

My college is like most colleges: up or out. After six years you're either promoted to associate professor and senior rank and tenure, or you're fired. Kate was out at the end of this year.

When my six years were up I wasn't made a professor and I wasn't kicked out. I have what is called *de facto* tenure. I've never found out for sure what *de facto* tenure means, but it keeps me working, so here's to it.

I passed the cubicle Kate has as her office. It's next to mine. She wasn't in. Or was she? Her desk was littered with papers and books. But it was always littered like that, always. It had been that way all summer, between the end of the spring term and the beginning of the summer session—as if she'd been deep into some immense research project and stepped away from her desk for a moment, then never returned. She was a poet, another teacher of writing who had been trying for years to get a book published.

I sat down at the desk in my own cubicle and looked over three memos our secretary had left. All please call me's. One from Gail. She never called at home though Janice was away every other day. Another from Fred, my chairman, asking me if I could switch our lunch from tomorrow to today. The third was from Andre. My god, was Andre in town?

I called Fred first. We made the switch he wanted. Then he said, "Jack, have you heard about Dorothy Dole?"

"What about her?"

"She's in the hospital; that's what I want to see you about. I don't know how serious it is. I thought you might know." He meant, would I call Thorpe and see what he knew. Fred and Thorpe weren't on speaking terms. Thorpe was another writing teacher.

We once had a lot of famous name writers teaching our writing courses, but all that had been pretty much during Dorothy Dole's time. She was a tall, gaunt, fierce woman who had cowed her colleagues. Since her retirement, the writing courses had gone downhill.

"I'll find out what I can," I said. "See you at lunch."

The next call was harder. Janice was on her twenty-four-hour shift this evening and Gail expected me for dinner. But if Andre was in town, it was probably for one night only and Andre knew no more of Gail than Janice did.

I called Andre. He was at the Drake and I caught him in because he said he'd called me at home just after I left. He got my voice recording, my own rasping voice saying I wasn't in and could be reached at my office number. It was eerie, he said. He couldn't talk about anything else for a couple of minutes. "How many of you are there? Is this a recording I'm talking to now? How do I know it isn't?" All this fake astonishment expressed in his familiar, genuine French accent. And then finally, "What's the matter with your voice?"

"Too much whiskey, I guess."

"Jack, listen . . . I'm only in town for today. You understand. You and Jan must come down and have dinner with me tonight . . ." Loretta wasn't with him. She'd stayed behind in Paris.

Then I called Gail. Her phone rang and rang and rang. Where the hell was she? I went down and held class.

From time to time, one of my students tells me he wants to get a job like mine because there is nothing, absolutely nothing he can conceive of, to match the career of being a writer and teaching writing . . . I never know what to tell him, because I often feel the only real preparation for a job like mine is to have been a stepchild.

We are a private college, never rich and getting poorer every year. Back when Metro had caught on as a mail-order college and then as a night school, we'd graduated some students who had become immensely wealthy. Their gifts, added to what the school already had, gave the dean a golden though warty hand. Our faculty had been small and famous, but few of those old boys had Ph.D.s. Those who did were hooked down from their balloons of retirement as they floated by. We were among the first to hire remarkable women passed up by other greater schools. Left-wingers, if they were famous enough, found haven with us. We were innovative then, even outrageous. Metro, for a while, stood on the upper West Side like a statue of liberty casting a flickering light on a dark nation, beckoning to the outcasts of other colleges, to students who refused to be regimented, to those who couldn't conform if they wanted to, to the dropouts, the egomaniacs, the troublemakers, the mother haters, the downtrodden of the garment district and the post office and labor force, to women suffering the miseries and boredom of marriage, to pool hustlers and men in pinstripe suits with black shirts and white ties, morgue technicians and canoe instructors, opera singers and photo retouchers, all sorts, all ages, some coming to get a degree, others to fill time—all in all, a stimulating lot. They sat in front of teachers who were an odd lot like themselves and measured the teachers against their experience on the streets and in the market and valued them in proportion to what their teachers gave them. Some of these students kept track of what their courses were costing by the minute and figured out how many concerts they could have attended, plays they could have seen, books and records they could have bought with the same money. Nobody in those classes slouched around in his seat and wondered when the hour would end.

For a while, before my time, Metro had thrived without granting a degree of any kind. Then they granted a B.S. In time, it was a B.A. It took a little longer to get a chapter of Phi Beta Kappa. Then they could grant an M.A. and finally a Ph.D. By this time they were no longer a small college. They had expanded, put up new buildings as they fought local citizens' groups for block space. Metro, in my time, had changed. Because they now granted advanced degrees, they could no longer hire teachers without advanced degrees: bad policy. To keep their academic standing, they had to see that holders of advanced degrees were thickly seeded in our catalog. For two years now, a completely equipped darkroom with seven hooded Beseler enlargers had stood unused because the college was still trying to hire a photographer with at least an M.A.—some said.

Others said it was because Metro wanted to eliminate the course and spend the money on something more academic. Metro had gradually become anti-creative and the whittling down of the writing courses was only one aspect of this puckering of the spirit. Not anti-creative because they hated creative things with the envy and bitterness of the non-creative, but anti-creative because they'd got infused with a Germanic philosophy of education. Although our students remained pretty much the same at our base, we'd sought and reached the ultimate in academic respectability. Good wishes to writers and artists, but let them thrive elsewhere. Art was the subject, not the business, of scholars.

But Metro was not yet economically ready for such a strict view of itself. We no longer had a faculty with great names. We were facing bankruptcy, looking everywhere for the money to keep going. Every time we raised our tuition there was a strained expression on our faces. There was much talk about returning to old standards and manners—the good old days—but nobody knew how to turn back. It was too late. What was saving Metro were all those old students we drew from the time the college was founded late in the nineteenth century. The old mavericks who had made it. It was their names, not any of our own, that would appear in stone—all those mean lives we'd changed. Trouble was, we would have to wait for them to depart one by one from this world, leaving all that behind which could not be smuggled through the gates of heaven or hell.

Hence, low salaries. Salaries so low that everyone who could quit had quit, left the faculty, gone to schools that measured a teacher's worth more handsomely. Or, rescued on occasion by former students now old friends, gone to the front lines of commerce. Those of us still left were too old to shift, too settled, sometimes too loyal, or too academically shabby to fetch anything for ourselves elsewhere.

Now that I think of it, we *were* all rather shabby. I had no reason to go about in a peaked dunce cap murmuring *mea culpa* in our graffiti-scrawled corridors. The great autographs of our past were retired and gone. Nobody still in our department had published anything remarkable. Some had published nothing. When we brought along a young graduate student, hired him and put him to teaching, nearly our only chance of keeping him would be his academic anonymity. If he published a scholarly book that got him attention, some other college hired him at once.

Metro's president and our dean did recognize that teachers were something of an asset, and so ground crews and janitorial forces were no longer as large. We had few guards. Typewriters were bolted down and we locked all the doors we could, even the doors to our offices when we were inside them. The halls were sometimes unswept for days at a time, old gum and cigarette packs lying in corners, Coke bottles gathering on window ledges. The rain leaked through the roof on the top floor of the building where I had my office. We put wastebaskets under the leaks.

Even the paint was beginning to peel from the walls in the faculty club, where I met Fred for lunch. We ordered drinks from one of the slow, sullen waiters, who were as underpaid as the rest of us; then Fred put his glasses on to study the menu. Fred's hair was thinning and going gray. We began teaching together, both of us right out of the Army. His face is getting lined too, but he's charged with a restless, ceaseless, purposeful energy that gives him a youthful manner and appearance. His eyes are gray-green and they have snap. He dresses as I do, carefully casual. Today he has on a white button-down Brooks shirt, a soft blue jacket and a checked bow tie. We do not, any of us, live sexless lives at our college. We live the kind of lives we're reported to in all the books and plays about college life, and Fred makes no secret about his attraction to a pretty face or ass. He doesn't though, by his own admission, make passes at his students as much as he used to. "I'm selective now," he once told me. "First they have to make it clear they want to get laid."

I think of that now as he puts down his menu. "Fred, how does a girl make it clear she wants to get laid?" My voice is weak and hoarse and I'm sending air up from my gut to set each word on. It's precisely as if we'd picked up the conversation from the last time we had lunch. He grins and looks out the window over the rooftops below. Sex is something he loves to talk about, and his grin is real. He doesn't, however, take my question seriously, and I'm absolutely serious. True, it's one of our congenital topics, sex, a safe topic, one of the world's safest. I think he also likes it when I try to get him to gossip about the department, the workings of which are endlessly curious to me —how do people get promoted, really, and how are raises figured out, and who influences what? But he keeps the mystery.

In any given year, I tell him, half a dozen girls will act irresolute about their virtue. "I mean, you're sitting at the desk, you and this student, looking over her paper, and you glance up suddenly, you know, and she's looking at you, more interested in you than she is in her paper. Is that all you need?"

But he wants to talk about Dorothy Dole. Dorothy, now into her eighties, has been living on the $10,000 interest from a trust fund that will go to our department when she dies, and Fred means to see we get it. It's supposed to go into fellowships to bolster the writing courses. He's talked to the dean and he's talked to Dorothy's lawyer and he's talked to Dorothy's doctor, all since I had him on the phone. Fred said . . . no disease to name. Maybe it's malnutrition. The maid who came to her apartment every day left a lunch for her which, after a time, she noticed was no longer being eaten. Fred lowered his voice, solemn: "She wasn't drinking." The apparatus, he thought, was frayed, coming apart, cells disintegrating, things popping apart, tiny explosions all over the brain and body. She wasn't our fearful dragon any more.

I had mixed feelings about going to see her.

Dorothy had written more than twenty novels, many of them book club selections, and I had never been able to finish reading one of them and often wondered if any were still being read by anyone. Nevertheless, she mattered to me. She had believed in me as a young writer. It was Dorothy who had hired me eighteen years ago. We had never been sociable outside school, but everyone in the department associated the two of us as literary kin—and I, as her protégé, was being asked, I clearly saw, to go down and see old Dot and make a departmental show of concern.

I told Fred I'd called Thorpe already, that it was all news to him Dorothy was in the hospital, and Thorpe, I said, had gone off at once to see her. I told Fred that he should go with me, but he sighed and shook his head. He and Dot had once staged a faculty club foam-flying jaw fight from which neither ever properly recovered. Fred had a lot of pride, acted on it, stuck by it. So there I sat, the drapes of duty closing in, Fred pulling the cords; I was lacily surrounded, all escape blocked off. I didn't want to go alone.

When I left Fred and went for the car, I thought of Gail, but it was no use picking her up. It would take too long.

I have no right to feel superior to Dorothy Dole. I am a middle-aged writer who published a novel and who was encouraged and who is still hanging in there trying to pick up where the first novel left off. I spent a lot of time after that first novel was published wondering why I couldn't seem to get another book into print, wondering where I went wrong, what went wrong. Time alone taught me that not just I or even a few but most writers stand as I do, or did, with that same baffled expression of frustration and indignation. The majority of first novelists never publish a second novel, but there was nobody to tell me what it was going to be like. Or if there was and they did, I wasn't listening, didn't want to, couldn't . . .

I drove down the West Side Highway, the Hudson River on my right, black thoughts in the middle of my head. Dot was dying, I was convinced of that. The whiff of death came to me. Another dying woman. I'd seen so many old women dying, my mother, Janice's mother, my aunt . . . all of them dying slowly, a tube in the arm, teeth out, mouth open, gasping for breath as if sobbing. What was up there waiting for me this time? I hate death. I hate the end of anything. I want to hold onto everything, everyone—one of my problems, I guess.

I managed to park the car. Inside the hospital, it was depressing, so many people, so much noise that when I spoke to the receptionist with my rasping voice, she had to lean forward to hear me.

Dorothy was on the seventh floor. The elevator was so goddamn crowded that the passengers spoke of disaster. I heard talk of the elevator cable snapping, all of us plunging. We made it.

I look for Room 707. Can't find it because it's a ward and they haven't stuck a number over it; then, in the ward, I can't locate her. I walk from bed to bed, one end of the ward to the other and back again. Maybe I haven't recognized her. I can't be sure. I go ask the nurse. She's busy, flipping cards. Death is hectic here. But the nurse takes me by the arm and points her out. Bed eight. It was the one I thought she might be in; I hadn't been sure.

The skin is white and tight over the bones of her skull, her head on the pillow as if dropped there when she fell back after trying to rise, mouth open: black, open mouth breathing lightly. Her face is so thin. Her arms are so thin. Is it cancer? But there is a kind of beauty about that old woman, in her great bones, in her great nose. The grand old dragon is not only toothless now, she's helpless. Holding the flowers I've brought her wrapped in their white paper, I call to her as well as I can: "Dorothy . . . Dorothy . . . It's Jack Fross." No response. What a time to croak my name.

I see by the flowers and card on the table Thorpe has been here and left a message—he will return, soon. I leave my flowers and a similar message and I leave, without expecting to return or see her again.

What the nurse had said was, "Shake her. She doesn't open her eyes, but she'll wake up." No shake of mine woke her, nor any word. I don't think Thorpe had any better luck.

We are all so self-centered, Dorothy too. What do I care about her, really? She was never a friend of mine. Thorpe, one of her former students, had been a friend. But I came and stood by her bed and leaned close to her head and said, rasping, to her closed eyes, to her open mouth, "Dorothy? Dorothy?"

I spent fourteen bucks for the flowers and I left them there. Maybe she'll know. It's done.

She's had a good, full life.

Heading uptown, I tried Park Avenue. I wanted to cry. Jesus, the traffic in this town.

Gail had never told me to call her before I dropped around and I didn't know if that was because she saw no guy other than me, or if she didn't give a damn what kind of situation I dropped in on. I think it was the second. But I was convinced she didn't expect to get married, that her life was her work, her work the theater.

She was young, so young that her face in the bed beside me now, eyes closed, looked like a child's, a troubled child's. She had coppery hair like the thinnest of spun wire. It churned around her face or seemed to, even when motionless. She combed it a lot, fretfully. I loved to touch it. It was mysterious.

She took acting lessons, singing lessons, ballet. She went to tryouts and sometimes got small parts. And she got a lot of rejections. It was rough on the ego, but her ego, like mine, seemed secure if not serene. She'd been in the chorus of a Broadway show and had gone on tour with another. But what she really wanted was a one-woman show as author, librettist, choreographer and actress on Broadway, followed by a standing ovation, nothing short of total recognition and adulation.

When she wasn't working in the theater, she was a typist-secretary. Because she was in a cast now, I knew she was home on Monday. Come Monday, I always dropped around. She'd never given me a key of my own. If she wasn't there, I just went away and took it hard.

Gail had a davenport that folded out into a bed and in the corner, at one end of the davenport, she had the portraits of her family: mother, father, four brothers, two sisters, and the heads of two nieces at the sides of the youngest sister. I studied them. Everyone in the family was smiling at me.

"I think," I said, "your family likes me."

"What?" Her head turned and she looked up at the wall where I was looking. Some of her hair hung over her eyes, and she lifted it away with the back of one hand. She didn't look like any of her family. Her face was so much smaller, her gaze so much sharper than theirs, her eyes deep brown. Because of her eyes her face would have definition at fifty, even a hundred yards. A lot of faces become a blob at ten feet. Her family all had good, average, healthy blob-at-fifty-feet faces—their hair dark or light brown.

"Don't you believe it," she said. She looked at the ceiling. "My father, I think, would like you."

"Why?"

"Just a hunch." She thought awhile. "My brothers would all say—there she goes again, involved with an older man. On second thought, they might be relieved if they knew about you. They took my divorce hard, all of them, but they took it even harder when I said I'd never get involved with one man again."

She got up and headed for the bathroom.

"Are we involved?"

She shut the door behind her with a bang.

I looked back at her family. They had those dead, gazeless eyes that local photographers are so good at catching, but even so their personalities came through . . . especially the father's. He wore a western hat. His shirt was open at the collar. Someone had taken his snapshot just as he turned his head, before he had time to set his expression and let his eyes go dead. Gail had blown up his face and framed the picture because it was the best one she had of him. He owned a wheat grain elevator in Nebraska, but this was the first time in his life he was solvent. He'd had a hard struggle, pulling himself out of debt, putting kids through college. This, or his, was not a face, however, that showed struggle and disappointment; no weariness or gaze of bitter vindication. His smile was the slightest and the best of them all on the wall; no teeth showed, it was perfectly natural—a look on his face of enjoyment, a relaxed man, one eye squinting, almost closed in the sunlight, the other merry and a little sly. His face solid and wide and not jowled. Only his head and his open collar showed in the frame of the photograph, but he looked tall as well as big, a heavyweight, a man you didn't mess around with. It pleased me to think he could like me. I hoped she meant it.

We got dressed and folded the bed back into itself. Gail was moving about briskly, virtually snapping things into order with her fingers. She had on a pair of tight slacks, blue jeans with bell bottoms. She wore jeans a lot, had the shape for them. I mean her ass was beautifully contoured. And she liked to wear wildly colored blouses. She was proud of her small waist and of her round small breasts and she obeyed a show biz principle an agent had advised her to follow: if you've got it, show it—so blouses got worn half unbuttoned.

She had put up her hair. Her neck was slender. I never tired of watching her move about.

"Gail," I said, "how does a girl make it obvious to a guy she wants to get laid?"

"Why? Do you think some girl you know is trying to send you a message?"

"No. It's something my chairman said. He said he doesn't fool around with his students anymore unless they make it clear to him they want to get laid."

"Is that what you teachers talk about?"

"Well, how does a girl? How does she do it?"

"Don't you know?"

"I don't think I do. I don't think I'd know if a girl was leading me on."

"Afraid I can't tell you. It was never my style."

Janice wasn't in, but I knew she'd been home and forgotten again to turn off the telephone answering machine. When I checked to see who, if anyone, had called, the first voice off the tape was Janice's—her long and melodic "Hello," then a man's voice: "Beans, beans, the musical fruit. The more you eat, the more you toot." Then Janice said, "Who is this?"

"It's Ben."

"Ben who?"

"Ben Wallace. Is that you, Alice?"

"No, this is not Alice," said Janice icily. "You have the wrong number."

They both hung up at almost the same instant.

There were no other calls. She didn't know how to erase the recording.

Janice does not have an easy life.

We drove downtown early, parked near Andre's hotel and walked around and looked in store windows. Art galleries make Janice impatient. She walked ahead to dress shops and shoe stores. About seven-thirty we seated ourselves in the lounge of the Drake. The Drake was lively for a Monday night. One of the Smothers Brothers, Tommy, I think, wandered by, first in, then out. The room was going to be too noisy for me to try to talk, but I thought I could probably be heard if I kept my phrases short and didn't try to say too much. Janice sat beside me sipping her sherry, looking stern.

Janice had never liked Andre from the time I'd met him. She thought he was bossy, vain, pretentious and worst of all a womanizer . . . no, worst of all, too much of an influence on me.

So—not to miss anything, she'd got out of duties that evening to come along.

We were seated on a padded bench with a small round table in front of us when Andre came through the door from the lounge. He wore a sleek black suit. He had good tailors. I noted at once he looked older than he had two years ago. There was gray in his hair, at the temples. And he noticed my mustache— took it for a fake, or pretended to, came up with a finger and his thumb out, squeezed it, exclaiming, "My god, would you look at that. A mustache." He said approvingly to Janice, "He is the real Howard Hughes. Howard Hughes never died."

I pulled a chair over from the next table but Andre ignored the chair and sat down beside Janice, squeezing against her, so we had her between us. He put a wrapped gift box in her hand. "It is my favorite perfume," he said as she, surprised and delighted, opened it.

The bottle had a wide neck. This seemed to surprise him. He took the bottle from her, glanced at the label and handed it back. Janice patted some of it on her throat and her wrists. Andre drew her to him, pushing his face down into the aroma, exclaiming, "Ah . . . ah, ah . . ." She laughed and squirmed. Once more, he had won her over. He always did. And it always annoyed me, as if she'd let me or herself down.

A bottle of perfume, a silk scarf, earrings, he made it seem so simple. But that was Andre, a Frenchman bearing gifts. Janice had always blamed him, in good part at least, for our earlier split-up. She did not know, but Andre had been rough with me. Basically a family man, a husband, a father, he said, "Jack, you do not divorce a girl simply because you do not get along. She need only be a good mother. Live your own life, do as you please. When she is furious at you, make love to her, buy her perfume. Why do you think you have to leave Janice? She is a simple uncomplicated woman who loves pretty things. Flatter her."

"And now," said Andre, "for dinner." He suggested a Japanese restaurant. There was this wonderful place just down the street. "The food is cooked for you right at the table. Come."

We strolled eastward, Janice between us. He took her right arm. I took her other arm. We lofted her along. But I felt depressed. I hardly knew where we were going. Janice was either happy now, or being a damned good sport. Once more Andre grabbed her and dipped his nose into her neck. The perfume, he said, was driving him mad.

But the restaurant, well, the restaurant was jammed. Throngs waited, they filled the barstools, stood against the walls, sat on waiting chairs, sat on the floor.

"This is impossible," said Andre. "No, this is impossible." We walked back toward the Drake.

Since I was scheming to grab the check, I suggested a French place across town we all knew, where I could afford the bill. Andre and Loretta had taken us to so many dinners, had had us to so many meals, had done us so many favors. They had put up the money, loan though it was, for the down payment on a house Janice and I had briefly owned in the suburbs. Andre shook his head. "No, that too would be crowded."

We came to a restaurant with plush carpeting and crystal chandeliers that was almost empty. Andre led us inside. At the five or six occupied tables sat white-haired executive types with their wives. We were seated.

"Andre . . . what are we doing here? It's either going to be ridiculously expensive or the food is going to be lousy. Let's get out."

"Jack, why are you so grouchy tonight?"

I wouldn't answer.

"Jan, what is the matter with him?"

I put it off on something else. I didn't want to be rude. "Do
you remember Dorothy Dole?" I said.

"He went to see her in the hospital today," Janice said.
"She's in a bad way."

He'd never met Dorothy Dole but he'd always wanted to,
and because I'd never brought them together he'd always
thought I was holding out on him. As a literary agent, he'd
wanted to handle her. She had a reputation for being hard on
agents, dumping them with regularity. Andre was convinced he
could manage the most temperamental and difficult of artists,
if they were women. He would have charmed her, I'm certain.

Andre ordered for all of us.

"Half of everything," Andre said gravely, "is attitude. In the
Army before I had learned to write a literate sentence in English, I was the editor of a camp newspaper. When I could not as
an enlisted man get security clearance to write training films, I
became an officer in Air Corps Intelligence. When I had published only surrealistic poetry in Parisian newspapers, I became
a partner in one of the best literary agencies in New York.
Then in Paris, forty-four years old, I thought, what will I do
next? I will make lots of money. Why not? So I went into mu-
tual funds. I have made money. Lots of it. Millions."

Janice, ripe with perfume, was smiling. I had begun to wonder if any one of us was real.

"Let me tell you briefly. Five years ago I was in a small office
with five men. Now I have an office with a staff of two thousand. I started the company with $125,000, and I am now sit-
ting on $150,000,000."

I had no reason or wish to doubt him but I did. He was, as I
knew, perfectly capable of anything. I guess it was hard to believe anyone my own age that I knew closely could ever be so
successful. We all have our dreams of love and glory, but we

learn in time to forget them and settle for what we can get. Not Andre. Other people's daydreams were his everyday reality.

I don't know what the bill came to, but he left a twenty-dollar tip. Then, as we moved from the restaurant to a taxi and to a series of East Side bars, I became convinced I was slightly crazy, as if my fan belt had broken and my head was overheating. Something was wrong with the night. Was it someone else's success, a friend's, I couldn't make real? I would hate that.

He was one of the most patient and durable friends I had and he would, I was sure, crawl halfway around the Eiffel Tower to help me if I needed help. I'd do as much for him.

At the end of the evening we sat in bargloom lighted by an imitation Tiffany lamp. A stereo set was playing with such hi-fi realism Andre went away to see if it was a live combo. He came back and said, "I like this place. This is a good place." He was trying to be upbeat. My lousy mood had him worried.

He tore a couple of pieces of cardboard from his beer coaster and stuck the plugs inside his sunglasses and stared at us, howling with mock laughter. Then he took off my glasses and put his glasses on me. He grabbed Janice by her shoulder, pointed at me and howled, "Look. Look. Look."

I just wanted to go home.

Four A.M. My teeth explode, one by one, like the boards of a fence. I think I hear someone running down a long hallway. Our cat, sunk between the desk lamp and the wall, sleeps on although something is moving under the fur in his stomach. My fingers are still. They lie across the open page of a book. When will I go to Samarkand?

July 20th. Dream and peril—

When the film footage I'd taken on our June vacation at the Cape came back from the lab, I called Judy and Norman, a couple of our friends in the building, and asked them to bear witness. I tried to make the home movies I took into little works of art, each scene a bit of heightened reality. Like my random worrying, it kept me occupied.

Judy and Norman arrived together. Judy, I saw Janice noting, had on a breast- and hip-hugging dress. Judy was delightfully stacked. She was our neighbor one summer on the Cape and we knew her before she met Norman and got Norman to divorce his alcoholic, seldom seen, seldom home wife. She then moved into Norman's apartment. Judy, when she moved in, was already two months pregnant—and it was three years before, as Norman put it, she dragged him to the altar of "marital honor." Norman was a bearded, cheerful, easygoing man with a kind of grand independence that was an endless aggravation to Judy.

He liked his clothes old and wrinkled, let his beard grow where it wanted to, figured out vacations he could take alone, read endlessly. He taught at Metro, my college, in another department. If he only worked at publishing papers and articles and books he could double his salary, but publication didn't interest Norman at all, not at all. He said if Judy would quit trying to improve him, he'd be utterly contented.

I had the motion picture projector set up on the table beside

the davenport, and right away I let them know they had a treat
in store—cast of characters to include myself, Janice and
offspring: our daughter, Perse, that is, and her children. Her
husband too.

They got seated. Janice snapped off the lights and I beamed
the images at a bare space on the wall (our old screen nearly
useless now, torn, difficult, moody). We sat and watched it all
again: the great sea, the great heavy sea and the seaside. Perse
running along the wet sand. Sea gulls. A child's bare hands cup-
ping sea shells. Perse's bare shoulder and slender neck—and beyond, where she stood gazing, whitecaps. More sea gulls. Sand-
pipers. Janice walking away from the camera toward the front
door of our cottage. Bathing suits on a clothesline. Garage windows reflecting sky and clouds.

Much satisfaction to this beholder, who sat with his hands
on the throttle switch, the hum of the past at his ear, the days
of a month ago spinning by, time snatched back, familiar faces
from another place in our dark living room.

All the way through.

"That's it."

Lights on.

As ever—looks of relief, and some questions such as what
were cottages renting for this year. Judy's folks had a small estate on the Hudson River and before Judy and Norman went
upstairs, we all agreed it would be fun if we joined them in the
country for sailboating this coming weekend.

I spend too much time in these home movies I make taking
pictures of people walking away from the camera, too much
time taking pictures of landscapes where nothing moves, taking
pictures of still life—when all that really remains of steady interest is the faces of people, the color and texture of the skin,
the lips, the hands. I guess I'm still interested in the camera

and in my own technique of using that miraculous device, an important initial interest that should pass, leaving the cameraman, or the writer, for that matter, with the only thing that counts, that everything else is subordinate to, his subject—and the subject, is people. It's people. It's you and I, it's them and me, face to face. It's all of us and Time.

Late Saturday afternoon as we sat drinking twilight in on the lawn chairs beside the cottage behind the main house where the folks lived and where Judy had grown up, little Francine arrived.

There were just the three of us at first, Judy, Janice and me, talking about nothing much but talking happily, bantering—and then Francine, Judy and Norman's ten-year-old daughter, arrived and kept breaking in, trying to change the subject of a nearly subjectless drift of voices, failing mostly because nobody really cared that much about the conversation. So Francine got up and went over to the lawn hammock and swung it and yelled at her mother that it needed to be repaired. Her voice got louder and louder and became nearly constant; Judy would turn her head once in a while and tell her to be quiet.

She was a scrawny kid with big, knobby knees and an awkward gait. Her mouth was so small it was almost unnoticeable under her long thin nose—but her high plangent voice could carry as far as anyone's I'd ever heard.

Off across the lawn, back in among the high bank of trees and leaves, a lot of birds were chattering in the twilight. I'd never heard so many birds. Francine's cries mingled with theirs. "They do that every evening," Judy said, then turned to shout, "Francine, I told you to be quiet." She had lost her hostess cool. "We're trying to talk, and I want you to be quiet. You can listen, but you're not to interrupt us."

"Those birds haven't seen each other all day," I said, "and they've got a lot to talk about." I took another drink and felt at peace.

Janice said, "How many are there? It sounds like thousands."

But we didn't have Judy's attention any more. Francine kept jerking at the swing and shouting at Judy until she was commanded to go over beyond the flower bed on another lawn area. She went, foot-dragging, and found there a bag of golf clubs. It was a beautiful set of clubs, chrome, all matched, her own—and she began to knock a ball around. I saw she knew something about swinging the club—someone had been teaching her—and I saw, uneasily, she was whacking not a practice ball, a little ball of knit wool, but an honesttogodgoodforthreehundredyardsonthefly hard little rubber rock.

Judy and I both saw her start a full swing in our direction, and Judy came up out of her chair screeching, "Francine, haven't I told you never to hit the ball toward people?"

Francine yelled back, "I was just going to putt."

That was when her father came up. Norman sat down with us and we listened to Judy and Francine shouting at one another across the flower bed.

"I don't care what you were going to do. I've told you never to hit the ball in this direction."

Francine did have a putter in her hands, so her argument had just enough validity for her to carry it on for some time. Norman listened with a cramped smile but said nothing. When Judy sat down again, she said sharply, "Norman, you still have your swimming trunks on. We're dressed. Can't you dress for cocktails?"

Norman stood up, spreading his bare arms in consternation, but he kept smiling. "You should have heard her the other night, telling me to go get dressed in front of her parents." He started the story, but he was interrupted by Francine wading her way straight through the flower bed to rejoin us.

Judy turned. "Francine, haven't I told you not to walk

through the flower bed? Haven't I told you? It's not our flower bed. I don't want you to do that anymore."

The kid had real style. She knew exactly what she could get away with, and she was entertaining herself with a good bit of enjoyment.

Norman went gloomily up the stairs to their apartment above the garage and Francine, as directed, went back to her golf practice—while we tried to decide if the potato chips we were eating, much thicker and crisper and tastier than any I'd ever run into, were made from potatoes or from an agreeable combination of soybeans and chemicals.

The chips were almost gone and Judy sent Francine into the cottage to bring down another bag. From an upstairs window, Francine yelled at us, "Norman isn't doing anything up here. He's just sitting on the side of the bed."

Then down came Francine and over to us. "There aren't any potato chips."

With a mild, barely controlled voice, Judy said, "There are. I put them in the cupboard this afternoon."

"There's nothing there."

"Did you look?"

"I looked everywhere."

"Well, go back and look again."

"There aren't any."

"Bring down something else then, some Fritos, anything." Their voices were beginning to rise.

"There isn't anything. I told you, there isn't anything."

"I want you to go back up there again," Judy yelled, "and while you're there tell your father to get down here."

"He doesn't know what shirt to wear," Francine screamed.

Francine made one more trip up the stairs and back again, empty-handed. Judy got up and went for the potato chips herself; Francine went off somewhere. Janice and I sat listening to the birds. They were now much quieter.

"Better a bull for an hour than a steer for a year," I said hoarsely.

Janice frowned and said, "Where did you hear that?" just as I saw Norman and Judy coming toward us, ten feet away. Judy had the bag of potato chips and Norman was wearing a fresh blue sport shirt. He was seething in his reticent way. Whenever he could, he stayed behind at the apartment in New York and Judy went off with Francine to sail the river and lie on the lawn beside her parents' stone house. The weekends he joined them were rough on him; then this otherwise amiable, talkative, scholarly man grew silent and testy.

That night, as the four of us sat at their dinner table, Norman refused to eat his lobster. "I just don't like gourmet food," he explained, scowling.

Judy took a claw off his plate and was ready to break it open for him, but he was desperately adamant. Norman didn't say anything, but he'd had it. He sat there, eyes closed, shaking his head, as if his head were wired to shake. He couldn't stomach lobster and she was trying to get it down him anyway, to enrich his life.

Sunday, Norman skulked around by himself. He sat most of the time in a garage, in an old wicker chair, reading *National Geographic* magazines. He looked so lost and miserable that as we drove back to New York, Janice, who finds divorce an unspeakable subject, said, "Maybe they'd be better off apart."

Was she thinking, maybe, of us?

The next morning as we sat on the balcony having breakfast, still reliving the weekend, I asked painfully, "Do you think he heard me say—Better a bull for an hour than a steer for a year?"

She shrugged.

"What's going to become of Francine?" Janice said. She was genuinely concerned and I tried to think of what would happen to her. I was concerned myself, but concerned for whom? For Francine? For Judy? For Norman? Or the man Francine married? The concern was like the weight of a general anxiety settling down on me.

I sorted through all the kids I'd known when I was Francine's age and I couldn't come up with another who had all of her qualifications: rich grandparents, a mother who gave her anything she wanted and a lot of stuff she didn't even know she wanted, expensive things, a wrist watch that must have cost a hundred dollars, a three-hundred-dollar guitar, an Arthur Ashe tennis racquet, a five-hundred-dollar ten-speed bike, and every game and toy that toy stores could dream up. She had it all. The closet of her room was jammed. I said I couldn't remember knowing any kid like Francine.

She gave me a look and said, "Some people think you're like her."

A sound of surprise came out of me. "She's a girl!" . . . really thinking that one over.

Was she just trying to bust me one again for the hell of it? I'd been in and out of analysis for any number of years and had learned to examine all clues that came my way, to turn them over and over in the sunlight like chunks of broken shard from my buried life.

Francine spent a lot of time upstaging her father, I'd even heard her call him "the dummy." She made cracks about how little money Norman earned, and her mother patiently let it pass. "I never," I said, "gave my father the business the way Francine gives it to Norman. But you used to let Perse do that to me before we broke up." Her look now had me worried.

Her lips curled down. "You had a good environment, but

you didn't let it shape you. Environment doesn't shape you."

"Who are we talking about? Tell me, how the hell am I like Francine, tell me."

"You always have your own way about everything."

"That's stupid. Listen, I stick to principles. I don't give in. Is that what you mean by—have my own way?"

She stood up, clutching the front of her robe, "You have to spoil things for everyone else, or haven't you noticed?"

It was time for Janice to leave for the hospital. After she'd gone, having got me off to another rotten day, I sat on at the table, looking over toward Broadway, finishing my cup of coffee. I didn't feel like writing. Another day was shot.

July 28th—

Sometimes I lie on the couch and stare at the ceiling for twenty minutes without a word. He plays solitaire. He says solitaire helps him listen, but I suspect it's another of his tricks. He wants to be a psychiatric innovator, and he's probably working on a paper. He'll break my silence by saying, "What are you thinking about?"

"I'm thinking about all the work I have to do this afternoon when I get home."

He shuffles his cards. It's a standoff.

What did he mean when he said, "Will the real Jack Fross please stand up?" Am I someone other than who I think I am?

Again, in lieu of a dream, I had only a story to bring him. It saves my voice to type them out, and they come forth in a kind of open-eyed dreaming. It saves my voice to hand them to him and he accepts them, although he still thinks my hoarseness is resistance to analysis.

"What do you make of it?" Newman asks.

"It means I want to go to Samarkand."

He snorts.

He's asking a few questions today.

"The girl, that's Gail. Or, I don't know. Maybe it's Perse or someone I wish I could run off with. It must be Gail. That old man on the island, I don't know who he is. No one in my family. Maybe he's my first editor. He died."

"Time's up for today," Newman says cheerfully.

The sonofabitch.

The day summer school ended I was walking down Fifth Avenue. I saw Cook's on the other side of the street, crossed over, went inside, sat down at a long counter and talked to a girl who had been sitting at a small desk behind the counter staring off at the traffic outside.

I said, "I'm interested in taking a trip around the world and I'd like to find out how much it would cost."

She got out a pad with a sheet of paper that mapped the world of Europe and East Asia. I pointed at Trieste and said I'd leave New York and fly there, and from there take a small boat down the Dalmatian coast. I drew my finger along the flank of Yugoslavia. ". . . down around here and over to Athens. Spend a little time in Athens. Then go up through the Bosporus. Spend a little time in Istanbul." She nodded. No sweat so far, but I was about to head into trouble. My finger ran off the map.

She got another, bigger map that had Samarkand on it, but Samarkand was way out of its geographical position. It was down below, or south of the Caspian Sea. I complained. She apologized. "This is just a sketch map," she said.

—Oh, well.

"I'd like to take a boat," I said, "from Istanbul across the Black Sea and then travel by train or bus over to a port on the Caspian Sea. If it's possible, I'll cross the Caspian by boat and then get a train to Samarkand. There used to be a train that ran from the Caspian coast to Samarkand. Does it still run?"

She shook her head because she didn't know how anybody traveled in that area. "If you want to go around the world, you'll have trouble getting from Samarkand to New Delhi."

"Could I rent a car?"

"Just a minute." She went off to check into a book on her desk and came back, shaking her head. "You might be able to get a plane, but in that part of the world you can spend anywhere from six hours to days on end waiting for the plane to leave."

So we skipped that little matter. From New Delhi on, everything went smoothly. We charted an air course from New Delhi to Calcutta to Rangoon to Manila to Hong Kong to Tokyo to San Francisco to New York.

"What would that cost?" I asked. "Do you have any idea?"

"Just a minute." She left the counter, went up some steps to an office, consulted with someone for five or ten minutes, came back. "Two thousand one hundred dollars."

"And how much," I asked out of curiosity, "is your standard trip around the world by plane?"

"Two thousand one hundred dollars."

August 20th. No safe adventures—

When I got to Gail's apartment on the New Jersey banks of the Hudson, I mixed us each a drink, took mine out on the balcony and sat at a table she'd set for dinner. A tugboat was moving up the river, sending back a long wake. It was heading toward the George Washington Bridge, riding low in the river, moving steadily, smoothly. Nothing, I think, moves as beautifully as a river tug, not a swan, or a duck, or any swimmer, no other boat. They're so low and small and powerful. They move with a kind of inevitable, invincible grace, with a purpose. And the purpose is to lend pure power to other, bigger boats. Isn't that absolute giving? A supreme benevolence? Perfect confidence?

It was time I made up my mind about a few things. Did I want to leave Janice and this time make it stick? Then go off to Samarkand? And what about Gail? Yeah, what about her? And Metro? Quit teaching?

It was a time for seriousness.

It was a time for decisions—or at least for one. By careful calculation and in-depth reflection, I figured the last serious decision I'd made was to see Gail on the side.

I drank and watched the boat and listened to Gail inside at the piano, practicing. I felt wonderful. Dinner was in the oven in the kitchenette and the odors were drifting out to me.

It was hard for me to understand why, with her voice, she wasn't famous. There had been a period after I first met her when I suspected she was—that she was concealing her stage name. She sang at benefits and weddings and danced and sang and acted in off-Broadway shows. A couple of years had passed since she'd sung anywhere but in a chorus. She had once sung a lead in a Hunter College opera. It was a world I could not understand and wished I could join. I'd never known anyone in my life to work so single-mindedly and so happily at anything as she did at her singing and acting. But I was aware that before her singing and acting she had worked just as hard at ballet, then sculpting, even writing. She was a talented writer, too. I was a judge of that. Now she had a small part in an off-Broadway play and half the time she wanted to be a serious actress and half the time she still wanted to be a serious singer.

She reached the end of her song. The piano went silent. She came to the balcony door and said, troubled, "How did you like that last number?" I knew she thought she'd started singing too late in life.

"Wonderful, just wonderful. I was sitting here watching that tugboat go up the river, listening to you and your song, the river, the boat, it was all an orchestration. It was beautiful."

"Jack."

"What?"

She came over to the table and sat down. "I was going to wait until after dinner for what I have to say."

I had the sensation of everything going rigid and timeless. "You're pregnant?"

"Nothing like that."

I waited.

"Is your wife a rather tall, bosomy brunette?"

"Why?"

"A hook on her nose right here?"

"Yes."

"I was afraid so. Big hips?"

A century or two went by. The tug moved no closer to the great bridge, and the ice did not melt in my glass, nor did the glass drop from my fingers.

"Has she been here to see you?"

"No. She was downstairs yesterday looking over the names by the elevators—and she took a good hard look at me when I went by."

So—I didn't stay over with Gail. I went home. Ah, ha. Janice was in the living room watching the late movie. She hadn't gone to Boston after all. I didn't ask her to explain herself and she didn't ask me to, but I knew she was waiting to hear where I'd been.

I said nothing. I hate to lie. It's an awful business, but I'll lie if I'm pressed. That's the worst part of leading a double life, there are so goddamn many lies I find myself involved in, whether I like lying or not.

I must admit my fits of unfaithfulness have been hard for Janice to bear or understand or forgive. And they are fits, because I don't usually have a girl around I know I can drop in on. When I do, I try to keep it all very discreet, but a number of years back the girl didn't. When put to it to explain myself to Janice I couldn't. I couldn't even explain the other girl to myself. It wasn't that I was all that tired of Janice. Girls are just an urge I live with, a need that sometimes gets the best of me. It's not a matter of do or don't want to, as I told her, not a matter of will power. We had a big scene.

As I fixed myself a drink out at the hall closet, I recalled my flimsy defense again—with pain.

"Not a matter of will power," she'd mimicked me.

"No, it's not. It's like alcoholism. Like some Rutter's Anonymous, goddamn it. And I know it's an urge that can destroy my life just as much as booze can a boozer's."

"Once in and you're hooked. I see, you go on binges with women. Is that it?"

I nodded.

"And I suppose it's an illness. It isn't love. Love is what you feel for me."

"For all I know, that's what love is . . . a binge . . . and then a godawful recovery."

"Well," she said, "I suppose I should be glad to get any explanation. Are you going to run off with her, leave me?"

"No."

"But you expect me to stay with you?"

"Yes."

"I see. And you're just being considerate and explaining that you're always going to be involved with another woman because you can't help yourself?"

"No! Not that either. But when I'm not involved, it's because I'm making it one day at a time . . . and passing up easy stuff all around. And . . . I'll tell you something else . . . I don't think I'm any different from most other men."

It was just an explanation to hold her, but she believed it. What is the tug and pull, the meaning of the *he* and the *she* of it? Janice doesn't know either. She knows this though—she isn't going to put up with it.

"Let me tell you this, Jack. I'm not going to suffer in silence. You hurt me and I'll hurt you, and I don't mean maybe. I'm no different than any other woman. Make me suffer and I'll let you know I'm hurting. Any woman alive can beat a man at that game."

She'd said this just before our first marriage ended, when I learned to take Janice at her word. I could only hope she'd mellowed a little with time.

I took my drink and went back to the living room. All friendly I said, "What's the movie?"

She kept her profile toward me and I studied the arch in her nose, her thin lips, the jut of her lean jaw. She never answered. I said nothing myself and watched the movie until I'd finished my drink. Then I got up to go to bed.

As I went out of the room, she snapped, "Your voice is worse."

Newman says briskly, "Time's up for today."

What is the sound of one hand clapping?
It is the sound of silence.
What is the sound of silence?
There are degrees and kinds of silence: silence as a lack of sound, silence as a concept of space, silence as an image: the universe without end. Silence as the music of the spheres. Silence as reality without a sound track. The silence of the deaf man and the silence of the mute. The silence of the tree in the forest that falls with no one there to hear it fall. No sound without someone to hear, no sights without someone to see, no surface without someone to feel. World without odors and sound and substance: this is the first silence, silence of the first and of the penultimate degree. The second silence is the sound of one hand clapping.
What is the loudest silence?
It is the silence of guilt unconfessed, the silence of suffering unspoken, the silence of desire unexpressed.

Yes, Janice is a tall woman, a Junoesque figure with a bump on the bridge of her nose that gives her a beaked or predatory look when anything has her alerted: dirt on the windowsills, a draft from a doorway, cigarette smoke, a noise she can't identify, a noise she can identify. She listens constantly to the engine of our car whenever we're out, calling my attention to sounds I can't hear, asking me when I last had the oil changed.

She's compulsive. Everything has a place and everything must be in its place. She'll tear a postage stamp off a letter she's put on upside down. If she turns off a faucet, she studies it to see if there's a drip. She remembers everyone's birthday she ever wanted to and still sends them cards. It used to bug me, now I pay it no heed. She can't help herself. She's made Perse into a fusser, too. In a way, it's kind of wonderful to watch them together. If there is a God, I think he deliberately created such people. It's as if they believe in perfection, in some sort of perfect life. They indulge in brand name idolatry, and they shop endlessly in stores whose names roll off their tongues in a kind of daily linguistic liturgy. It's a religion with them. Their faith is in electric toasters, Mixmasters, freezers, kitchen gadgets of all kinds. They both believe in the well-organized bureau drawer and closet. They sniff the air in unison at any offending odor. A cockroach will send either of them into hysterics; any kind of insect sends shudders through them. A fly on the loose in a room will pull their otherwise attractive faces into ugly contortions.

When we broke up years ago, Janice went to see my psychiatrist to let him know how uncaring I was—but he told her, as I learned later, that it was she who had busted up the marriage. This shocked her. It bewildered her. It could even have been the jolt that reunited us. Anyway, since we've been back together, she's talked to a marriage counselor and read enough books about marriage to be less demanding now of her husband than she is of the faucets.

If I left things lying around these days, she picked them up and said nothing. She usually took the garbage out now; the only time I did was when I thought of it. She didn't keep after me to get the car washed. She took the car for its bath herself every Saturday morning. That was progress—but she had learned to do most of those things anyway during the ten years we'd been out of touch with each other.

I still did not measure up to Janice—or Perse. I simply tried a little harder. We all did. I even found a curious comfort and security in their fussing. I didn't ridicule it any more. It went on around me like the sounds of our insane world.

But what a strange long way we'd come—or fallen—all so strange a transformation for two nice kids in school screwing on the ground and drinking gin and setups on money orders that came from home.

August 25th. Fletch and Samarkand—

I saw someone today walking up the street who looked from behind like Fletch. He had Fletch's sloping shoulders and long arms and big hands—and his suit jacket didn't fit him right, was a little tight, the sleeves too short. He walked with long strides, a country boy's lope, and he wore a fedora set squarely on his head. Seeing him I thought at once: it's Fletch. But Fletch is dead. Even so, I caught up with him at the corner and as we stood waiting for the light, I took a look at him to make sure. No, it wasn't Fletch. This man was black—and that was ironic because Fletch might as well have been black for all his ticket of whiteness bought him.

So I've started to think about Fletch again, trying to remember how old we were when we decided we wanted to go to Samarkand.

I can't remember who came up with Samarkand first. Perhaps it was Fletch. He was a couple of years older than I and he read a lot, too. So he could have read about Samarkand.

I think I was somewhere between eight and ten years old when we sat around rubbing the pot we found in the pile of junk behind his barn. What we both wanted from our genie was a trillion dollars. Were we earnest? I think we were. We were earnest, I know, about the three wishes. Suppose the first wish or the second wish or the third brought us some bad side effect? The third wish, and this was Fletch's idea, would always have to be reserved for three more wishes. We rubbed. We rubbed and waited. Nothing. We also snapped chicken wishbones and sought out the first star of the evening to wish on. With time we dropped the trillion and got more reasonable, but the search itself became more complex.

It was our impression, through reading, that the streets of a faraway place called Samarkand were paved with golden bricks, that its buildings were studded with jewels. We were going to go to Samarkand and, at the risk of our lives, snatch fortune in one quick, brilliant raid.

When I was in bed at night trying to imagine the terrain between Michigan and Samarkand, I'd have little trouble seeing my way to the Atlantic Ocean. I'd been with my folks on a trip to New York. I could imagine the ocean easily enough, and the boat. I'd seen enough photographs of Europe to imagine France and Switzerland. But then, beyond the Alps and Heidi and Swiss cheese, things got murky. I had a glimpse of a Turk slumped at a water pipe, a camel, a spear, a mountain pass with a Roman soldier. What lay between the Alps and Samarkand? I still have trouble imagining my way to that city at the center of, what, my known universe? And it was the same with all the other journeys that Fletch and I planned. The first part of each later journey, to dig gold in Alaska, to uncover gold in the fallen temples of the Yucatan, to dive for pearls in the Pacific, to fight as mercenaries in Latin America, always began on real enough ground and then dissolved into the landscape of a dream. Finally, we were planning a trip no more complicated than hitchhiking to Traverse City to pick cherries. And we couldn't get organized enough to pull that off.

By then we were dating girls and our fantasies had turned to conquests and forays closer to home. That once remote, romantic city in Asia had moved as close as Grand Rapids, its rubies and diamonds and bricks of gold now transformed into payroll checks and what they in turn turned into—a late model secondhand car, cases of beer, a girl friend, a house with a yard, furniture. But the furniture and the house came after the conquest of the girl: in most ways Samarkand had focused down to the girl. It did for Fletch. Marriage for him followed a brief courtship. I went off to college. But I never got over the thought of our big adventure, of Samarkand, couldn't get it out of my head, the thought at least of journey and danger shared with a friend. I hung on to that dream, and after Fletch was married still wanted us to make some kind of a trip before the demons who protect the treasure at the end of the road had bewitched us out of the road itself.

The girl Fletch married lived near us, one of the most attractive girls either of us had ever known. He had no job, was working the farm for his father for little more than room and board, but he married her. It was the only honorable thing he could do and Fletch was brought up to accept responsibility.

The summer of my junior year in college, when their second child was well on its way, I decided Fletch and I ought to drive up to Harbor Springs and back . . . have that adventure. The time had come. I'd pay for the gas.

I dropped over to his place on a Saturday morning and caught him at home—or rather out in his workroom. The workroom was in the old granary under the hayloft. The door was locked, but I could hear Fletch inside hammering at a piece of metal. His thing was mechanics; for the last year, he had been secretive about his work. I rattled the door. The hammering stopped. I said I wanted to talk to him. Then I walked to the open barn door and waited.

Fletch was no longer farming those eighty acres he lived on. The only hay in the barn had packed down and rotted. The last cow had died. It amazed me how fast a place could go to pot. Since I'd gone off to college, holes had opened in the roof of the barn, and while I stood waiting for Fletch a pigeon flew in through a hole the size of a window and lit on a rafter. The trees in the orchard could barely sprout leaves. The grass and alfalfa in the pastures was waist high. He worked in town now. It paid better. Anything he could get, he said, paid better than the farm. He was still in debt for the first child and did not know how he would ever get out of debt—unless he hit it big with an invention. That's what he was at in the granary.

When Fletch came out, he locked the door behind him. He looked discouraged, depressed. We sat in the doorway. I told him I was on my way to Harbor Springs. My mother's brother and his family were taking their vacation there. He made a lot of money, this uncle, and it was routine for him to give me ten or twenty dollars whenever he saw me. My mother said it was because he'd been wretchedly penniless as a young man. I wasn't sure we'd find him, but I had enough money anyway to cover the gas if Fletch would drive me up and back.

He thought it over. I knew he wanted to go, but something was holding him back. Then he sighed and said, "Okay," and we walked down the driveway from the barn to the back of the house. Norma was at the kitchen sink, just inside the back door. Fletch said to her, moving out of the kitchen toward the stairs, "Jack wants me to drive him up to Harbor Springs."

Norma was then maybe eight months along. She was a small girl, slim legs and arms. She lit a cigarette and blew the smoke out of the side of her mouth in a thin fast stream. She leaned against the wall, resting her stomach against the sink, frowned and stared at me.

"We're just going straight up and back," I said because she didn't look full of consent.

Her lips were turned down at the corners. She brought the cigarette back up to her lips, nodded, and went back to the baby bottles.

When Fletch came down the stairs, he was dressed in his

best suit. He had on a shirt, a tie, and his light tan fedora. We were in the living room when Fletch said to her, "I need some money."

She looked at him, eyes big and rueful. "You know there ain't any."

But Fletch said there had been six dollars, at least, in her purse last night, that he wanted some of it and he didn't want to hear any more shit about there being no goddamn money and where the fuck was her purse, and she started screaming and she turned around, found me and yelled, "What are you trying to do coming around here making trouble?"

I said, "We don't need any money, Fletch."

"Don't you know he's married? He can't just take off when he wants to." It was an example of my natural-born blitheness that I stood there staring at both of them with genuine surprise while she screamed on, "What about me? When do I get away? I'm stuck here with the kid while he's off having fun. I'm stuck out here in the country every day of the year. How do you think I like that . . . ?"

They were both furious, full of energy, jerking around. Fletch was picking up things, shirts, dresses, magazines, newspapers, kids' toys, throwing them around without looking where they went. Norma danced behind him, trying to hold his arms down, and their cries of recrimination and outrage had become a duet, words over words; even the baby was joining in.

They went up the stairs. She had him by the back of his coat jacket, but he was in the lead. I went through the kitchen and out into the yard; even out there I could hear them in the room just over the kitchen, because the window was open. He had, my god, gone up to break open their piggy bank. I stood under the window, under their cries and grunts and growls and wails and tried to think what I ought to do. Hell, I should leave, but I didn't want to go without saying good-by.

Fletch came to the window and said calmly, very calmly, "I'll be right down, Jack." He had one of those clay coin banks in one hand and he cracked it against the window ledge. It broke and spilled coins on the ledge and out over the ledge as well. They fell on the ground around my feet, mostly pennies, a few nickels and dimes.

In a minute Fletch came out the back door and started grubbing around in the dirt. She stayed inside.

"Ah, look, Fletch," I said miserably.

He never turned or responded. When he had all the coins, jamming them down in his pocket, he headed for the car, and seeing I didn't move toward the car, he stopped and gave me a long, hard look.

"I don't want to start anything," I said.

"Then, don't you give me any crap," he said. "Let's go."

I still hesitated.

Fletch got behind the wheel, and I stood looking at the car for maybe another minute—until he started the engine; then I went over and got in slowly.

Fletch said, "We have to make this trip. She can't tell me what I can or can't do. Not in front of other people. Blowing up like that. Giving me orders. I *got* to go now. If we don't go and I give in, she'll start running my life."

He swung the car around in the clearing behind the house and we took the driveway, two worn wheel tracks in the grass, out to the gravel road.

In those days the countryside got primitive north of Petoskey. Beyond Petoskey the road was unpaved. When we weren't passing through land that had been lumbered off, the woods came up darkly on each side of the car, and the sky was thatched with a cover of leaves and pine needles. Where the land had been cut or sometimes burned off, stumps remained:

a strange sight—great forests cut down and lugged away. Where acres of flames had burned, the stumps stood like black and broken teeth rooted in the ruined ground, here and there a tall trunk by itself. We passed swamps where the trees grew in black water. Our road ran north through the small town where my mother and her family had lived. I was born in that town.

No one in my family was there any more; even so, I asked Fletch to drive around a few streets so I could look at houses I knew, set back from the road, separated by familiar side lawns.

The streets had been paved within the last five years. The old wooden sidewalks I swore I remembered had been discarded; the old home was changed; the porch was gone.

Because of the way our trip started, my feelings and thoughts were still unsettled—although I should have been used to family brawls. My first parents, my grandfather and my grandmother, had been a scrappy pair and well matched. I'd never seen a picture of them shoulder by shoulder in an oval frame, immortalized in the fashion of the period in which they lived together, because they were probably unable to tolerate each other long enough to be photographed. None of the men and women in my family had been able to live together compatibly. They seemed (aunts, uncles, cousins, mothers, fathers, grandmothers, grandfathers) to live in hobbles and clanking chains, all of them struggling in a sucking swamp of home life, lurching across an endless, treeless world, complaining but hanging together.

Yet my grandmother and grandfather must have been happy for a while. They had three children in quick succession. By the time I was born, however, those children were grown and my grandfather was beginning to hack off the chain that held him home. He sometimes slept on a cot he kept in his law office. These departures to this office were issued as public proclamations, his words like banners he carried aloft. Sometimes it was my grandmother who kicked him out, threw his clothes on the porch, sent me upstairs, locked all the doors. Once she said he got her down on the floor and sat on her and choked her. "Until I was blue in the face," she told a divorce court.

When I was born, that was my early world. My mother and father had already separated, temporarily. My grandparents were bringing me up while my mother was off finding, she hoped to god, some kind of better life for herself. For that matter, my mother hated her mother.

We all lived, as best we could, our impossible lives in that very small town in northern Michigan, a town so small that nothing exciting ever happened that wasn't talked about the next day by everyone—so that all that happened in my family was happening, so to speak, on a stage under floodlights; and the only thing that made town life endurable was the comforting knowledge that other families lived as badly as we did. What we had was life: thick, rich, passionate life.

Harbor Springs was another hour or so farther to the north. We came to Little Traverse Bay and Petoskey in time; by then we were talking freely again. I'd spent the previous summer working as a busboy in a hotel in the Harbor Springs area and, as we drove along, I told Fletch what life was like at night. The girls who worked as maids and waitresses outnumbered the boys; they went out every night in pairs and groups. The girls were easy to meet. They all seemed pretty and carefree, looking for fun. I told Fletch we ought to hang around the bay long enough to look in on a few nightspots before heading home, and he said he thought we should, too—as long as we'd come this far.

We came to Little Traverse Bay. Harbor Springs lay across the water from Petoskey, most of its hotels and homes under green shade, leaf hidden. The water was blue, as blue as a sky-flooded valley.

Northwestern Michigan was then and perhaps still is one of the most heavenly places on earth, a summer lap of luxury and contentment. In winter, everything closes down; merchants, satchels heavy with the summer's swag, head for Florida and California and Arizona to spend it or make more. The brand name families of Chicago and Detroit, the sovereign rulers of plants that make and distribute automobiles, farm machinery, bandages, beer, chemicals, the throned rulers of hotel chains and taxi fleets and newspapers and hospitals, send their families to the hotels and summer homes around Little Traverse Bay to provide the local people with the silver and gold they spend in their own gardens of the Hesperides.

There were big hotels along the road going out of Petoskey, frame structures, windows facing the bay. At the end of the bay, our road turned left.

I didn't know what hotel my uncle and his family would be staying at, but I started looking for him at the best hotels. There were only three in that category, and he wasn't in any of them. I tried several smaller ones and finally found him at a rooming house on a side street behind the main street stores. I didn't think he was pleased to have me find him in such humble accommodations, but he took Fletch and me out to lunch —at a diner—and insisted we order steak.

My uncle Bob said fondly, "How you kids fixed for moolah? You traveling on credit?" Then to me, "Here, take this . . ." shoving a bill in my hands. I took it, but not so blithely as I had at other times, nor with the satisfaction I'd anticipated on the drive up. Usually he loved to give me spending money and I loved to take it; but I felt guilty this time. Maybe he wasn't as rich as I'd thought.

When we pulled out of Harbor Springs an hour later, the

sun was edging toward the lake; I had twenty bucks in my pocket I hadn't had before. We took a small road down the shore of the bay. We got out and walked the sand at the water's edge. Dunes lay ahead of us and to our left, and beyond the dunes were the tops of trees. The water was shot full of golden flecks of sunlight. A few people were still swimming and sunbathing. We sat down to watch a girl about seventeen or eighteen paddling offshore in the shallow water. She was with a woman in her thirties—her mother? A friend? We squinted and watched, sitting together in silence.

Fletch took off his suit coat and folded up his sleeves, but he kept his hat on. He was in a good mood. "I wish," he said, "we had some swimming suits, because I'd sure like to teach her how to swim."

"The breaststroke?" I asked, and Fletch rolled over on the sand with delight, the funniest thing he'd heard in years.

I said, "Let's flip for who gets the old one." He got out his coin purse that was bulging with the treasure from the busted coin bank and found his Indian head. Fletch checked the date on every coin that went through his hands.

The Indian head fell on the sand between us. Fletch won the old dame. I tried to shove him to his feet and start him toward her, but Fletch rolled away, delighted by the idea though. I grabbed the nickel and Fletch grabbed my wrist. I let the nickel drop. He was strong.

We took off our shirts and lay back on the sand, chests up. Fletch had tilted his hat over his eyes. The brim was stained with sweat. He was almost bald, and he wore his hat indoors and outdoors, summer and winter.

The girl and the older woman moved down the shore. They were wading in water around their ankles, carrying their clothes. We watched until they left the water and went up a path between the dunes and out of sight.

The afternoon was over and we drove back to Petoskey, had a hamburger, then walked the street looking for a liquor store. We came to a drugstore and Fletch stopped and began to look over the postcards. I looked them over myself briefly and walked on, but he stayed behind. I went back.

He stood, turning the card rack. "I want to find one for Norma."

When he had the card he wanted, he went inside to the counter and started to write a message. He wrote it carefully, thinking it out line by line. I sat on the end stool of the fountain. "Fletch," I said, "you're crazy. We're driving back tonight. She'll get the goddamn card next week while you're at work."

But Fletch wrote his message and signed it. Then he stuck on a postage stamp. We went outside and, at the corner, dropped it into the mailbox. The lid went *clunk*.

The first bar we stopped in had a couple of girls sitting at a table. We took seats at the bar and ordered beer. We talked and from time to time prospected. One of the girls was tall and thin, the other was sunburned, her skin mottled where she was peeling. She seemed depressed and she was telling a long story to the skinny girl—or perhaps she'd been telling the story so long she'd grown tired. She rested her head in one hand. The other girl was lulled by her words, her eyes closed, her head bobbing from time to time. Once the listening girl smiled wanly, then opened her lips to laugh. The other smiled and opened her eyes to witness this moment of perfect understanding. They hadn't looked at us since we sat down.

When we finished the beer I said, "Let's go." Fletch looked surprised, but he got up and we went out to the street.

"We can do better," I said.

But we didn't do any better. We checked every roadhouse

between Petoskey and Harbor Springs. Nothing. Maybe it was too early. We checked the joints in Harbor Springs, but not even the dance hall on the pier had any girls to spare. So we headed back for Petoskey, where the girls we had seen earlier now had two guys with them. Meanwhile, the evening was about as interesting as a front porch after dinner. Fletch was already driven to the friendship of our car bottle.

"Hell," I said, "let's head home by way of Charlevoix. Maybe there's something doing along the way." Fletch just nodded. He'd stopped talking to me. He'd got sullen. I felt I'd let him down. At least I felt he felt I had.

Between Petoskey and Charlevoix we came to joints beside the road that had five or six cars parked out front—inside, nobody. Had the cars been parked there by the roadhouse owners as lures? Or were there five or ten single girls in the ladies' room? Waiting for us to leave?

Fletch's face was strained. Night had long ago descended, and Fletch drove with the lights of the cars coming toward us brightening and dimming his face; the face I saw in those passing lights was the face of someone enduring the night and life itself . . . and me. The cool air off Lake Michigan and the dunes blew in at our windows. The engine hummed us on eternally.

About twelve-thirty we stopped at a place in a small summer town. Over in one corner of a big plank-walled room, an electric guitar, an accordion and a violin were working. At least twenty people sat at half a dozen tables. There was a small dance floor. But no single girls. We took a table, ordered a pitcher of beer, drank and waited.

"A couple of girls could still come in," Fletch kept saying. I think he believed it too, and I know I tried to believe it. We kept digging into the change from the twenty and going to the can and watching the girls who got up to dance until the call came for last rounds. And that was that.

Pulling out of the parking lot behind another car, our headlights lit up the heads of a couple in the back seat, their lips locked, their eyes closed in rapture. The car ahead turned down a side road after a few miles, but the kiss never ended.

Fletch said, "There's something, Jack, I want to be sure you understand."

"Yeah."

Long pause. "I love Norma. I don't know what you've been thinking . . . but the fact I wanted to get laid tonight has nothing to do with what I feel about her."

"Sure, I know that," I said quickly enough.

He shook his head. "Naw. Everybody knows I knocked her up and then we got married. I could have got out of it, and I didn't want to. But things are rough now, Jack. I can't find a job I can stand. They're all dead ends. I've worked on construction, in gas stations, all for peanuts, for money to pay bills I can't catch up on. Sometimes there'll be months between jobs and I'm ready to take anything I can get. I got this job in a paper mill and there's these tiny paper fibers in the air all the time. I breathe them in and out of my lungs. You know what that can do to your lungs? I can't live this way. If I was trying to have some fun picking up a girl tonight, it's because I don't get much fun."

We drove south, following a highway that took us as close to the shore of Lake Michigan as we could get, but the lake was never easy to see. The moon was bright enough, but private land lay on our right, not water. A stretch of road came along where only a high dune lay between us and the lake. We pulled over and got out.

The moon was brilliant and I held my hands out to throw shadows on the sand. I looked at my hands. They were like

marble. I showed them to Fletch and he looked at his hands.
Then we took off our shoes and started climbing the hill. The
cold sand grains slid between my toes, and I sank in up to my
ankles. About halfway to the top we stopped. The radio in the
car was playing, but the car lights were out and the music
seemed to be coming from some place miles away, a fourteen-
piece dance band at a big summer pavilion. Fletch had brought
the bottle along and we each had a drink, looking toward the
crest, music behind us.

At the top the lake lay out front, but away and far below,
under the dome of night. The wind blew up the brim of
Fletch's felt hat and he put one hand on his head. There were
waves on the lake. We could hear them hit shore. Nothing
grew on the dunes except a little grass. "Looks cold," Fletch
said. There were no boats on the water, no cars on the highway
below, no lights of houses. "That's one cold lake," he said.

The wind chilled our guts. Even the stars were freezing us.
We stood squinting into the wind, looking out at the black
lake that stretched to the horizon: it could have been an ocean.

"Well . . ." he said.

"That's all," I said. As if we'd scaled Mount Everest.

We turned and started down, sliding a foot or so every step.

Then we drove without stopping through little towns lit by
streetlamps, where no one was out walking and only an occasional car kept us company. The dawn was breaking when we
drove into his yard. Fletch stopped by the barn so we could sit
a minute. We sat looking toward his house, where his roof was
beginning to brighten with a pale light.

We'd been talking about a night we'd taken our girls to
Grand Haven for a party on the beach, remembering how cold
the sand could get after the sun went down, even when you
and the girl had a blanket wrapped around you. If you and she
stayed by the fire, it was warm—but if you wanted privacy, the

two of you took your blanket back into the dunes and found a hollow to lie in. We'd had some good times we agreed. Fletch could play the guitar and he'd played for us. We had sung and drunk spiked ginger ale and eaten what the girls cooked and brought along. We'd tossed a football around and swum bare-assed and drove around fast enough to scare each other.

Fletch said after you get married, that fun ended; not just for him it ended, for everyone. "Don't get married too soon," he advised me. "I got married too soon." He shook his head. "What happens? Why does all that fun we used to have come to an end?"

I had my door open and was about to slide out when he said, "Have you got a buck you can spare?"

"Sure."

I had about eight dollars, all singles—and I counted off four.

"A buck, that's enough. I'll pay you back," he said. "Give me your address at your school. I'll send it to you."

"Oh, hell," I said, "it's just loot." I gave him the eight bucks. "Keep it."

"No," he said, but he took it, and I knew just how he felt, his mixed feelings. I'd had them with my uncle. "I'll send this to you," he promised.

We both got out of the car and shook hands. The windows of his house were dark, the grass around our feet steely bright in the morning light. "See you," I said. Young bucks parting.

I cut across his front yard and took the gravel road home.

Fletch and Norma kept having children until they had four-teen. He never got out of debt or found a job he liked. By that time, Norma later told me, Fletch was a hopeless drunk and all she wanted was out, so she left him seven boys and went away with seven girls and she got a divorce. Very soon, because she was still a good-looking girl, she found a man who wanted her, children and all. Fletch tried hiring a housekeeper to care for the kids while he was at work, but he couldn't make enough money to take care of the kids and the housekeeper, too, so he went on welfare and raised the boys himself. He also joined a church and finally quit drinking. He told a couple of his closest friends he hoped Norma might come back to him. Then he had a couple of heart attacks. He wouldn't go to a doctor and spend money he needed for the kids. One day he dropped dead and all the boys moved in with their mother.

I think of Fletch's question a lot. You're young, having a good time, everything's in control. Then you're married and it's all gone.

What happened to Janice and me?

What happens, Fletch? I don't know what happens.

Janice would say we just couldn't shape up.

August 27th. A week before my scheduled operation—

Monday it was—with Gail expecting me for dinner—

Paul Johnson came out of the West and brought along both his kids in his Bronco. His wife had been killed in an auto accident and he was roving around looking for solace. He had stopped at his mother's house in Detroit, at his mother-in-law's house in Cleveland, and sent us a card from a friend's house in Albany saying he'd soon arrive in our parking lot.

Paul was someone I knew in college and now that I think of it, the oldest friend living I have. I was really glad to see him. Neither of us ever had any ambition higher than our writing. A lot I felt and believed about writing I'd learned from him. He wrote a complex prose style. The mere reading of it left me giddy, as if I'd been staring steadily through a magnifying glass at a Christmas tree ten yards away. I was far from being the only one of his readers convinced of his genius. Around campus anyone who cared about writing considered him with awe: a budding Proust. In addition, he was as tall as Thomas Wolfe, as hard as Hemingway, as wild as Saroyan. He was tense and sure of himself . . . an exciting and stimulating guy to be around. I don't think any of us were wrong about his potential or stature. Two publishers had him under contract for a novel, and not the same novel. Both publishers thought if they could bring him into print, it would be the literary event of the year. But Paul's response to their pleas to shorten and clarify his work was outrage. His revisions would come back longer and more obscure. He could not shorten and clarify.

That refusal to compromise extended throughout his life, and that integrity plus the seething passions, the joys, the rages, the sorrows also made him a prickly guy to be around. He did not save it all for his work. Sometimes a garage mechanic, a passing car, a stray dog, a loose bolt got the full exposure. I enjoyed him, but I watched my step. He scared Janice. She thought he was a moral idiot, a liar, and a petty thief. Worst of all, he refused to find a job. But she liked him.

Everyone works. Paul had a corner in his house where he filed clippings, wrote extensive notes, and elaborated the outline of an immense book he had been working on for years. The outline alone ran something like 1,200 pages. Now and then he'd send me a piece, a scene from some kind of catacomb life under the streets of New York, or another scene about an encampment of feebs and idiots somewhere in the desert of the Southwest.

Understanding Paul's life was like trying to understand his writing. The understanding depended on an interpretation of overlapping events, times, places, intentions, inferences. There was usually something out of focus to my simple eyes. I could ask questions to help me with my interpretations, but it took effort to reach the genuine perspective, or truth.

With Paul's arrival I anticipated focus, a reduction of impressions and expectations and blurred meanings, if not a clarification, a simplification of Sally's death. And that sort of understanding, I suppose, belongs with art and nothing else. It's not life. The simplification of ourselves, the people around us and the events that happen to us is the art of life.

After Paul arrived, we took the tire off the top of the Bronco and carried it upstairs to store it on the balcony, where it wouldn't get stolen.

He had this yellow western shirt on for dinner, had ironed it himself in the study, pearl buttoned cuffs and pockets, a shirt that Sally must have bought for him. He was dark and lean and grim. His hair was still cut short, a close gray brush cut; but he'd said that since Sally's death, he'd had his first "store-bought" haircut in years. He wore faded blue jeans and high boots with leather laces. He now ironed all the children's clothes as well as his own.

"Why, Paul, where did you learn?" Janice said.

"I had to go back," Paul said, "to the time I watched my mother ironing. I didn't, you know, pay any attention then. I had to remember it and watch it again, closely this time. It came to me. It came to me."

It was appalling, he said, how much he'd taken for granted what Sally did. "There was never any whining or complaining from her, and she got so much done. She had a heavy load." He wasn't, he said, getting much writing done any more. There was no more leisure time.

After dinner, out on the balcony, sitting with Paul, just the two of us, he said his main problem was loneliness. "You can't imagine what a gap Sally left behind her. It's incredible. I miss simply having someone around to talk to." He leaned forward, a thrust to his head, pressing his hands together. "I've learned this—I can't live without a woman."

I asked him if he had another woman in mind, if there were any around him at the moment. There were several, he said. Who was in the lead? Still leaning forward, looking forward, he said without hesitation but in a lower, quieter voice, "Ann." His head nodded slightly.

But there were problems. He seemed to have seen enough of her to know life would not be the way it was with Sally. She'd put more demands on him, on his attention, on his personal time—he wasn't specific, but he wasn't ready to give up that much. His resistance had been stated quietly and with genuine sadness, even gentleness. This was not the old aggressively implacable Paul.

"She has her own problem with loneliness," Paul said.

"Do the kids like her?"

He nodded. No problem there.

She was twenty-eight years old. Paul looked late forties. I gathered one of their problems was Paul had no job and he still wasn't about to get one . . . of any kind. "Oh, I might," he said, "get a part-time job in the afternoon while the kids are at school, but to hell with this full-time job and baby-sitters for the kids in the afternoon, and then the cooking besides. No, I don't want any part of that."

He owned his house and some property, and he'd had his first checks from Social Security for the kids. He spoke of renting his place and taking the kids to Mexico. Mexico had been Paul's goal for twenty years. Although Mexico, for gringos, had been transforming itself from a cheap, primitive land replete with colorful mystery into an expensive Disneyland, Mexico still drew him, powerfully. His kids, two well-mannered or at least restrained girls, were bright. They could even miss a year of school, he said. He could tutor them himself. He and a writer friend in Denver were planning an excursion into Mexico to look the situation over. He'd leave his girls with his friend's wife, then they would have everyone come down if they could find a house to share at the right price in the right place.

Paul was amazed I was still having trouble with my voice. How long had I been having this now—two, three years? He had his own theory about my problem. "Quit teaching and get out of New York," his blunt advice. "Your body is sending you messages. You ought to listen. Come to Mexico."

"No," I said, "I'm going to Samarkand."

"Samarkand?"

"That is, I think I'm going to Samarkand."

He saw I was serious. "Why Samarkand?"

I told him about Fletch. "I've been thinking about Samarkand for some time now. I believe the imagination needs a nourishment of its own . . . we ought to pay attention to it."

He nodded, listening intently.

"I just want to go, that's all, make a big beautiful gesture . . . the gesture itself a poem."

Paul slammed his fist against his leg and came an inch out of his chair, "Do it."

"It's not all that easy."

Over on the elevated section of track beyond our buildings a graffiti-covered subway train rumbled slowly by. He pointed at it and said slowly, "All you have to do is get on board."

On Saturday afternoon we all drove out to Larson's digs on Long Island. Larson was one of my former students, a tall lean man with a gruff manner who liked living alone with a couple of Malamute dogs. His home was the pump house on an old estate. He had fenced it in so his dogs had roaming space. I thought Paul would like him because Larson also refused all forms of traditional employment. He made his living in a way Paul could only envy. Larson played the horses and had been living off what he made at the track for several years.

Saturday was an overcast day and Larson was worried his barbecue was going to be rained out. We'd arrived late and even so there were only two couples ahead of us. We joined them, vacant chairs all about on the lawn beside his house. Larson went around glaring at the sky, on thoroughly bad terms with the overcast.

Paul's kids were good. They sat side by side in chairs, silent, observing. Or they wandered around the yard, occasionally whispering to one another. Larson told them how to get down to the shore of the bay and off they went—and after a while came back, excited, showing us mussel shells.

Just before dusk another couple, who had two children, arrived. All four kids, strangers and shy with one another at first, were transformed at some moment we were hardly aware of into friends and playmates. We sat on plastic webbed lawn chairs, looking off into woods and green leaves where an old weedgreen road, unused for years, ran past the woods and turned in among the trees. A touring car with a tattered roof and rusting hood was parked off the road down near the turn. Larson said it had been parked there for a couple of decades.

On Sunday we drove down to the bottom of Manhattan and onto the Staten Island Ferry. Paul and Sally had taken the ferry ride on their first date . . . so Paul wanted to take that ride again. He didn't tell the kids what it meant to him.

I told him Andre had been in town and had made the making of millions sound easy. Paul said he was glad to hear it, and I think he was, but we couldn't think of anything else to say for half the ride.

Paul had been another of the writers Andre hadn't been able to get published before he gave up being a literary agent. Paul used to console Andre and tell him not to get discouraged, because to Paul everything was fate. Paul never sent any of his work to publishers and no longer had an agent. Once when I'd asked him how he thought he'd ever get published, he said in effect, what will be will be.

From Staten Island we drove into New Jersey by the Bayonne Bridge and, swinging back toward New York, stopped in Hoboken at the Clam Broth House. Paul and I went into its old waterfront bar and ordered a quart of clam broth and some sandwiches. It was tradition for the men at the bar to throw clam and mussel shells in the sawdust on the floor when they finished eating. The shells lay everywhere around our feet. Paul liked the place.

Then we drove to the little park in Weehawken above the Hudson River where the lights of Manhattan across the way lay shimmering on the water. Below us Alexander Hamilton and Aaron Burr had dueled at the foot of the cliffs. Paul said, coloring history, "Hamilton shot first and missed. Then Burr lit up a cigar, took careful aim, and shot Hamilton dead."

We didn't notice there'd been an accident up the street—a car had hit a lamppost, knocked it over; the cops were still around, but the crowd had gone. The car was a wreck, a shell. Glass all over the street. Volkswagen glass. We were thinking of the Volkswagen Sally and Jenny were in when a car came over the crest of a hill and sideswiped them. There hadn't been enough of the car left to salvage, not even the baggage rack on the roof—and there wasn't a lot left of this one either.

The park wasn't much of a spot for a picnic, but you bear up, as the saying goes. We sat on stone benches, ate our sandwiches and drank our clam broth. We gazed over at Manhattan, that beautiful island. I thought of Gail. Far down the river, haze-blurred, the lights of the Verrazano Bridge.

Paul's tenderness for the memory of Sally did not seem strange—although I could not remember their getting along at all well. They'd fought most of the time and she was constantly on the point of taking the kids and leaving him. Yet he missed her. He was grieving. And I was transferring the vague grief I felt from Sally to Gail—knowing one of these days I'd lose her, already suffering. These little affairs on the side seldom end well. When we left the park, the cops and the smashed car up the street were gone.

Sally's death had shaken Paul. He was gentle and considerate to the kids. Around the apartment he was helping, volunteering all he could. Paul had even washed the dishes after dinner on his first night with us: I came in from the balcony and there he was at the sink.

The kids slept in the study. Paul slept on the davenport, reading and falling asleep each night with the light burning, the light still burning each morning when Janice got up and went into the kitchen to start breakfast. He had hay fever and Kleenex lay wadded and scattered around on the rug. Our liquor supply got steadily lower. Janice took it all pretty well, for Janice.

I had to check into the hospital on Monday and Paul wanted to be on his way again. That morning, when Janice left for duty after breakfast, she clutched each of the girls and gave Paul a good-by kiss.

Paul and I carried the spare tire from the balcony down to the parking lot and tied it to the rack on top of his Bronco. Then we brought down the girls' red luggage that once was Sally's.

A lost cat was running around under the cars in the lot, someone's pet. There was a collar around its neck. I'd seen a couple of kids with a worried cat a day or so ago. The same one? I thought it would either starve or get run over—and I wished I could do something, the way I imagine everyone does, but doesn't do anything. Paul could have put the cat in the Bronco and taken it West, or I could have carried it upstairs and had us another animal; but we didn't do more than glance at it.

The sky looked like rain and they were heading for the Pennsylvania Turnpike, no tarpaulin over their luggage. Coming East from Seattle, Paul said they hadn't used a motel once. He liked to drive steadily through the night, through day, through rain—non-stop through everything. He strapped the luggage down: "I'm just going to assume it's not going to rain."

He shook my hand good-by with a sustained firm grip, "Samarkand if you can . . . Mexico if you can't."

About six o'clock in the morning, the nurse came in and stuck me with a hypodermic needle. It burned. It smarted. She went away. Gray light at the window, light that fell on the curtain between my bed and the bed by the window. The needle in the ass, I thought, is always the worst of it; the worst was over.

I tried to go back to sleep, but couldn't. The mattress was hard, and under my white sheet was slippery plastic. Breakfast came for the man in the other bed. None for me.

I heard the surgical cart clattering down the hall. It came in the door: my carriage. I took off my glasses and eased over on the wheeled cot. My chauffeur took me out of the room and down the hall. I watched the ceiling slide by, heard rustling, heard heel sounds, heard a murmuring. I felt tranquil, not at all doped. It never seemed to me the shot I got had much effect.

We rode up on the elevator and I watched the ceiling of another floor slide by. The operating room wasn't ready for me yet, so I got pushed into a big closet. On the shelves beside me were tanks of gas.

In a while Baker, my doctor, came in. He had on a green gown and a green cap. He said we'd be ready in another ten minutes. He went away. Another doctor, gowned, came in. He introduced himself. He would deliver my anesthesia. The anesthetists always introduced themselves. It was a different man each time, as if something kept happening to their jobs.

Then my doctor came back, and the three of us waited. My doctor looked alert, poised. He always did, even when I saw him on an office visit. In my blurred vision he waited now like a highly conditioned athlete on an Olympic track-and-field team—a man in a state of relaxed tension.

I made a joke about the main event. They smiled. I was feeling nice and loose, just a bit impatient.

Then across the hall and into the operating room we went. I moved over on the table with the straps, and the straps went around me. My left arm went out on the little ledge and got taped down. When the needle went into my arm, I started to count. I counted backwards from ten, but I didn't get far; I never got far.

That needle had gone into my arm nine times in the last four years. No, there was that office procedure when Dr. Flint removed a node using a local. Eight times then. Often enough so I wondered if I wasn't getting to like the sensation of going under. It was a trip.

This time, when I came out of the trip into and back from oblivion, my teeth were chattering and my body was shaking. I couldn't move. I couldn't stretch out a finger. I was paralyzed with drugs, half saturated with chemical coma. The bars of a bed were up, bars on each side of me. I tried to move my arms. Someone was yelling my name into my ear. I blinked. The nurse went away. I tried to speak. Something was wrong. I couldn't get a voice out. I didn't think the cords were gone, but they weren't working. I tried again and got out a tiny rasp, then I sank away from the room and bed and surfaced again with Dr. Baker beside me, leaning over the bars: green shape, eyes behind glasses, a Chaldean figure. I managed a little voice to show him I could make a faint raspy sound. He went away. My head got somewhat clearer. The nurse came back and threw a couple of blankets over me. I was getting something from a tube and bottle. The tube was in my arm. Postoperative shock? My teeth were chattering. I sank away and woke wheeling down a long hallway, took that as a good sign, slept, woke again in my room. What was it I'd heard Baker say in the recovery room? That this would be the last time he operated? This time should have done it, he'd said, but if it hadn't, and he didn't sound sure it had, he'd have to try something else.

I usually spent one night in the hospital: one day and one night. I arranged, every time, to check into the hospital in the afternoon, then got a pass to go out for dinner. That way I taught my last evening class of the week and Janice drove me back to the hospital. I'd have the operation the next morning. After all the other operations I'd always felt good by lunchtime, ready to check out. But this time Baker had reserved the room for two nights. When my lunch came, I didn't want to eat or even sit up. It was the first time I'd felt any pain after an operation, and it was the first time the operation hadn't improved my voice. I'd never got my old voice back, but I always got some of it back, got a voice back that was at least usable for a while.

Later I sat up and tried to eat my lunch, but my throat hurt when I swallowed. The whole throat was raw. It felt as if he'd stretched his head and shoulders down it. I guess he thought if it was to be his last chance at the cords, his last shot at scraping them, plucking them clean, he wanted to do a good job.

Rigmarole. It's all rigmarole. I'd reached the point where I was going through the motions, doing what I was told, listening seriously, that is, to what I was told, but I didn't believe any of it. I was in a state of calm most of the time. I would marvel at how my body stood it all. Life is serious, but it's a game all the same. One doctor says: Stand on your head every day for twenty minutes. Well, why not? Another says: Drink a glass of salt water while you gaze at the moon. Well, why not? An old woman says: This is holy earth; rub it on your throat. And why not? What difference did any of it make to me?

What I had was inscrutable.

Back home again—

"Guilty as charged," I said.

"What did you say?"

"I was talking to the cat."

"Why? Why do you say something like that to a cat?"

"What else do you say to a cat? It's what he's been waiting to hear. He's glad to get the news. He's glad to get news about anything."

I thought my voice sounded worse. Both Janice and my daughter did too. It usually sounded better after an operation, but not this time. At least I could still speak.

The cat was giving me his nothing look.

Twice a week, every Tuesday and Thursday morning, rain or shine, in sickness and in health, I took my trip to Newman's office. I scheduled those appointments early so they didn't break up my day. I'd leave our apartment at eight o'clock, walk to the subway, climb the steps to the elevated platform and catch the downtown local. At Fifty-ninth I'd change to the IND and at Seventh Avenue I'd grab the E train to the East Side. On Lexington Avenue I'd follow the sidewalk down to Fiftieth Street, then cut east until I came to First Avenue. A long trek. That's where Newman and his wife lived and where he saw his patients in a long narrow leafy room with a threadbare orange couch, a careworn pallet of a couch that sometimes had a blanket on it and sometimes didn't; and there was that big plant at the head of the couch shading window light for his patients, crouching over me, my pinwheeling thoughts rising bucket by bucket from the muck of my past, my mind a virtual mud-filled old cenote full of ancient relics, the bones of sacrificed virgin things, the nose of an old idol, a bracelet of gold, a dagger with a blade of jade, little bells.

It took me an hour to get there. He came to the door, a short, wide man getting wider every day. Nothing fit him, nothing ever had. He had an energy that was going to explode. I sometimes thought of how it would happen. BAM: pieces of rubber inner tube and balloon rubber and Styrofoam and splinters of steel and copper wires all over the walls and floor. When I lay on the couch and talked, I had a sense of the silence that was listening to me, constantly swelling with what I said—that noise of his shuffling and slapping cards, a kind of feeding sound. What all of us patients fed him was our restive agitation that he fed back to us as healing rays. If only we lay there long enough and fed the appetite beyond the green plant's leaves, we would be strong and mean again—like him. Ready to take on anybody, anything. That's what I wanted. Then I'd be ready for Samarkand.

But it wasn't easy. I'd long ago exhausted everything in my past, in my childhood in particular, not only with Newman but with half a dozen other psychiatrists or psychiatrist types over the past fifteen years. I wanted to find someone who could help me realize my potential—that is to say, get me published again. What was the matter with me? I had skipped in and out of clinics that kept the rates down to something I could afford—and kept me in the hands of novices all the way. I never knew if they were good or bad. How can a patient tell? The doctor says so little.

It's hard to measure silence.

With some I thought I'd improved; that is, I'd learned a little patience. I didn't blow my top as much any more. I wasn't as jittery around authority figures. I was still working, holding down a job. So I wasn't a hopeless case. But with some of the professional listeners I'd made more progress than I had with others. Some I'd made no progress with whatsoever —and I was beginning to think Newman was one of them. On the other hand, maybe I was as cured as I was ever going to be.

Not that I understood everything about myself. Far from it. Why did the football on Gail's grand piano bug me? I brought that up now with Newman. He was at least a close listener. Sure, he had personal problems. He was a congenitally angry man. He fought a lot with his wife, I knew that. He rarely said a complimentary thing about anyone when occasionally we discussed public figures, politicians, artists, actors, TV repairmen, and the like. When I told him about the people who were giving me a hard time, mostly at Metro, he sprayed his hostility on them with little cyanide sentences. Talking to Newman was like hanging around a mean older brother. He played solitaire and listened and shuffled cards. I know the card playing was supposed to mean something parabolic and profound. He was crafty, full of subtleties.

One day, years ago now, sitting up, session over, I said something about the plant at the head of the couch to Newman. He had stood up by then and was putting away his deck of cards.

"It's a dieffenbachia," he'd said.

I put on my jacket, staring at it. It had green leaves, long and fairly wide, more like blades than leaves. "It's also called," he said, "the mother-in-law plant."

"Why?"

"If you chew on one of its leaves, it's supposed to paralyze your vocal cords." He saw I was staring at the plant, very curious now, and he said, "Try it."

It is very hard for me to resist a dare.

He said, "Break off a piece and chew it."

I did. At once. Not a big piece; a small piece about the size of my thumbnail. I sank my molars into it, lightly, bit it a couple of times. It felt cool, tough, slightly sour and acrid. At that point I spit it out and stared at it in the palm of my hand. I heard Newman laugh. I tossed the piece on the earth beside the plant, wiped my hand, and we both knew there were limits to how far I'd go on a dare—if that was what he was trying to learn. I never knew.

I saw Newman again on Thursday, and the following Monday, when I told Dr. Baker about the episode with the dieffenbachia I'd all but forgotten, he was thoughtful. "Why," he said, "did he have you do that?"

"I don't know. He raises a lot of plants. His office is all hothouse at one end. Have you ever heard that story about the dieffenbachia? That it can paralyze the vocal cords?"

Baker shook his head. "Never."

"Nobody else I know has either."

Baker looked stern. "You should ask him why he did that. Why would he do something like that with you? You're too suggestible."

"Then you think this trouble with my cords could be psychological?"

"At the beginning, perhaps. But not now. You have polyps on your cords and they're spreading. This time I think I got them all. But I want you to rest your voice as much as you can. Keep it low and don't talk when you start to get tense. Watch tension. Use your amplifier in class. Are you using that amplifier?"

"I'm going to."

"And don't lecture. That is, don't go on talking to your students for five or ten minutes at a time."

"I don't do much of that anyway. These are seminars, and the students do most of the talking."

"I know, so you've told me. How many operations have you had?"

As he glanced at my records, I said, "Nine."

"Nine," he said, and stared hard at those papers.

"Yeah, nine."

"If the polyps return, we'll have to try another procedure."

"X-ray?"

He shook his head. "No. X-ray therapy does not work on the cords. I can tell you that from experience. The treatments would ruin your voice completely."

"Then what else?"

"There are a couple of procedures that have been experimental for a long time that I now have more confidence in. One is freezing the cords; the other is transplanting the epidermal layer of the cords."

I must have looked alarmed. He glanced at his nurse. They took a long look at one another, then he said, "You might as well know there's been a cell change. But there's nothing to be alarmed about. There are three kinds of cells. Cell A is a healthy cell. Cell C is cancer. Cell B is something in between. That's what you've picked up, we think, some of the B cells. Our pathologist isn't sure what they are. Anyway, I've sent the slides off for another opinion." He glanced at his nurse again. She looked away.

"How long will that take?"

Baker shrugged. He was frowning hard.

"I would guess then, if I'm to spare my voice, talking endlessly on the analyst's couch about my problems isn't exactly the best thing I could do."

"No," said Baker, "it isn't. Talking while you're tense is bad."

"No tensions?"

"No tensions."

"Okay."

When I got back to the waiting room, Gail was sitting in one of the easy chairs. She'd said she might be there, but I hadn't let myself count on it. With Gail, everything was might and maybe. She didn't like being pinned down, but her maybe was as good as I will. We went downstairs to the street and walked around, wondering where to go. She had the afternoon free and though there were a couple of things I had to do, I forgot about them.

Baker's office was in the east Seventies. We walked toward Central Park and the Metropolitan Museum, the sun of a summer's end slanting the air around wrought iron railings, the pale lids of trash cans, and gray buildings with high windows. She took my hand as we walked along, something I always liked although I was too big for all that. I'd never had another girl who'd take my hand. Sometimes she'd just hold onto a couple of fingers.

"Well, what did Baker tell you?"

"He says I should be okay now, but my voice is never going to be much better than it is . . ." Then I said no more about Baker. It was too hard to talk on the street with the horn sounds and drumming motors around us.

At Seventy-ninth Street we cut into the park and headed for the slope of a hill, dogs all around us. At least twenty people were out with their dogs. I admired their guttural barks and wished I could make one. A basset hound trotted beside us, morose faced.

Gail asked a man in shorts, wearing sandals, "What are you having—a dog show?"

"No. This is dog hill."

We walked over the crest of the hill and down a walk, still holding hands. "The hill belongs to the dogs?" she said.

"As the streets belong to the people."

"That's wonderful," she said. "That's one of the nicest things I've blundered onto. Do you suppose there are other hills like that, I mean hills for cats and turtles and gerbils and all those pets we keep locked up in rooms and cages?"

"A hill for turtles and another for gerbils?"

"Why not?" she said. "There are bars where writers go."

"And teachers have their faculty clubs where they drink their faculty drinks and think their faculty thoughts and cross and recross their faculty legs and blow their faculty minds."

"That's right. And newspapermen, their press clubs."

"And senators, their cloakrooms."

"And priests, their priesteries."

"There's no end to each kind seeking out his own."

"No. No end," she said.

When we got as far as the boathouse on the lake, we bought a couple of soft ice cream cones and found a rock to sit on.

"That woman I saw plucks her eyebrows. They were narrow and arched and her eyes were narrow. Did you ever find out," she said, "if that was your wife?"

"No. I never asked her. And she hasn't said anything."

"Doesn't it bother you?"

"No more than a dozen other disasters."

"It bothers me. She looks as if she could be mean. Is she?"

"Mean?"

"She looked like a four-lane highway to Hell. Does she carry a stiletto?"

I laughed. "That sounds like her. But I doubt if it was. Janice has Sicilian ancestors. She's got vendetta in her blood, but that's on her father's side. On her mother's side, she's German."

"A methodic killer."

"Well, if she killed anyone, it would be me, and if she was ever going to kill me she'd have done it years ago. When we split up and got divorced, there was another woman involved. She left me pretty much unharmed."

"She kept you from visiting your little girl."

"I didn't say she doesn't get mad."

"What else did she do?"

It all came back to me, but I said nothing. I said nothing.

"Well, I'll tell you this, Jack, if it was, if she was your wife, she has a hard jaw. She's never going to let you go. I mean—in case that's what you're waiting for. Her blessing as you set off."

"Ah, Gail, I don't know what I want. I never know what I want until someone tells me I can't have it. But why would she want me? I'm not even sure what you see in me."

"That's easy. You're a dreamer's dreamer."

"What's the appeal in that?"

"You're a dreamer's dreamer. There are actors' actors and writers' writers and swimmers' swimmers. Just the way Lotte Lehmann is a singers' singer, you're a dreamer's dreamer. You draw dreamers from everywhere, all of us run-of-the-mill dreamers, just to watch you dream. But what do you see in me?"

"You're pretty and cute."

"I want to be something more than pretty and cute."

"You're fun to be with. I miss you, you know, when I'm not with you. I think about you."

She squeezed my hand. "Do you?"

"Oh sure. And when I'm with you, a part of myself that's been buried for a long, long time seems liberated. I'm not at all sure what love is, but I think it has a lot to do with feeling liberated. It gives lovers, I imagine, a certain proprietary feeling about one another. That other part of my life"—I paused—"is a closed system. Nothing is going to develop there unless I publish another book. With you, my options are open. With us, anything could develop."

She was waiting for more.

"What I think is so great about you," I said, "is how you've managed not to be trapped. All your options are open everywhere. That's the way we all ought to live."

"Then why don't you?"

"I don't know."

"Jack, why did you go back to your wife? Why did you marry her again?"

II

Survival

October—

My throat crumbled a little more. Its ragged edges clawed the wind of my words. It was hard to get enough air under what I said to finish a long sentence. When I spoke, I spoke slowly, reminding myself not to speak for long and not to raise my voice too much, to give my cords a chance to heal. Another operation could do my voice in. I carried my amplifier back and forth to class. In class I spoke softly into the mike I carried in one hand. I tried to take care of myself, to stretch myself out, but even so, about three weeks into the new semester, I started telling my Thursday night class about Samarkand, preparing them for my departure—or dreaming?

Budar said she thought I was going to be disappointed if I expected to find old Persia on my way, old Persia's mud huts, the old Persian people. She's from Teheran, and recently.

Her hair is black and straight. A brownish tinge in her eyes keeps them from being as black as her hair. Those dark eyes, round and direct, are steadily receiving, receiving, tabulating. She sits very straight at our long conference table. When someone is reading a story aloud, her eyes move, watching all our faces, tabulating our listening; I can't even guess what goes on in her Iranian mind. What I know about her I've had to find in what she writes; until her last story came in, it was hard to find her in her work, hard to say what she was like—but in that story she seemed real and complex, responsive. She was more honest than she'd been at any time before, more open.

Budar's beginning to trust us. Budar's emerging. In our last conference she'd said she was afraid of being as truthful as she could because she was afraid if she let herself go far enough to say everything, to hold nothing back, she'd lose her mind. I recalled another student who knew Budar well saying she'd had a difficult life. But the Teheran experience was far behind her now, far enough so that she was beginning to write about it: the girls' school, her childhood companions, their talk, mostly talk about boys and her eagerness for passion. I still didn't get much sense of street life in her work, although once, from her story's window, I saw a man publicly whipped, once I passed through a marketplace and heard a merchant crying his wares. After that story had been read, I said, "Budar, what happened to Persia?"

She leaned forward, her round eyes getting a little, just a little larger, saying, "Persia?"—almost thrown by the question. "Persia? It is Iran now. Since 1935." Her lips moved carefully to enunciate each sound, each word getting the same emphasis. "It is not Persia anymore."

"But what's happened to Persia?"

She was sensibly trying to answer a crazy question asked in all earnestness. "It is gone."

Borrowing from what another student at the table had told me, I said, "But don't the Iranians call their written language Persian?"

She nodded.

"So then Persia isn't entirely gone."

And then she spoke of her country, now calling Iran Persia, and I could see that Persia was still there, still in the heads of all those Iranians.

And the next week, when I came to class, I found myself talking on and on about Samarkand. Microphone to my lips, I spoke softly and slowly and they listened.

Someone else in the class, an American boy, had lived for a while in Iran, working for the Peace Corps. The next Thursday night, when he came to class, I saw he was carrying a large heavy book, and when class was over, while everyone was getting up and putting on jackets to leave, he leaned forward from the other side of the table and turned the opened book around to show me a photograph. It was a color plate of an oriental rug. Didn't it look, he said, like the one the class had seen in my study at the party last spring? I agreed. Yes, they did look alike. Yes, perhaps the rug came from Iran.

I was fitting my tape recorder and mike into a blue flight bag. He and one other student had stayed behind. Art, the other student, was a young published poet who had recently kicked a heroin habit—and that's what he wrote about: nights of skag and horror. Parson wrote about Iran. He couldn't wait to get back there. We brought our hopes and nightmares into class, all of us.

The rug, Parson was saying, came from a very small town, a town too small for most maps to bother about but there it was on Parson's map, up in a corner of old Persia by the Caspian Sea—along the very route I wanted to take to Samarkand.

I said, wheezing, "That's all mountainous country in there, isn't it?"

He nodded. "Very." His eyes squinted and he drew his head back. A sudden vision of that remote world was blinding him. He turned a few pages and stopped at another map. His fingertip tapped the right then the left side of the map: one tap up by the Turkman Republic, or maybe it was Afghanistan, the other tap over in the west.

"Here and here," he said, "were the passes the invading armies used when they attacked Europe." His finger tapped again in the area just to the east of the Caspian Sea. "The people here have an oriental cast."

I heard Art say earnestly, across my shoulder, "Isn't it dangerous . . . traveling through that countryside?" He was an ex-college football player, a lineman, and it seemed strange to me he worried about danger.

Parson thought about the question. He thought about the question so long I answered for him. I said, "No." But I wasn't sure. Would it be? I got worried. Could there be any place on earth more dangerous than New York City?

"A few years ago," Parson said, "it would have been . . . everything is changing, all over the world."

—Damn, I had to get there soon.

In among the photographs of Persian rugs were a couple of shots of village streets. The houses were made of mud.

I got excited. "Do the towns look like this?"

"Yes. The towns are very picturesque."

"Why," said Art, "do you want to go to Samarkand?"

Should I explain about Fletch and his farm and the magic lantern, the whole bit? No, it was too much. All that. "I'm curious. It's another reality. I like other realities."

Parson nodded. Then Art nodded too, the two of them nodding me on my way.

I put on my suit coat, took my flight bag with the tape recorder by its handle, and we went out of the room and up the stairs, out of the building into the night air.

I croaked my good-night to Parson and Art at the subway kiosk. Downward they went, side by side, sinking from my sight between walls scrawled with the names of all our inarticulate, frustrated child poets who sum up their short lives in their nicknames and the numbers of the streets where they live; down between those livid letters and swirls and strokes Parson and Art went—into the underworld of the Great God Damn.

I walked on home, taking my nightly chances on assault and robbery. Oh, it's not that bad. I think the papers overdo the muggings, but the streets are too dangerous, for a lot of reasons. I used to think New Yorkers went insane, many of them, as soon as they got below street level to a subway platform or train, because that's where I'd see most of the mad ranters and shouters. Sometimes it was a well-dressed guy with a brief case giving us all hell as he hung from his strap, a man who, I thought, probably regained his senses as he reached the street. But now the nuttiness had spread all over town and got ugly. Nuttiness hung over us all like an enduring smog.

I walked by the curb's edge, still feeling good from class. Usually I leave a class with a feeling of euphoria—as if I'm not such a fool after all. It would be very hard for me to give up teaching; I really don't know if I could.

At ten o'clock at night there were still students and faculty and staff people out on the streets walking around; a couple of blocks from the college the sidewalks got a little darker and there were fewer people in sight.

The light was against me at the corner, but I didn't wait. Targets should keep moving. I crossed the street and saw I was alone. Six blocks to go. Nobody could hear me so I began the vocal exercises: ma, may, me, my, mo, moo . . . stressing the vowels, holding the vowel sound, breath coming up evenly, steadily from down deep, nothing wasted, and it passed my teeth packed with all the sound I could give it. I intoned: "And this is the way the world ends, and this is the way the world ends, and this is the way the world ends, not with a bang, but a whimper," trying to get through all of it without taking another breath, but I couldn't quite make it. I was developing the lungs of a pearl diver, but my cords weren't happy. "And this is the way the world ends, and this is the way the [breath] world ends, and this is the way the world [breath] ends . . ." Someone was coming toward me. I quit talking, but he'd heard me, because he had an apprehensive look; when I glanced over my shoulder, he had turned his head to stare at me. I tried a sustained hum, pitching it up into my nose and making my lips vibrate. By now I was probably a neighborhood character.

Over to my right across the street, teen-agers were spaced around on the unlighted terraces of our neighborhood school —standing in a lovely tableau, artfully arranged, people in some dream—no, more as if the lights of a mansion and patio had gone out on a staged party. They drank cans of beer or soda pop; they chatted together, girls and boys, thirty of them at least. Where the streetlight dimly hit the side of the school I could see the same spray can art that decorated the subway platforms and subway cars and buses all over town: names, initials, street numbers. They covered the side of the school to the height of some six or seven feet and they covered the rocks on the slope between the school wall and the sidewalk. The school was new and it had several terraces, all of them desecrated, and still I looked forward to the nights the kids stood in the dim light, talking quietly, all of them relaxed, cool. They were as cool as the characters out of *Last Year at Marienbad*. I crossed the street to walk slowly past them, propinquity being all.

Two blocks beyond the school stands River View Gardens: seven twenty-story, cubelike brick towers looming in a U formation around a park with cement walks. It's all fenced in. We have our own guards. We're an island of safety, a middle-income co-op haven surrounded by student rooming houses, dormitories, college-controlled apartments with senile superintendents and broken mailboxes, slums, welfare food stamp spenders, whores, pimps, addicts, winos, old ladies with swollen ankles, retired ministers and professors, black faces, short Spanish women. Almost no one in the nearest ten-cent store speaks anything but Spanish and right beside River View Gardens, matching us for height, brick for brick, are low-income apartments.

I crossed the street at the high corner of our turf and ahead of me were the towers, the brick towers. Our peeling, mangy balconies gleamed dimly. We have a card table and chairs on our balcony; some balconies are enclosed; most stand open. Ours does.

Before we had blinds on our bedroom window, at the very beginning, when I lived there alone and the bed was the only piece of furniture I had, I'd wake in the morning and look out the window and across the balcony railing toward Broadway and think I was living in the canvas of a contemporary meta-physical painting. Beyond the balcony was the flat space of the next building, a billion cells of precise bricks around eighty pre-cise windows, and beyond that, taking up most of the picture, rose a giant. He was wide-shouldered and flat-chested, a narrow warrior, no neck at all. His head, a water tower on the roof, I suppose that's what it was, his helmeted head; behind him sky, cobalt blue. He was one of our neighboring low-income apart-ment houses, facing north, a sentinel's head—as if trouble, when it came, would come from that direction.

I'd got about halfway down our walk when one of our guards came past me from behind riding a motor scooter. I think our co-op cops have worked out a strategy of buzzing all of us as we come across the grounds at night just to show us they care.

The lights were on in our apartment. Janice would be home safe. She was followed home one night from the subway by two men that our guards intercepted.

A place like this exists only with a co-operative effort by all the tenants. Not only every building but every floor has a repre-sentative. We have a newsletter. There's a committee that plants flowers every spring. We have a workshop, a darkroom, a ceramics group. We hold regular meetings. The meetings are usually held on nights I'm teaching, so I seldom get to them. But they have my good will. I like this area of town. At Christmastime these buildings are canyons of colored lights. The poor people over in the city housing outdo us every year. On a December evening, as I walk home from class, Christmas cheer flashes and burns at the high banks of windows. *Love, love*, or something like that, the message in the cold and the night and the (sometimes) snow so overwhelms my senses I nearly melt around my bones with delight. I've seen the lights of Las Vegas but what we have here at Christmas beats them. Where else is there such a sight?

I once asked Sean if he put any decorations in his windows at Christmas. He said yes, that he put up lights that spelled H-E-L-P and they flashed on and off. I wonder if he made that up himself. He says great things. He says of people and their careers—we are attracted toward that which we cannot do. I'll come to Sean: he helps me get through the year.

Walking across the paved space in front of our building, I got out my keys. There are two front doors that seem part of an expanse of glass, the left door permanently locked and without knob or handle any more. I let myself in. One of our elevators was out of order again. They keep breaking down. I arose—homeward; heavenward?

Janice was in the living room sitting on the davenport, watching television. I said hello but she didn't answer. Didn't turn her head, just gave me her crooked smile. That meant trouble. I put down the flight bag and went into my study and looked at the rug, but I couldn't remember any more what the rug Parson had shown me looked like. When I walked back to the living room, Janice turned her head, that small, bitter smile on her lips. What was up? Had there been a call I didn't yet know about? She still hadn't said hello.

I was too tired to play. I went down the hall to my study to see if I had any messages. I threw the rewind switch. Vibrations came up through my fingertip. Somebody had called. Then I heard Mrs. Ketterick's voice, her cultured, easy lilt reminding us we were expected for dinner the day after tomorrow at seven sharp. The next voice was my chairman's. Fred wanted me to call him in the morning, that request followed by some news. Old Dot was out of the hospital and back in her apartment and apparently in great shape. He wanted me to see her on a peace and courtesy visit. Well, neither of those messages could have troubled the waters of Janice's serenity.

When I turned, she was at my shoulder. Buying the machine had been her idea. She was all for any new gadget. But she could never remember how the buttons worked. I'd shown her how to turn the machine off, but she often forgot it and would make a call, then get in about five words before my recorded raspy voice broke in on her conversation with the hospital or a friend, telling them nobody was home and to leave, at the sound of the beep, name and number or a brief message.

I said nothing to Janice, who had heard both messages, and I headed for bedroom and bed. Our sex life had fallen off considerably in recent years; I let the radio lull me to sleep.

Lying in bed, I put on my headset and tuned in the news. I listened and listened. I didn't know what I was waiting to hear, but the news of the world rattled around in my skull and my head expanded to the size of a circus tent to make room for everything. My head, as my eyes closed, expanded to the size of the universe with all the events of the day, the knifings, the clubbings, the hijackings, the strikes, the revolts and wars; even Con Edison's latest rate hike became me by miraculous transfusion. I became a vast solar silence stretched across suns that were points of light. When Janice slipped in beside me, I felt the lurch and tilt of the universe.

I woke up at two in the morning. The news was still pounding away, the blinds were open and in the distance I could see the shape of our guardian giant. The cat, Tucker, was pacing across my chest.

I took off the headset, turned off the radio and lay awake looking out of the window. It probably had been Janice that Gail saw snooping around her building. I knew I wasn't going to get back to sleep.

I got up and put on my robe, got my little packet of pot and wandered down the hall, the cat following me. He wanted to be fed. I dished out a serving from his can of catfood, then went into the living room and sat down on my stool in front of the television and turned the screen on with the sound off. I lit my water pipe.

Smoking was bad for my throat, but what the hell. I didn't think I took enough chances or had enough new experiences. I settled my elbows on my knees and watched some cowpokes sitting around in a corner of someone's barn. They were talking. They all had short haircuts, and that dated the action at once.

My mind began to wander. I wondered if I could get away with going into the study, closing the door and calling Gail. I also considered going downstairs without calling and taking our car across the bridge, dropping in on her, and driving home again in the fine dawn light.

But suppose I found someone spending the night with her, some other guy, what would I do? What could I do? Forget that shit, I thought. That's for moody reckless kids. It would hurt all right if someone was with her, so I didn't want to know—the way Janice didn't want to know about Gail. But she knew. Perse knew. They both knew. Janice just didn't know who the girl was. Or was that it? Had she just found out?

I sat watching my silent show until I felt the pot hit, started to feel sleepy, then I turned the set off, drank some milk out of the container in the refrigerator and went back to bed. Janice hadn't moved, but she was awake.

Love is a kind of trip along the edge of an abyss. It's like the ride I had that wonderful night Janice and I were invited by one of my students to Mark di Suvero's studio. Up on Di Suvero's roof he'd made a merry-go-round out of beams and planks and it revolved out, part of it, over the edge of the roof. One of his sculptures: he called it, "Love Makes the World Go 'Round."

If anyone felt up to the ride, to the odd thrill of it, he sat on one of the seats and someone got the merry-go-round swinging, sending the riders out over the edge of the roof four floors above a black side yard, spinning them out and back again, out and back. We all took turns over streetlights and darkness, carrying our drinks in one hand. Except for Janice. She wouldn't. It was a roller coaster thrill, a kind of chance taking, a kind of gambling. Who really knew how safe the damn thing was? That merry-go-round on the roof of a loft on the Lower East Side was the only one of its kind. I've often thought of it since and wondered what Di Suvero did with it. He was an artist making Truth manifest. Making Truth a piece of Reality—a work of the hands and the imagination. Maybe he only made it for himself, for the hell of it. I have never been able to forget that night; the other people who were there, for the most part strangers to me, were from a neighboring culture, not very talkative people. Probably on drugs. They had visionary eyes. Some of the guests were black, some oriental, some were dressed in jeans and no shirts and wore beads. The oriental girl I can't forget was tall and thin. She seemed to be dressed in several long colorful scarves. She sat in a swing in one of the big vacant rooms, rippling with a dozen or more different hues. She was spotlighted and all alone, not I suppose a living exhibit, but nevertheless a work of art in herself. It didn't occur to me to speak to her. She was too goddess-like and detached —unapproachable. At some point during that evening, the sculptor, whose legs were then paralyzed, climbed a long rope, hand over hand, to a roof beam.

Love has its dangers; at its best it does. It's a ride along the edge of an abyss, and like gambling it's a tempting of one's fate, an act of faith, an act in which losing is as sweet as winning.

Who said what everyone wants is a safe adventure? Some advertising man, no doubt. I see it offered to me in all the ads. When that sexy blonde lights her cigarette, it isn't just sex juxtaposed with a brand of cigarettes; it's the prospect, in a lush glimpse of throat and breasts, of a safe adventure that makes me want a cigarette myself.

Everyone has a problem with boredom. I do. And so what I long for is adventure, for Samarkand, or if that's impossible, then I want some other adventure close at hand.

When it comes to Gail, I feel the abyss. I'm aware of the abyss as I sit around with Janice. I don't want her to know about Gail, but she will find me out. She will know it first intuitively, by subtle signs and clues neither of us is aware of. If and when her suspicions become unbearable, she will look for something more substantial to match Truth with Reality. And then the abyss will not be beside me any more. It will be below me. And below her, too.

I don't really want the abyss to gulp us up.

And so now with Janice, and with Gail, even with Perse, the need simply to survive takes hold.

I may not understand why I remarried Janice, but I know why we got married the first time and it wasn't love alone. I'd knocked her up—and I thought I ought to marry her. On our second date, swinging out over the abyss I put my hands under her skirt, up above the nylon, holding the heat of our passion in one happy hand. The next weekend we checked into a hotel in a nearby town feeling all the virginal giddiness that goes with that sort of adventure—drinking gin and ginger ale from a paper cup, pouring the gin out of a pint bottle, necktie and shirt over the back of a chair, both of us dauntless and urgent once the lights went out; only the shade at the window beamed its Saturday light at us like a dying moon. It was all a lot newer to us than we let on under the sheet and blanket. We left that room hours later blissfully hooked on sex. We spent two years screwing in the snow between our coats, in back seats of strange parked cars, in bathrooms, vestibules, and every other imaginable practical and impractical place. Our sincerity was such that when she was knocked up, we talked as if we didn't want to look up an abortionist, but we did a lot of looking and asking. We rode fifty miles on a bus one weekend to talk to a doctor we'd heard might help us. He told us to get married. But that night at a seedy old hotel with sagging corridors of linoleum, she aborted naturally. We held each other, Janice and I, tightly all night long, tightly and tenderly. The next weekend in a small Ohio town, we lied about our ages and got married by a justice of the peace.

We could have just shaken hands with relief and forgot about it, but the curious thing is I don't think that crossed either of our minds. She was still in school and I was in the

Army. We kept it all secret; then a little over a year later, when I got out of OCS and had more of an income, we got married again, in front of her folks and my folks and a lot of other people.

So much for being honorable. As soon as the war was over and we were back together, I was, like Fletch, wondering what happened. Janice changed; she seemed to see everything differently, through a different set of pupils; she was able to see me now, she said, for what I really was: irresponsible, selfish, lazy, vague, a liar.

But we did have some happy times while Perse was a baby. I can remember them. The child was fun. I had a teaching job I liked, one I had fallen into by chance.

So much of my life has evolved by chance. I was stationed in New York when I got out of the Army. I'd been writing and producing movies for the Signal Corps; a documentary outfit in town was ready to hire me when they could get some cameras. Because of a shortage of equipment there'd be a wait, and while I was waiting, said they, why didn't I get a job teaching freshman English? I had a novel coming out, didn't I? That would be all the credentials I needed. There was a shortage of teachers.

So I went over to Metro, starting with a small college, and they hired me. They gave me a fiction class. Dorothy Dole was impressed with my book. "We can tell," she said, "you're not going to be one of these one-book authors. We want people here who will make a career out of writing."

At semester's end I no longer wanted to make commercial movies. It was as if when I walked into that classroom, I walked inside my head. I felt completely myself, and out of me spilled my personal fantasies, my thoughts. I talked the only subjects I really cared about—imagination, stories, mine, other people's, love, glory. I talked and, unbelievably, those beautiful faces, strangers, all listened and encouraged me. They opened notebooks and wrote down the random things I said.

But Janice wasn't all that sure I had a good job. She had her doubts. There were other things I should care about besides the inside of my head. And it wasn't, well, a *real* job. She could hardly call what I did work.

I'd sit in our dining room, where I had my desk, writing something, and she'd come up beside me and say over the clack of keys, "Take out the garbage."

I concentrate when I write and so I could only look up at her and say, "Huh?"

"I said, take down the garbage."

We had some hard words about the relative importance of garbage. I know it's a standard joke, the garbage, but we lived that bit and we got worked up about it. After a while I think I impressed her that I should not be interrupted, so she would put the garbage sack down beside my legs, where I couldn't miss it when I stood up. She would put it there and I wouldn't even know she'd done it. Getting up, I'd kick it all over the floor. But . . . that wasn't what broke us up.

The day I knew I had to make a break was when we moved into that house in New Jersey. After the furniture was shoved into place, I remember sitting on the side of the bed in the bedroom thinking, "I'm going to get old and die here."

Out in the yard the lawns were not yet seeded; there were no curtains on the windows, the gleaming floors were the color of hardened ear wax. I sat on the bed on the bare mattress and looked around the bedroom, Janice's and mine, and I thought, "This is the room I'm going to die in."

I never think of that house with affection. It was haunted from the day the roof went on, a mean and evil place.

That summer I went up to Peterborough, New Hampshire, on a writing fellowship. The bliss of having every day free to write with no bitching, no fighting, no errands, no frowns over-whelmed me. I couldn't go back to that again. I wrote from the colony and told Janice so. She read my letter, left Perse with a neighbor, got in our car without suitcase or toothbrush, and drove up to find me. I was sitting in the local movie theater with some other colonists when she broke in. I went outside and we sat in the car. I loved her. I just couldn't stand the way we were living. She couldn't stand it either, she said. I wept with her, tear for tear. Things would be different now, she said . . .

But things got worse. So the following summer, at the Mac-Dowell Colony again, I decided to make the break good. I wrote no letter of parting. I went silently back to New York and moved in with a girl. She was a fine girl with a keen sense of outrage who listened to all my complaints and decided to help me break up a destructive marriage.

Janice couldn't find me. She didn't know where I was. School hadn't started yet. Andre knew, but he lied to her and said he didn't. Janice flipped. She packed a suitcase this time, grabbed Perse, calmed herself with two or three seconal capsules, and headed off for Grand Central Station convinced I was holed up with my folks.

While she was some eight hundred miles away, sobbing and being soothed, I borrowed Andre's car, drove over to New Jersey and let myself into the house to pick up a few things. On my desk was a message: "Welcome home, darling."

It has thundered through my *ho head* ever since. That house was, after all, my *home*, awful as it was.

What was I doing? What had I done?

Our Lady of Letters:

When I got over to Dorothy Dole's, the first thing to strike me was how clean she had the place. The table in the dining room alcove, where she always worked, was unlittered with manuscripts and books and coffee cups and glasses and letters. It was cleared, and in the center of the round tabletop lay a white doily; on it, a glass vase of fresh daffodils. The rest of the apartment, including what I could see of the kitchen, was also immaculate, as if organized for a beginning—the beginning of a day, a meal, a visit, or the rest of her life.

The maid, a black woman, answered the door, let me in and departed down a narrow hallway. Dot was settled on a big blue chair; another armchair had been pulled around in front of her for me.

I sat down and smiled but got no response.

Her eyes were barely open, and the way the slits of her eyes slanted gave her an oriental appearance. Age had carved her a scary, evil old mask.

To keep from talking too much, I had a list of questions in my head to ask her; when she'd answered them, I meant to go. She sat leaning forward in the chair, her back hunched, her bony elbows resting on the chair's padded arms. I told her how great she looked. Perhaps I overdid it a little, but I meant well. She did look better than I'd expected.

"Oh, I'm all right," she said. Her voice sounded as gravelly as mine. "I'm all right. I thought I told you to bring a bottle if you wanted a drink."

"I brought one," I said. It was only ten o'clock in the morning.

"Where is it?"

"Your maid took it."

She bellowed, "Agnes." Steps came down the hall. "Serve us a drink."

"Yes, Miss Dole."

"Goddamn it," Dorothy said, "they won't let me keep anything around the place."

And then we were both silent again, face to face, staring. I wanted to start talking about myself. As if this were what I'd come to do. It was like an itch, unbearable to resist. To recite my whole history, in a way I never had with Newman, spill out all my problems and frustrations; jammed tight with the need to, beyond anything I'd ever guessed. But I wasn't supposed to talk and her mind was half gone anyway.

"Jack," she said suddenly, "go out and help her make those drinks. She puts a drop or two of . . . what did you bring?"

"Scotch."

"Go out there and pour us a couple of drinks."

I did. I went out and loaded her glass and loaded mine and brought them back. Agnes said nothing. Agnes shook her head and went away—down the long hall. I got the feeling Agnes liked old Dot and if someone else broke the rules, why, what could she do? Even so, she took the bottle with her.

"The department," I told Dot when I sat down, "wants some sort of record on how the writing courses got started at Metro."

"I started those courses," she said. "I got the whole thing started. There wasn't a college in this country then that taught creative writing. We were an extension college, night courses, no, that was later—correspondence courses first, then night classes. I talked them into letting me teach a class in how to write fiction."

Nobody at Metro cared how the creative writing courses got their start. I just wanted to get her talking.

And it got her going. The venom sparkled at the corners of her lips. About eight years ago, retired and teaching part time at the age of seventy-five, Dot had been dropped from the department, as she and everyone else knew, to get rid of her; and word had gone out that no one would ever again be made a senior professor without having earned a Ph.D. Then, with old Dot out of the way, the department's Ph.D.s had swung their hatchet at the vine she'd planted in their midst, a vine so powerful and extensive it was strangling the literature courses by its size alone. It had grown too big. The professional writing teachers were beginning to outnumber the academicians. Now, what kind of English department was that? The hatchet had done a good job. I was the only one left who taught a full program of writing classes.

Still, the college wanted her money. The dean promised it would go toward fellowships to support writing students of talent and promise, but old Dot didn't believe it. She soon got around to that money, too.

Three funds were arrayed around her. One had already been established by a dozen of her former students, all now relatively famous writers. The second would be set up, it was hoped, out of any money she left the college in her will. The third was sunk in a trust established by a deceased friend and fellow teacher at Metro, a trust on which Dot was partially dependent. She was spending it anyway. But on Dot's death that trust would fall into Metro's hands—all prearranged by lawyers before the college had shoved Dot into retirement.

Whoever Dot left her own money to was still for Dot to decide. It consisted of real estate and royalties and she might well leave it to her maid, to anyone.

"Metro," Dot said, "will get Florence's estate, but they will not get mine, not a cent. I've seen too many funds misappropriated in my time. I tell you now, every penny left to the school marked for our writing students will be spent for something else. Nobody gives a damn what the donor wanted; it's what the school thinks it needs. Money's fine, but the donor's a nuisance. So I am not leaving any of my money to Metro."

She began to thrash around in her chair, and to change the subject I asked her about her childhood in Wisconsin. We came from adjoining states and, when we got together, we invariably talked about the Middle West.

"That's my new book," she said, startling me. A smile had appeared on her face. She leaned back. Her drink was empty. She rattled the ice in her glass. Half my drink was left and I poured it all into her glass. She said nothing. "I can remember," she began after a long drink, "the early settlers. My grandfather and my grandmother were early settlers . . . people who made this country what it is today."

"Is this a novel?"

"No."

"How much of it have you done?" I still wasn't sure she was actually writing another book.

"It's coming slowly," she said. "I can't work on it long at a time. My publisher's deadline is next March. What are you working on, Jack?"

It was the first personal question she'd asked, and this startled me too. "I guess I'm writing a journal. I don't know what to call it."

While moving around in her chair, her skirt had hitched up and her legs were showing almost to her crotch. They were good-looking legs and did not match her scrawny arms and comedy mask of a face. She made no effort to pull her skirt down, and I had the goddamndest suspicion she knew her legs were showing and liked them that way. Her legs reminded me of posters preaching the evils of syphilis. That is to say, I was curiously attracted and frightened, not disgusted, just a bit scared. I wanted another drink—and wanted to get out, at once.

"I've thought about doing nonfiction too. I don't know if you remember, but I spent a couple of summers in the Yucatan, mostly in Mérida . . ." I said, conscious of the hoarseness of my voice, of my pauses for breath. "I did a book about that, the Yucatan. A kind of travel book. . . ."

"Who published it? Was that Random House?"

"Well, it never got published. I may rewrite it."

She spread her legs and gazed straight at me, leaning forward. Leering, leering, leering. "Send it to my editor. I'll give you his name."

"It's already been to your publisher."

"They didn't take it?"

"Everybody seems to think the subject lacks appeal."

"Nonsense," she snapped. "Write the books you want to write the way you want to write them. If you're a good writer, anything you write will have appeal."

Good advice. The same advice I handed out to my students. But it never seemed to work, or rather one simply wondered after a multitude of rejecting editors had passed it by, if he or she was all that good a writer. Her books had been tailored for salability; her heroes and heroines were decent, sympathetic human beings with clearly defined problems each overcame in his own way. She drew her characters from life, her relatives, her friends, the people on the faculty. Each book was about someone in an interesting occupation or about someone in an interesting environment. Four of her books were book club selections. Although she no longer had the vast audience she'd once had, although she was a bit old-fashioned, she was not forgotten. No, I won't say she hadn't followed her creed. That's the way she wanted to write. Perhaps her books were not written for someone like me. She had written the best books she could, and had told Thorpe not too long ago she was convinced her books would be read long after people had started to ask, "Hemingway . . . who's Ernest Hemingway?"

"Did you read that diary of Anaïs Nin, where she talks about why a writer writes?" said Dot, fixing me on the sour point of her gaze—accusatively. "I never read such drivel in my life. What does she know about writing? She's used that little talent she has for an ego thing, ego trip, whatever they call it, all her life. That's why she writes, to pretend she's important and famous, and the only people she fools are the people who've never read her."

I was both curious and defensive. I liked Nin, what she stood for as a struggling artist. "Why did she say people wrote?"

"Oh, some nonsense about creating a world for the writer to live in better than the world around her—the writer transcending herself . . . all ego froth. That's what's wrong with all her books."

"Then why does a writer write?"

"A writer writes to make a living. Everybody wants to be famous. It's not enough to want to be famous, but anybody can make a living, or has a right to want to."

"Didn't Edmund Wilson admire her?"

"He liked one of her books, and then never again said a word in her defense—that I ever heard about." Her voice was a steady, operose growl. "She keeps a lot of little friends around her telling her how good she is and she tries to cultivate all the critics she can to get them to say nice things about her. It's the people who don't know her, like Elizabeth Hardwick, who tell the truth in print, and she can't stand to read it."

"Henry Miller said her diary will be one of the great works of our age."

"Miller? What does he know? They lived together and split up. Anyway, who sees her diary? Safe thing to say, for him. That thing she's publishing now is just excerpts. You don't see anything in it about her love affairs, and she's a female spider. Lies, all lies, everything she writes. Miller's done one, maybe two books, and the rest is all self-indulgence. Norman Mailer is another example . . . whatever's good in his work is made rotten by his vanity. You see that everywhere, in writers like what's his name, that Marvin Woldman, where is he now?—masturbating in a madhouse, driven mad by his own self-importance. A lot like that. It's not enough to want to be a writer."

And so the conversation continued, Dot giving me her blunt reactions. I asked her, "Did you ever write a book that the publishers wouldn't take?"

"Of course," she snapped. "What writer hasn't? But they were all bad books and I knew it later and I'm glad they weren't published. I rewrote some, some I threw out. I published a book every year for years, did you know that?"

"Didn't teaching ever get in your way?"

"Never. I wrote my first draft in the summer and polished it up over the fall and spring."

I sat there thinking she must have been a great comfort to her students because she had a quick answer to every writer's problem and she delivered the answers with conviction and authority. I was beginning to feel convinced myself, though I had no respect for what she wrote, and Mailer was a writer I admired—a guy willing to risk looking bad to find his own beat and feelings. Dot had a different kind of drive.

One of her old students told me she opened her classes each fall by telling them how many thousands of dollars she'd made writing in the past year. This ex-student, who went on to become a fiction editor at the *Saturday Evening Post*, heard her say, "I made twenty-three thousand dollars last year, and I'm going to tell all of you how you can do it too. So listen to me and do as I tell you."

The students who would eagerly listen to that are nearly gone today, because the short story market is virtually gone, and novelists are overcrowding the diminishing novel market. Most of my students write out of literary ambition; art for profit's sake is scorned. A few of my students have even declared they don't want to get published; they scorn even that.

Dorothy Dole had one more surprise left for me. When I got up to leave, she arose herself. She walked beside me, hunched and slightly unsteady, holding my arm in a hard grip. Her fingers began to knead into me, steadily, rhythmically. When we stopped at the front door, I understood at once she wanted a good-by kiss. Her eyes had opened wider; that is, they were now half open. I could see her dark, moist pupils, could feel their gaze as a hard force. I aimed my mouth for her cheek, but that's not where she wanted it. She drew my mouth against her lips into a moist, tongue-probing kiss that left my knees weak as I went out the door.

I draw no conclusions from any of this. I grow more weary by the hour of conclusions.

This morning: a postcard from my uncle Sam. Some hunter with a high-powered rifle shoots Sam's next-door neighbor dead. The man's reshingling his shed, gets picked off the roof like a squirrel. Sam, who hears the shot, is first on the scene—to keep him from being skinned? To skin him?

Saw a guy this afternoon pushing his cart around our supermarket, his hair up in pink plastic curlers.

The Salvation Army has a thirteen-piece rock band. How do you save the soul of a Times Square junkie with a rock rendition of "Onward, Christian Soldiers"?

Or how do we take care of all the poop on the top of our highest mountains, dropped there by mountain climbers—turds and other junk, organic and inorganic, dropped by the climbers along their way to the summit? They're flying the shit out by helicopter, and park rangers with scoop shovels trail along behind the climbers. The National Park Service is going to build a shithouse at the 14,410-foot peak of Mount Rainier in Washington. Climbers on their way to the summit stand in line now to use the two outhouses at the 10,000-foot level.

Listen, it's a serious problem. What's happening to us?

I drop such notes regularly into my "life" file. Today I took out a few, looked at them and thought: But these don't reflect me, they're not me at all. I'm not a brooding fellow who files cynical observations. Fact is, most of the time I feel fairly cheerful—well, a lot of the time, and where's my record of that?

For some reason, the stupid things people do to one another come more quickly to mind than the generous and beautiful things. Then, too, the style of our times is cynicism, doom thinking, gloom, and taking ourselves very seriously. I find myself caught up in it.

I've got to start making notes about more of the poetic things I've heard of or seen or been involved in—like that visit to Di Suvero's studio. Things of beauty, things of beauty. Reality. Leave Truth to the philosophers.

Over at Gail's I rang her bell and a man answered the door, something I think I had always dreaded and been prepared for. He was a short, squat fellow in a baggy suit, and all I could say was, "Is Gail in?"

"She's out," he said, and stood there. We stared at each other. Then he said, "I'm the piano tuner."

"Oh," said I, huskily. "I'm a friend of hers. I thought she was expecting me."

"You're a Mr. Fross?"

"Yes."

He let me in.

He had his bag open over by the piano bench, where he sat down again and began to plink at the keys in a solemn, methodical manner. He was like a doctor, a piano doctor, making the piano say ohhh, ahhhh, eeee. I wandered around. Occasionally, he did some chording that was mellow and beautiful.

That grand piano was Gail's object of adoration, a Knabe. She had bought it after her divorce. Like me, she bought something to console herself following or during a disaster, spending money she would otherwise never have let loose. Since she'd bought the piano, she had lived in five apartments and she took it everywhere. Had it carried up narrow stairways, hoisted up from sidewalks and swung in through windows, and I could understand how she felt about the piano. But not the football. There it sat, in a blue glass dish, smack in the middle of the Knabe. It was a nice new football, pumped tight with air—and over its bright orange skin were scrawled at least a dozen signatures.

Because of the piano, the room seemed crowded, but the balcony extended the room, and beyond the balcony was wide open space indeed. All in all, she had a pleasant place, a place I liked to come to and felt at home in, a kind of luxurious tree house with a view of the river and Manhattan.

"When did she say she'd be back?" I asked.

He paused, his finger pointing toward the football. "I half not seen her."

Low bookcases extended along two walls, meeting at a corner, and while the tuner labored over the ivories and among the wires, I tried to find a book to read. That wasn't easy at Gail's. I don't know where she got her books. From Third Avenue secondhand stores? There were few recent titles and not much poetry, although she liked poetry and had a poem tacked up on her kitchen bulletin board, one about recovering from the hurts of love. Once I tried to educate Gail by giving her a collection of Wallace Stevens' poems only to learn she had heard him speak at a Phi Beta Kappa dinner and didn't like him. When she told me this, I made the great mistake of intimating she was a literary idiot and got shaken up with a barrage of very hard-edged words. Gail had a quick temper. There was the time I mildly criticized a painting she had hanging on the wall by the kitchen door, something I decided an old lover had given her or even painted—and got told in two words to "Fuck off." I learned later she had painted it herself. She got over these slights quickly, but I handled her with care now. That football though. Christ, why did she keep it around?

I went out on the balcony with a two-day-old newspaper and sat down. I left the paper on my lap and stared at the river for a while. Over across the water cars were moving along the West Side Highway. A bank of grass rose to the east of the highway. The leaves on the trees at the top of the slope had only begun to turn autumn brown. That's all New York trees

do as winter comes along, turn brown. Last spring I'd watched
the forsythia yellow from this same balcony, amazed when a
couple of cold spells hadn't killed it off. I wish I knew more
about plants. I'm convinced they have a sensate life. Watch
them tremble in a house when there's no draft. They have simple needs and simple sensations; they have a reality, and everything that experiences a reality has its truths, its opinions.

Where could she be? What was keeping her? I was getting
anxious now. Did I have the wrong day? How could I? The
tuner knew my name. She'd said only a few hours ago she'd
meet me at her place. That was at the lunch hour theater.

She was appearing daily in a kind of showcase set up at a
church north of Midtown. The performers got fifty dollars for
two weeks of work, about enough to cover their cab fare. But
that would be enough if a producer dropped in and saw them
and liked them. Mostly her audience consisted of office workers
on the loose who paid a dollar contribution and got a free cup of
coffee along with the show. I'd paid and got my coffee and
carried in a sandwich, sitting at one of the tables, eating with
the others in boarding house style, watching Gail up in the spot-
light on the stage. That's my girl, folks. Though I couldn't really see her well. The room was crowded. I watched her
reflected in a sheet of glass. An open glass door? What was it?
She shimmered like reflection on water. Made me uneasy.
When I got too uneasy, I stood up, moved away from the table
and joined the standees. She was leaning against the piano, telling the audience how great the piano player was, earning him a
hand. Her last number coming up. Wearing a short dress and a
hat with a big brim, a piece of costume from one of her more
triumphantly untriumphant off-Broadway musicals. I knew all
her songs, all those offbeat, sophisticated lyrics, from hearing
her practice. And I was right about her face. It was clear and

sharp from where I stood at the rear of the room. She projected physically. She was going to be famous. I was sure of it.

Was someone telling her *that* now—prolonging his lunch hour—in a gypsy cab going around and around Central Park? Show business exposed her to so many impressionable, impulsive people.

Across the river and above Riverside Drive and the trees, I could see the three highest floors of our apartment house. The top balcony would be Judy and Norman's. I could just make out the crates of books Norman stored there. He loved his books —ol' Norman, who complained that Judy was driving him to financial ruin buying clothes for Francine that Francine didn't need. Judy's folks came to visit in a limousine, but they were no help to Norman.

I often amused myself trying to figure out where Gail got all the money she needed to live in the style she did. Her ex-husband paid no alimony, or so she said. Her father didn't sound so well off he could support her, dotingly, in such comfort. There were no signs that anyone was keeping her. My friend Sean, who knows about everything, once told me a man never had to ask a girl if she had any money because a girl spilled everything about any money she had in the first ten minutes you were with her. Not Gail. She never explained and I tried not to pry. Yet she must have a ready supply of cash. Her apartment could have cost around $75,000. Even its maintenance was high. When we went out to dinner, she insisted on paying her half of the check—a gesture of independence. She drove a BMW 2002. She wore mod clothes and expensive suede jackets. She couldn't do all that on what she made singing a song or two in off-Broadway musicals—or even as an executive secretary, a job she seemed to be able to pick up when she needed to. That must be a good portable job.

I'd once thought Janice had a good portable job. Back in college, when I'd decided I'd like to be a writer who moved around from New York to New Orleans to San Francisco, wherever he chose, Janice's job had seemed ideal for that kind of life. My income as an author might be irregular and uncertain, but her paycheck would be steady and she'd find work wherever we went. She was not just a nurse: she was a nurse with a graduate degree. But that's not how things worked out—they might have—but they didn't. The thought of quitting a job ate her up with panic.

In about half an hour the piano tuner left. He leaned out onto the terrace to say good-by with European formality. We even shook hands. Then I was alone.

What did Janice know? I knew one thing, I did not want what I had with Gail disturbed, so I'd better be careful.

Fletch drifted into my thoughts—and out. Then I found myself recalling two people I'd met during my first year in college. I had not thought of them since I'd graduated. One was a girl, the daughter of the owner of the largest motion picture theater in Grand Rapids; the other, the son of the owner of the sporting goods store on Main Street. The girl was attractive, the first I'd known who wore eye shadow every day. I don't recall dating her more than a couple of times. I thought now—staring at the swimming pool below—I met her too late. If I'd only met her in high school, think of all the free movies!

She was the daughter of a local merchant satrap. The guy I'd met was regal too, an aura of privilege around them both.

And then, as I sat on the terrace, staring at the river, Fletch was back in mind and I remembered our three wishes, original wishes, as we sat behind his father's barn in the morning shade, teapot in hand. The first was for unexpiring passes to all the movies in town, the second for unlimited, free-for-the-asking hunting knives, guns, tents, baseball bats, mitts and sundry treasures in the town's one and only sporting goods store. The third wish was for a renewal of our first three wishes.

I had met the girl too late—yes—because once we'd given up on help from magical powers in teapots, we'd wished for a girl whose father owned a theater—exchanging *quid pro quo* a teapot genie for a girl with a movie house. Although after that the things we wished for changed a lot, the girl remained in the foreground. In time, more practical or realistic, we would wish for a girl who had inherited a million. Interesting—the way we mixed the movie-sporting goods wish into a sexy, attractive girl. The ideal youthful life: money equaled booze/cigarettes/sex. Everything we'd been told was bad for us. That's what we wanted. What was bad and fun. Just what Fletch and I had looked for on that only trip we took.

My god, Fletch even married an usherette; but she came with no free passes. Only Andre had married a girl with a fortune; and everything else he wanted came with her. Strange—all fairy tale stuff—yet it happened. It happens. Now and then.

But I did not want to marry a girl with a pot of gold any more. Those opportunities come along to a teacher from time to time . . . Or—perhaps I should say I did not think I did. Maybe I was only sensitive about appearing middle-aged and poor with mighty little to attract and hold the daughter of a merchant nobleman—except a quasi-academic position in a small, obscure college.

Where was she? I waited another twenty minutes, then decided to call Sean at his paper and see if he was in. He worked in Hackensack, not far away. Maybe I'd drive over and we could have a cup of coffee. That way when she turned up I wouldn't be just hanging around waiting. But Sean wasn't in, and I'd just hung up when Gail came in through the front door pulling a cart of groceries.

"Jack," she said, "I hurried." What a beautiful smile.

We went to bed at once, leaving the groceries where they stood. The orange juice melted.

Things of beauty—

Not just objects casting shadows, like fence shadows or grass or a hanging plant of small blue flowers turning in the breeze, but people arranging themselves on park benches like flowers, arranging themselves to get all the sunlight that's coming to them, and old ladies smiling at babies rolling by, and young girls walking slowly under tall trees, and men and women in white shorts in a tennis dance on each side of a net, their contact a small yellow ball, and dogs with alert brown eyes sitting beside their masters. Look for beauty in breathing things. Believe and trust in beauty. Care about breathing things and celebrate joy.

The next evening—

We parked the car on Fifth Avenue, on the Central Park curbside, locked the doors and crossed the street. Janice had said little since we'd left home. Trouble was brewing still. She walked with her elbows bent, close to her sides. I hated us when things got like this, but I still didn't want to show I knew anything was wrong. She was all set to snarl and lash, waiting for me to start something.

The doorman at the Kettericks' apartment house unlocked the big iron and glass doors. Inside, a couple of uniformed attendants guided us to the elevator, where an elevator man, studying us as carefully as, let me hope, he studied any strangers, took us to the Kettericks'.

The elevator stopped at what was both the Kettericks' floor and their wing of the building. The elevator's gates shut behind us and we stood alone in their foyer. I rang the bell and almost at once a butler opened the door and let us in.

Mrs. Ketterick, tall, auburn-haired, with a calm, attentive manner, had been a student of mine. That was some time back, five years anyway. She didn't register for class any more because my classes were in the evening and she was afraid of our area once the sun had set. With reason. Once the sun set, terrible forces took over. You shut your doors tight on them. Just ahead was 1984. The time of Clockwork Orange was almost at hand.

We had drinks in a small study, dinner in a proper dining

room, and coffee and brandy in their living room. We sat on Chippendale chairs and looked out over the lights of the park. Servants entered the rooms or answered the telephone or removed our scraps and glasses at nearly invisible, inaudible summonses.

The Kettericks bought art. On their walls, one picture crowding another, hung Picasso, Dufy, Gauguin, Rubens, Vasarely . . . and fine sculpture stood about the eleven rooms in which they lived.

Mr. Ketterick was a financier who had inherited a fortune and then tripled it, at least. Mrs. Ketterick had brought to their marriage a fortune of her own that had come down to her from some vague European source associated in my mind with international cartels. It was not that Mrs. Ketterick was reluctant to talk about it, no . . . it was more that the explanation was complex and subtle beyond belief, out of a wholly different world—and Mrs. Ketterick did not understand it well herself. Her father was simply an immensely important man, almost unknown to the press and media of his times. She had seen him at dinner sometimes—or he came on occasion to her room for brief, fatherly chats. Then one day he died and left her everything. Millions. She was more than knowledgeable about art. She spoke four languages fluently. She had published a poem in *Harper's Bazaar*. She had studied piano with several masters. She had raised four sons, all married, sane, healthy and prospering—but all her life what she had wanted more than anything else was to write a novel. All she could do was get one started and that's as far as it went. Once a year she asked us to dinner and always after dinner, in the living room, she asked what she should do, as if this time I would have the answer.

Hell, I never knew. "Just write," I told her. "Write until you get it finished, then sit down and rewrite it. Do that about seven or eight times." What would old Dot tell her?

"But I can't," she cried. And there was a real cry in her voice.

Meanwhile, Mr. Ketterick, a polite reserved man, occupied— I think that's the word—Janice in conversation. He was a polite, careful listener. I think Janice enjoyed our visits there. She was not a smiler, but once we were inside the Kettericks' door she smiled almost constantly and her voice assumed what struck me as unusually cultured intonations.

The Kettericks had recently come back from a vacation in Turkey. I heard Mr. Ketterick say, "It's too dangerous to drive your own car anywhere in Turkey."

I swung my head around. "Why's that?"

"Why, they'll apparently let anyone have a license to drive who buys a car, and the country seems full of people who are learning how to drive."

"It's the trucks," Mrs. Ketterick said. "The trucks are the worst."

"The trucks?"

"They come at you straight up the middle of the highway."

"And if there's any kind of accident," said Mr. Ketterick, "the police put everyone in jail. An American can disappear into those jails and never be heard from again."

"We had our own driver," Mrs. Ketterick said, "who couldn't speak a word of any language but Turkish. Nobody speaks anything but Turkish. We had to have a guide, a personal guide, all the time."

"Aren't there phrase books for tourists?" I said.

"I had one. But it wasn't much help, and the language is so impossible to learn. Latin and Greek won't help you as a foundation. Turkish is so complicated to speak. If you're planning to go through Turkey on your way to Samarkand, Jack, a phrase book will be small consolation."

"When you leave Greece and cross into Turkey," said Mr. Ketterick, "you'll be on the edge of another world."

Janice, still smiling, was studying me closely. "Since when has Jack been interested in Turkey?"

"Hasn't Jack told you about Samarkand?" Mrs. Ketterick said with surprise. "Jack, did you make all that up about Samarkand just for your students?" She turned to Janice. "I thought it was the dream of his life."

Mrs. Ketterick looked so disappointed I had to confess it *was* important to me. I said to Janice, "You've heard me go on about Samarkand."

"I don't think I have. This is all very interesting."

"I suppose I elaborate on it in class, you know."

"Yes, I can imagine," said Janice.

"Another brandy?" said Mr. Ketterick, coming quickly to his feet.

"Please," I said.

"I might have known," she shouted on our way home, "what that money you keep in an account of your own is for." She was screaming really. I didn't argue with her. There was no need to. She'd always understood the money was my security, that if I ever decided to blow everything again, I could—and knowing that made my life more tolerable, the college, Janice, New York, my unpublished books. But the savings account was also Samarkand, and until now she had no idea Samarkand meant that much; now she had the account personified. Samarkand? Was I crazy?

I said nothing. Should I have told her if I were carrying that money down the street and some addict said his incantation—your money or your life—he'd get my life? I said nothing. I let her rant all the way home. I'd never spend it anyway. Who ever goes to Samarkand? These days?

Two nights later—

    Sean turned up with food and drink, coming straight from the newspaper where he worked as a feature writer. He brought a bottle of rum and a carton of orange juice, a couple of sandwiches and a box of Fig Newtons. The rum was for the two of us, although he didn't drink much any more. He said it made him maudlin.

    Janice had intended to be home when he arrived, because he was one of my friends she genuinely likes, but a little after our dinner she got beeped over to her hospital. Just as well. For the last two days she'd been kind of hysterical, as if a mental virus had hit her.

    When I came back from the kitchen with a drink for myself and some of his orange juice in a glass for him, Sean had started in on a sandwich. He was eating thoughtfully, a huge man in his early sixties, white-haired. He had played football at Notre Dame under Knute Rockne. One of the few things I knew about him. Nobody knows Sean. He nurtures more privacy than anyone I've ever met. I only know him intuitively. Really to know someone you need specific details, especially about the big moves he's made in his life. All of this Sean kept to himself.

    I respected his privacy and didn't probe, and he did very little probing himself; what he did, he did tentatively and cautiously. So it took him awhile to get to the question that was on his mind, but a direct question always deserves a direct answer, and finally he leaned back on the sofa and said for his opener, "Jack . . . ?"

"Yeah?"

"What would you do after you got to Samarkand?"

Janice had told me she'd called him, and she must have sounded as if I'd be departing any day now.

"I'd have to see. After I got there, I'd decide."

"Would you give up your job?" He was still trying to decide how serious things were.

"I wouldn't have to. I have summers free . . . and I can take a year off without losing my tenure. A year and two summers would give me plenty of time to get there and back. I've been thinking about it."

"I hear there's not much left to see anymore. You might be disappointed."

"It's just a trip I feel I have to make."

He let his breath out through his nose and thought awhile and said, "Would Janice go with you?"

"I don't know. I doubt it. It just sounds crazy to her."

He was glad I'd got back together with Janice again, and I knew he didn't want me to louse up my life. He thought I had a good deal and he worried about me. "Would you write about the trip?"

"I don't know." I laughed. "I might write about why I want to go there *before I go*, you know, to get the money to go. It's occurred to me that the people who wrote about their travels seldom said why they wanted to go wherever they went. Why did Lawrence want to go to Sicily? Why was he interested in Etruscan places? Why did he go to Taos? I know, I know, Mabel Dodge sent him an invitation. But it's not that simple. What's this impulse to begin with, to make a journey? We all have it, or most of us do. It's more than escape, a looking for change, a hope that things will be better somewhere else. We all have some built-in mechanism that drives us down the road."

"I don't," Sean said. "Just give me my bowl of porridge and a quiet corner near the fire."

"But you used to travel. You went to Ireland and Europe on your wedding trip, the first time you got married."

He nodded impassively.

"I've heard Freud thought the urge to travel, and it's a kind of urge, was a search for one's lost mother. I'd like to know where he said that. Ever heard that one?"

Sean shook his head.

"I suppose it's all those mountains in the distance, those great big mother's breasts . . . mother earth all around . . . I wonder if he had that in mind, Freud? That could have been part of it: Lawrence looking for his lost mother."

"We do a lot of that," Sean said.

"What?"

"Misplacing life."

"Yeah."

"Misplacing mother . . ." He laughed, that is, his chest and stomach heaved a couple of times. "Misplacing wives, children . . ." Sean, a Catholic, had been married twice and divorced twice. He had three children by his second marriage, two girls and a boy. "You look around and you can't find them, can't remember where you put them. We do a lot of that." He was both looking and speaking impassively—and it was, as always, hard for me to know what he really felt. Once when I asked him what he did when he was alone in his apartment he said, "Oh, I sit around and cry a lot." And then he said more seriously, "Well, I drink cup after cup of coffee and stare. I replay old scenes in my life as if I had them on a movieola . . .

run them back and forth, back and forth, slow the scenes down, take some of them a frame at a time, study them over and over."

I could see him doing just that, as he'd described it, and I'd laughed. Still, he probably did spend much of his waking life under a heap of guilts and regrets, and that was why drinking made him feel depressed. He was a poet, one of my first students, very talented. As far as I knew, he had not written any verse in years, although patches of poetry went into stories he wrote for his newspaper. Perhaps he thought I had a good life, only three classes a week to teach and a wife who was working, but he had an outlet for his writing—he had readers.

"Lawrence," I said, "could have been looking for his mother. Unconsciously."

Sean nodded. He seemed tired these days. He tried to sleep all he could. Whenever I called him at home, I woke him up; no matter at what hour I called, I woke him up. And still he looked tired.

"Being a romantic," he said, ". . . that probably has something to do with the need for travel."

"How do you mean?"

"Oh"—he paused awhile—"I think romantics believe a literary myth about a happy life on earth, and they go around, Jack, looking for island paradises, villas on the Mediterranean, ranches in the West, a log cabin in a forest, or adobe houses in Taos that are, preferably, outside town." He paused again. "All of them trying to match a myth to life."

"Can they?"

He shook his head. "No. About all they can do, you know, is recreate a myth."

"You think that's what I'm doing?"

"In a way. In a way. But there's more to it than that, what you want or need. There's more."

Sean thought about it and so did I. We sat in silence for something like five minutes, no record for us.

Then Sean asked how Judy was. Judy loved Sean. I'd never known a woman who didn't. And she'd have married him, I think, if he had been looking for another wife. He wasn't, and Judy finally married Norman. I told him we'd been to her folks' place up the Hudson and he listened with interest to my account of that day. "We didn't think," I said, "they were very happy."

"You know," Sean said, "men don't get married. They get windburn."

So we thought about that awhile—and then, seriously, I asked him, "Do you think marriage is a natural state for men and women?"

I had never seen him take so long to think over any question. At last he raised his great head as if he were scenting the wind. He gazed across the room. He stroked his cheek with one finger. He was puzzled. He stared at the rug. I waited. At last he said, "No." That was all he said. Just "No."

"Then why do people go on getting married?"

"It's women," he said. "They want to get married."

"But why?"

"Because they're freer than men, freer from everyday matters, more ready to take chances, more willing to."

At that moment Janice arrived. She gave Sean her usual big hug and kiss. Sean lost most of his slack and pensiveness. She wanted to cook some scrambled eggs for him, but he shook his head and opened his box of Fig Newtons.

"Put those away," said Janice. "We have cake in the kitchen."

"I love Fig Newtons," Sean said. "If it hadn't been for Fig Newtons, I'd probably have got married again."

November 12th—

I went down on the elevator and up the street to the deli for
a half pint of coffee cream and saw throngs of people gathered
on the sidewalks about a block ahead. People gather like that a
lot: maybe a couple of cars had banged into one another, or
somebody had been hit by a car while crossing the street, or
there was a fight, or an arrest, or it was a part of a crowd going
to some big shot's funeral. Whenever the cathedral up the avenue threw a funeral for someone like a senator or a baseball
star, the furs and bright jackets on the streets were everywhere,
as if we'd been caught in an undeclared holiday. But those people ahead weren't dressed up. This was something else.

I bought the coffee cream and went back to the apartment.

6:50 P.M.
Walking up the hill to class, carrying my portable voice
booster, I saw the crowd still on the sidewalks on both sides of
the street. Those who weren't standing in front of the school
with the spray can lettering on its fine brick walls were on the
far side of the street looking across. I went past a woman and
heard her saying, "He was left lying there for an hour and a
half before they took his body away."

10:30 P.M.

Our neighborhood has made the news again. A prominent official from the UN, visiting a friend, was robbed and stabbed to death by three half-grown children.

The following Monday afternoon—

While we were still in bed, our arms around each other, relaxed, I talked about Samarkand. Gail thought going was a great idea. She couldn't understand why I hadn't gone long ago. Didn't I get sabbaticals?

"Creative writing teachers don't qualify."

Gail looked surprised. "I know professors who spend their sabbaticals writing poetry and plays and novels."

"I know . . . but that's a regulation. I've gone into this with my chairman and he's explored it for me. I'm just telling you what I've been told. Well, look, if Metro had a writing department, then as an officer in that department I could qualify for a sabbatical as a professor of writing . . . but attached as I am to the English Department and without a Ph.D. in English and teaching only creative writing as a lecturer, I don't qualify. It makes sense. Writing courses no more belong in the English Department than they do in the French Department or the Philosophy Department. And that, baby, is why I can't get a sabbatical and go to Samarkand."

"I think it's rotten."

"I think it's life."

"How can you laugh about it?" She started in on Metro again. "Why don't you quit that job?"

"And do what?"

"Do what you're doing now, but do it somewhere else.

Teach and write. It's what you want to do, but why go on the way you do at a college that can't make a place for you?"

"Because it would be pretty much the same anywhere else. Anyway, I can't switch now. Why would another school hire me? I haven't published a book in eighteen years. I tried to get into the state system when they were going strong. Jesus, they paid well, but nobody showed any interest in me. I'm no asset except as a teacher. I haven't a name, a reputation a college can trade on . . . and no matter what you've heard about the importance of the good teacher, the good teacher is not rewarded, that is, he is not promoted and given pay raises just because he's a good teacher. From what I've seen."

"Then what gets him a promotion and raise?"

"Having another school trying to hire him away with the offer of more money and a better title. Everything depends on my getting another book out—and I can't."

"Jack, listen to me. I think you're letting this job at Metro get in the way of your writing. You're giving too much and getting too little back. It's crushing your spirit, your independence. That's why you can't write. It's a vicious circle. Can't you quit teaching and then turn to writing? Just be a writer. Forget teaching for now. It's killing you. I tell you, it's killing you. Listen to your voice. Quit."

"I would if I could. I would, but . . ."

"You go to a psychiatrist. Hasn't he told you to get out of that trap?"

"No. I think he's afraid I couldn't pay him anymore if I quit."

"Why haven't you applied for an NEA grant or one of the state's CAPS awards? They give away money to all kinds of writers. I don't know how much. At least four thousand dollars. That would pay your psychiatrist."

"Those awards aren't for writers who haven't published any-thing in eighteen years."

"What do you mean?" she said. "They're set up to help writers like you." One of my students, she pointed out, got a CAPS award last year, a young man who had published only two short stories. He'd got it on the merit of his work.

I sighed. "I haven't told you this . . . but I've tried for every grant around, CAPS, the Guggenheim, NEA. The year you speak of, or the grant you speak of, that CAPS thing . . . Gail, I never made it through the preliminary screenings."

"Then they're crazy. Those awards are fixed."

"No . . . no."

She wasn't relaxed any more and neither was I.

"What does your wife think of all this?"

"All what?"

"Your job, to begin with. Hasn't she encouraged you to get out?"

"Not really."

"I don't understand."

"She thinks I worry too much about things that aren't that important . . . like writing. She's sympathetic but she thinks writers overrate themselves and their role in the world . . . and those awards just encourage us in our self-deceit. She may have something. Anyway, I have my own solution."

"Which is what?"

"What I'm doing. I'm going to get that next book out, and I'm going to do it my way. It's a painful way. It's a dull way. It's even stupid, but it's the only way I know . . . asking no favors, no grants or fellowships anymore, no writers' camps. What I've been doing is learning how to be a writer, I guess—and me, I'm a slow learner. I'm a late bloomer. I'm a stubborn guy."

"Jack, I can't watch you doing this to yourself. If you'll just take a chance and pull yourself out of that trap . . . if you really want to write, I'll fund you. If I knew you were really writing, it would be all I asked. Just do your thing."

"Hey, would you?"

"Any time."

"Would you go to Samarkand with me?"

"Of course."

I lay quietly awhile, thinking. She got up on one elbow and looked at me. "What's the matter?"

"I suddenly feel like a bride," I said. "I was about to say—I don't even know you."

"What do you want to know about me?"

"Where does all this come from?"

"All this what? This apartment? I have a little income."

"You mean a lot of a little income."

She lay back and laughed.

"Where's it from?"

"Fate gave it to me, that's all you need to know."

"Tell me."

"I'll tell you when you tell me why you remarried your wife. I think you remarried her because you loved her and I think you still do."

"Nonsense."

"Let's get dinner on the table," she said, sitting up. She began to feel around for her earrings. "Move a little. I think one's under you."

I got up and sat in the chair beside the bed and watched her put both earrings on again. The sheet was across her legs now, her small breasts were glowing in the late afternoon light from the terrace. I realized that she was so young her body still had a nubile, childform voluptuousness.

"I'm way too old for you," I said hesitantly, hoarsely.

"Nonsense."

"If we went to Samarkand, I suppose you'd want me to marry you."

"No, I wouldn't. I told you I don't want to get married again, and I mean it. It's a foolish institution. Anyway, I would hope you'd not be fool enough to marry again—after two bad marriages to the same woman." She got up. "Now come on. Let's get this bed put back together so it's there for us to pull out tonight. Are you staying tonight?"

"I thought I would."

We pushed the bed back inside itself and I spread colorful pillows around while she went into the bathroom. I heard water running from a faucet. Was she taking her pill?

I don't know why I worried about her, but I did.

After we'd both showered and dressed and served ourselves drinks, she said, "So you don't think you know me?" She seemed amused.

"In some ways yes, in a lot of ways no."

"In what ways no?"

I stared across the room at the football on the piano. "Well, I don't get that for one thing."

"It's a football," she said. "People kick it."

"Oh."

"Was that what you meant?"

"But you're not a football fan. Is it because it's something you won?"

Her face got a little gray, as if some of the light went out of it, and she said, "Okay, what else don't you understand about me?"

"Like you're a very bright girl, Gail. You were a kind of *Wunderkind* in school, a magna cum laude, right? But you don't have any intellectual interests . . ." She shifted restlessly in her chair, so I paused. "I mean, you're very talented—you sing beautifully, you're a good actress. You dance. You sculpt. You can play a guitar. You love art and music and plays . . . but these are all things of the imagination. What about things that engage the intellect?"

"Like what?"

I shrugged. "Philosophy. Philosophical things. Reading philosophers and people handling ideas."

"Like who?"

"Have you read Susan Sontag?"

"I read her for one of your courses, don't you remember?"

"Well, you know what I mean," I said. She had fixed me with a hard look.

"You mean I'm intellectually deficient because I don't give a damn about Susan Sontag and keep a trophy football on my grand piano and stay out late Saturday night having fun."

"I don't know what you do Saturday nights."

"I'm glad you don't."

I back-pedaled fast. "I mean you're a mystery to me, Gail. I'm mystified and enchanted. You're full of surprises. You're forever new."

"That's from a letter of Keats to Fanny Brawne," she said. "I'm not a total loss."

I realized I'd been sounding like a wheezing, tired old character actor, an aging Andy Devine trying to be serious, and I shut up.

She came over to me and kissed me on the forehead. "Let's get the table set."

I laughed. "Well, you jumped on me because of Metro. You don't understand about me and Metro."

"Or you and your wife. Come on now. Why did you remarry her?"

"All right," I said. "Let me try."

She went and got her drink and returned. She sat on the arm of the chair, poised and waiting. "You went back because you found you were an incurable homebody? You needed a home?"

The guess was too close for comfort.

"But, listen, I didn't go back to Janice just to have a home. That's the point. I think it was my daughter, Perse, that got under my skin. I think my daughter put things on a quite simple basis: If I loved her, see, then what did any problems her mother and I had have to do with her?

"I remember once walking around in a department store with Perse. At Christmas. Aisles of soft homey things, pillows and bedspreads around. She had hold of my hand, the way you sometimes hold my hand by a couple of fingers. She was looking very serious. Janice and I had just split up. I wasn't living with them. She said, 'Don't you want to live with us anymore?' And I said, 'It's not that.' Anyway, I couldn't explain. How could I explain? She couldn't understand it didn't have anything to do with her.

"And then the visits to see them. They were a kind of hell and humiliation; the television set got snapped off—or on—whichever would bug me. That's Janice. Sure, she's mean."

"I don't know if I want to hear any more of this," Gail said.

"Janice's mother was alive then, living alone. She moved in. Did I ever tell you about that old bitch . . . taking up the air space I'd vacated? She hated me. Never wanted Janice to marry me. Glad I'd gone. She'd come into the living room when I was there on a visit, and she'd give me her horror mask looks to scare me away."

"And you decided," Gail said, "you just had to go back."

"I wanted to see Perse grow up."

"Did you have to get remarried?"

"Those were Janice's only terms."

"You mean that daughter of yours was bargaining power?"

"I guess so. Some of my friends had kids Perse's age, and I'd begun to take them to museums on Saturday and Sunday. Everybody who knew me knew I was substituting. They gave me sad, attentive looks. Years passed like that. I wasn't getting anywhere with my writing. I was feeling rotten, you know, tired of going around acting like a goddamn genius who lives only for his work, his writing. I felt bad about Janice and Perse. One day it occurred to me how easy it would be to go back and square everything. All I had to do was show some interest, not in Perse but in Janice. It worked. We got remarried. It was that simple."

"I believe it."

"I think that's your answer."

"You got hooked back."

"I guess so."

Gail went to the kitchen. She came in with plates and silverware and began setting the table. I got up slowly and went out to help her. Was this girl setting the silverware by the plates the one I should have been married to all my life? Impossible. She was only twenty-six.

Seated at the table—

"Okay," I said. "Now, what about you and your small income?"

"Oh, that," she said. "I won it in the New York State lottery." She passed the celery.

"Come on. I told you about me and Janice."

"I'm a lottery winner," she said. "Look it up. Why would I kid you?"

"But why keep it such a secret?"

"I would just rather not have everyone know. Think about that."

I gave it some thought.

"And keep it to yourself," she said. "Now, is there anything else I should know about you?"

I gave that some thought, too.

While eating, I did bring up Janice's strange smile and jagged silences. I brought them up as casually as I could—and I thought Gail took them well. But the prospect that Janice had focused in on us at last began to prey, though I played it off as inconsequential.

"People," she said suddenly, apropos of nothing, "become addicted to their poison."

"You sound as if Janice remarried me to get me back in her clutches. To kill me off at leisure. As if somehow or other my throat trouble is a kind of curse, one she's leveled on me that will do me in."

"It's not impossible." She sat rigidly, staring out at the river.

"It's also the theme of a famous short story: revenge by remarriage—Katherine Anne Porter." I was getting even for her crack about Keats and his letter.

"Don't take it lightly. There's a universal truth there. We exact revenge for the dirt that's done to us."

"Well, she more than got even, Gail."

"That woman's rage is depthless."

"You also make it sound as if I sought atonement. As if I were making myself a willing victim."

"It adds up, doesn't it?"

"You ought to go back to writing, Gail. You have a genuine schematic instinct. First-rate."

"You won't be serious. You have this way of making a joke of everything." Gail stood up and started to clear the dishes from the table on the terrace. She was really upset.

She cleared away everything except my beer. The day was gone. Lights were on across the river, all over Manhattan. I waited until I heard her dishwasher start before I wandered inside. She was leaning against the kitchen wall by the window with that defeated look she sometimes gets.

She looked around with a quick little movement of her head. "You asked me once," she said, "what I saw in you."

"And I remember. I'm the dreamer."

"What absolutely fascinates me about you is how you simply will not give up even when every sensible head around you has fled. You will not give up writing, you will not give up Metro, you will not give up a daughter who has no interest in you, you will not give up a destructive marriage, you will not give up me. And really, you know, for all my harping at you, I admire you. I think you're crazy, but I wish I could stick to things the way you do. I wish I had just a little of it. I give up too quickly. We should trade a little of our characters. It would do us both good."

She softened then, she always did, and she put her arms around me and said, "Help me, Jack."

"Help you what?"

"Help me hang in there."

The next morning—

I got up and put on my pants and shirt and in my bare feet walked into the sunlight on the balcony. The cool air blew under my armpits and over my hands on the cold iron of the balcony railing. The sun was rising behind Manhattan.

Whenever I stay overnight with Gail, I try to get out on the balcony as the sun comes up. She asked me the first time what I was doing. Sun worshiping, I said. Did you know, I'd asked her, that for the Mayas God was Time? God was Time and that was all. If you loved and feared time, God was mysterious and real. —Better, she'd said, than thinking of God as Money.

"Coffee's ready."

I turned around. She stood, a classical study of nudity—rusty red hair lying loose over her small shoulders, breasts to the rising sun, one hand held leaf stiff across the ultimate secret. Slowly her hand moved. She gazed at me with resignation and mock modesty, her treasure revealed, a gift to me and the New York skyline.

I laughed. "Don't you worry about someone seeing you?"

"Who? The sea gulls? You got a lot of male middle-aged hangups, know that?"

She turned her ass on me and walked inside. I followed her. Much scratching of matches. She stood with her back to me, shook her head to get the hair out of the way, and lit up, then turned slowly and fell back on the bed and stared at me, smiling. She held out the joint to take.

"What are you thinking?" I said.

"That I'm glad you made me drop your class."

"Is that really what you're thinking?"

"Don't you wish you knew?"

"I never know what you're thinking."

"I'm thinking we've got all Monday ahead of us and we can do anything we want to . . ."

Gail, Janice, Andre, Paul, everyone—

And the need to prove something. Everyone, moment by moment, out to prove something, trying to work magic, to convert truth into fact.

A fact and a truth not the same thing. Truth a conclusion about reality, reality the domain of facts.

That inner voice who talks to us about reality, the voice of Truth.

The reality of work as man's salvation because it lets him distract himself from Truth?

Reality not a distraction, but the main problem of the pioneer or savage.

The forest, the earth—the pioneer's reality. The savage also part of his reality, and vice versa.

The dreamer—as never a realistic man.

Reality not a daily problem any more in America.

God, as we know him, not a reality. God virtually truth/beauty/love—a response to reality, an emotion.

It's our own truths we're all out to prove. No one needs to prove reality.

Reality dependable; truth isn't. Truth can let us down.

To love truth? That's easy—so long as it's mine and not yours.

Reality the source of truth. Reality the creative force of life.

To love reality: an ideal.

Truth as love?

Love as All.

Thanksgiving—

Here it was nearly the end of November—still no word from Baker. And my voice was worse. It got worse day by day. It was splintering and chipping.

The day before Thanksgiving I took the car out of the garage and pulled it up beside the curb near the entrance to our building. I went in and got Janice and we came down carrying our suitcases. The drive to Boston took six hours, so we left before lunch and as we drove the turnpike, ate sandwiches.

I never made the trip without a mixture of urgency and dread; whatever I ate never settled. At the same time, I drove along convinced that this time there was going to be a miracle of understanding all around. I also knew it was going to be another hopeless business of derelict incompatibility. I had not given up trying to convince them, I suppose, that I was the only compassionate and right-minded person in the family.

The trip was good for both of us, spaced out as we were on the daily suffering our jobs or our ambitions brought us. Janice had her own real and imaginary quota of slights, insults and treacheries, being a member of an innovative setup at her hospital. She delivered children without the presence of a doctor. That meant she counseled and attended patients long before their labor pains. She got to know each woman, saw her through labor, held the baby up to light herself. She took her work seriously and a lot of her patients treated her with the accord due a doctor, just as a lot of my students treated me as if I were a professor. But we both knew we were peripheral professional people. We shared similar anxieties in that area. Those problems rode with us down the highway. Most of our troubles did. Yet it helped to get them out of New York.

These days the turnpikes seem to run off through the wilderness that vanished somewhere in the tranquillity of the eighteenth and nineteenth centuries. As if the endless forests had returned, that's how the turnpikes out of New York look: evergreens on each side of the cars. We drove alleyways through the primordial forest of an otherwise unmolested planet, hurtling along above the soft, sucking murmur of radial tires. I'd set my seat back so I could drive with my arms straight out to the wheel, racing style, eyes scanning the road, scanning the dashboard dials: oil pressure, okay—water temperature, okay—no warning lights flashing—3,000 rpms and holding steady, all systems GO.

Janice sat secretly counting off the exits. I'd see her fingers move and try not to let it bug me. If she thought I was taking notice, she'd count them off by moving the tip of her tongue against the sides of her teeth and it kept her silent for hours at a time as she sat motion-lulled, her mind wandering, her life reeling around inside her as the earth reeled by outside our windows. When she spoke, it was usually to report on her interior revisitations, her voice a narrative comment on the descent into a Christmas past, or some November morning when the frost of the year lay glittering on green glass-blades. She, like Sean, was a captive of spinning time spools and old aches and regrets and occasional joys—sharing some of them with me. I knew the worst harm I could do my voice was to talk in a moving car. So I listened to Janice, scanned the dials, submerging into my own reappearing past until our separate replays made montage images in my head: her voice spoke above some cement pier in the Yucatan where I knelt gazing down through thirty feet of water, clear as ground glass, at schools of orange and blue fish swimming above her grandmother's sunken face spread limply over rocks and sand and anchor chains.

Then I'd change lanes and pass a car and she'd gaze around, recovered to the perils of the present, and say, "When we get there, you would do well to say nothing more to Bob, or Perse for that matter, about Watergate, or even the last election. I mean that in no uncertain terms. It would be the worst thing you could do for your voice."

My daughter lives in a duplex about ten miles out of Boston. That is, they live upstairs and rent out the downstairs. They have a white frame house with a big lawn. Being on the edge of a wealthy residential area, they aspire to a place at its center. They'll make it. Her husband, an electrical engineer, is beginning to collect fees as an industrial adviser. He's also a teacher at MIT. In addition, his family has money. That helps. His family put up the money for the down payment on the house, and bought them most of their furniture. Janice and the boy's family are in a kind of competition, and Janice hasn't a chance. Janice regularly puts aside as much as we can spare from what she makes, and that's her war chest. Janice bought Perse her dishes, Tiffany china. I wanted to buy her some Haviland at auction for about a hundred bucks, and had the chance, but Janice was horrified. Neither Perse, she assured me, nor any other woman who cared about her house wanted anything in it that had been used by someone else.

"What about a nice thousand-dollar Queen Anne table?"

"That's not what we're talking about."

"Or would she rather have a hundred-and-fifty-dollar imitation?"

"She simply does not care to eat off plates that some other family has been eating from."

"Or tables they've been eating off, right?"

"There's no use talking to you. You'll never understand."

I really lose all those arguments because I wind up suspecting there is a world alongside me I don't understand and it leaves me uneasy. Everything in my daughter's house was as new as my daughter and her mother could make it. They were perfect consumers. They believed in enjoying life here and now. The place was pleasant enough: a comfortable sofa and chairs in the living room, high-pile wall-to-wall carpeting, beige with yellow stippling. The TV, a color set, gift of his parents, was in the recreation room in the basement off the garage so that the people in the living room could talk. Only we never had much to talk about, and I never went to visit them that I didn't make my way down to the recreation room to see what was playing. I'd watch anything the kids wanted to.

I never said much on our visits and let it be understood I was saving my voice. Curious thing. Perse's husband never heard my old voice although they'd met, got engaged and married about a year before my trouble started. They'd met at college and I'd gone to the wedding, but we'd never said a word to one another. None of us can quite figure out how that could be. It has sometimes crossed my mind Perse was keeping me hidden.

Perse and Bob were waiting. They and their kids came down the lawn that sloped to the street as we opened the car door. Perse was carrying the baby and Bob had a kid by each hand. They walked through fallen leaves.

He was a handsome boy. I could think of two or three TV and movie personalities he looked like, strong hero types. It was easy to see why Perse had fallen for him, but she must have had to date him up herself, because he was astonishingly shy.

Perse threw her arms around her mother and gave me a kiss, but Bob stood back, grinning. He nodded at Janice and me, and as soon as he could, turned his attention to his children. I did myself.

The two older ones, a girl and a boy, remembered me. The oldest is a girl, about four years old—just the age Perse was when, as Janice put it, I ran out on them. Walking up to the house with the child gave me the strangest damned sensation. It was mostly elation. I felt dizzy, slightly disoriented.

Bob came along behind carrying our suitcases. After we'd settled, he sat with us in the living room, two of the children squirming on his lap. He said very little except to the children. Company made him uncomfortable, and I sympathized. I liked him. It was hard to dislike a man so devoted to Perse and my grandchildren. But discomfort or shyness makes me uncomfortable, and pretty soon I got restless and then kind of desperate. I couldn't talk to him about his work. It was full of random references to things like RF and IF circuitry or radar threat signal processing and analog design. I got a trapped feeling and began to pace around the house looking out the windows. He disappeared into his study, where he stayed for most of the rest of our visit.

I worried him. He was not sure what to make of me. He'd heard too many stories from Perse and Janice, and I think he saw me as a Satanic messenger running between hell and bearded, bomb-hurling, die-hard Bolsheviks. He was the only young man I knew who still worried about Marx and Lenin. He had an American flag on one of the windows of his car and on several windows of the house. He subscribed to *National Review*. He had supported Nixon to the end and still admired him. He went to church with his family every Sunday—to mass,

I should say. He believed in prayer. He had once, I heard, lit a candle for me. But he was hard to reach. I liked to play with the idea that we were each of us secretly hoping to save one another. I know I knew, and Janice knew and Perse knew, to their consternation, that I in my self-centered fashion wanted to save him. But aren't we all trying to save one another?

I went to the kitchen once for a beer and, opening the can, looked out the window. There was Perse a few feet away raking leaves. "I want to talk to you," she said quietly without looking around. How had she seen me? Had she heard the can pop? She and Janice had had all the time they needed for a long talk and I'd been waiting for this. Even so, for all my apprehension, I stood leaning on the windowsill, thinking what beautiful arms she had, and hands. She was delicate yet sturdy. I was proud of her. Such a serious girl though. Very serious about everything.

She rested the rake against an elm tree, came over and made a little gesture that she wanted a sip of the beer. I gave it to her. Twilight was just beginning to color the sky, and the shadows on the lawn were all long and soft. "What's this I hear about Samarkand?" she asked with a small smile, a cheerful but enigmatic smile, as if she were asking me, now, what are you up to?

"Ah," I said, "you know Janice. She thinks I might go to Samarkand and blow a little money."

"The way I heard it, Jack, you are going." She seemed merely curious and not out to back her mother up. It always surprised and pleased me when I got any indication they weren't absolutely allied in mind, thought and action.

"Do you really want to go?" she asked.

I hesitated. "Yes."

"Does it mean a lot to you?"

I started to tell her about Samarkand but she said, "Save your voice. How many times have I told you that when you get tense you use your voice badly?" She handed me the beer. "You're not thinking of taking some girl along, are you?" She paused. "I'd watch my step."

"Watch my step?"

"Yes."

He made doors all night in his dreams, small doors, big doors, wide doors, narrow doors. All hand-carved doors, all of them, all of them. He'd wake up exhausted, saying he never wanted to dream of carving another door again. He would tell his dreams to his wife, how the wood last night was too hard to carve and how he kept being called away to the phone (in his dream) to take orders for more doors from people who pleaded with him when he said he could make no more, that he had thousands of doors on back order and could take no more orders, but they kept calling, the door needers, begging him, keeping him away from his work so that he had worked, or it seemed to him he had worked, all night and hadn't finished one door. He went to work exhausted and then could not rest when he went to bed at night because he had so many doors to make and was so far behind. The phone kept ringing, more and more orders coming in as if he were the only doormaker in the world. Why doors? Why did he dream of doors? If you do not pay your phone bill in your dreams, his wife told him, the phone company will cut off your dream service. And, said he, if I swear into the phone and use every filthy word I can think of? Yes, she said, it could be cut off for that, too. She wished she could be of more help to him. He was exhausted. Too many doors to make, too many doors.

"But if I know you," Perse had said, "you'll never go any-where."

December 1st—

"Jack. When you give me this business of how you've made an emotional commitment to Janice, or is it to your marriage, and how you have to be true to your sense of reality or is it your goddamn truth, I can't stand it. I don't think you've ever made a commitment to any woman, to any woman in your life . . . except for your daughter. I think you love her. But that's something you weren't prepared for. I think your mother probably ruined you for women for all time. America is full of men like you, men who can't bring themselves to trust a woman . . . until they have a daughter. You don't trust me, I know that. But you've got something incestuous going between us you like and I don't think I like it anymore."

"You mean you think I may love you and you don't like that?"

"I don't know if I want the responsibility. It's a drag. Anyway, I'm not your mother and I'm not your daughter. Give me a cigarette."

"I don't smoke. I'll have to get some."

"What time is it? You've got to go."

"Jesus Christ. What are we talking like this for?"

"Well, I don't know. It's no fun. I'm tired of you slopping your guilts all over my bed."

"You got me talking about Janice. I didn't want to."

"Do you still screw her?"

"Oh, you know . . ."

"You do?"

"Sometimes."

"Enjoy it?"

"Look, no more now. No more. Oh boy, oh boy, it's been a heavy night."

"Go home. I want you to go home."

December 7th—

I sit on this, the anniversary of Pearl Harbor, dreaming of underground places, caves, to begin with, all the way from little holes in the sides of embankments to deep passageways under the earth—like the tunnels left after the tree of heaven has been uprooted: moist tunnels narrowing down, down, down into a shimmering wormworld and icicle silence.

I hear the subway rattling out of its tunnel and rolling by on its stretch of elevated track on Broadway.

I sit in this chair by the window and imagine a caravan of subway cars pulling into Times Square station, say. One of the cars, a club car with curtains on its windows, inside its door, thick piled carpet, a bar, a color television set, all of it air-conditioned. Leaning on the bar like an airline hostess, a girl in shorts and black net stockings. Only a flicker-vision of this as the train pulls out of the station. Have I imagined it—or was that a private subway car? If so, whose?

A few days later, in class, my students talking about the same curious phenomenon—or do I imagine this, too? Apprehensions set scenes loose in the mind. I'm full of apprehensions when I take the street stairs down into a subway station. I sometimes think I leave a good part of my rational self behind. Anything can happen down below. But a private club car on a subway train of cars?

Then others have seen it too? There may be one or several of these cars. The transit system is in financial trouble; is this a gimmick to help them out of the red? I can believe anything after I've left the upper world. Once, riding on a local under lower Manhattan, a young man in a pinstriped suit, carrying a black attaché case, began to scream at all of us, "What are you staring at? Do you think you know me? Do you think you know who I am? Are you seeing all you want to?" Screaming to get his voice up above the sound of the subway's wheels, and screaming because he was so goddamn outraged, too. Who knows what it was all about? I sat there looking around for what it was he was screaming about. I couldn't tell.

I know a lady who said she saw the floor of her subway car split open at her feet—like a crevasse in an earthquake. It swallowed, she said, two men.

And then one day I'm standing at the Fifty-ninth Street station waiting for the Broadway local, and in it comes—carrying with it the private club car. The club car stops in front of my feet. And as the doors slide open, from behind me appear several people; one of them takes my arm. It's my old friend Paul Johnson. He's wearing blue denims and smoking a cigarette, flaunting all subway regulations. He doesn't seem to care. He doesn't seem to have to care. He's looking fierce, full of plans and confidence. He grabs my arm. Into the club car we go, followed by his two silent children. The doors slide shut. Off we roll toward upper Manhattan. He and I sink into a couple of soft leather chairs and the gal in the shorts with the net hose takes our orders for two Mai Tais on lots of shaved ice. He's wearing muddy work boots.

"It's too long a story to go into," says Paul. "I couldn't tell you when I saw you. I've gone partners with Andre. In the last three months things have been happening fast. The kids and I just moved into my New York pad and I'm having a small gathering on Friday night. Why don't you and Janice come up?" He quickly writes an address on a card one of his kids hands him. I can tell they're his assistants. Then he excuses himself and confers with the two children at the other end of the car.

When the drinks come two stops later, they return and Paul takes a glass. As the doors open, Paul and the two girls leave. He waves to me. The train pulls out of the station. He is walking along drinking his Mai Tai. The girls are licking ice cream cones.

"You're a friend of his?" ask my hostess' wondering eyes.

On Friday night, Paul's little gathering turned out to be in an old building that had until recently been a National Guard armory. He'd had the place completely remodeled. It was a castle in the middle of New York, a heliport, three swimming pools, two bowling alleys, one very intimate and private with, curiously, mirrors on the ceiling. A motion picture screening room, two kitchens, forty-five bedrooms, eighteen bathrooms (a roman bath, two steam rooms), nine assorted living rooms, a wine cellar with 30,000 vintage bottles, and an endless supply of liquor and liqueurs. Decorators were still around. In one of the conference rooms, Dali himself was at work on a mural. There was also an indoor racetrack and a stable of horses we did not get to see.

With a party in full swing it was hard to get Paul aside long enough to talk to him. I finally managed. I got him alone in one of the castlelike turrets in his old armory. We stood looking down at the streetlights and apartment houses below us. "Don't tell me," I said, "you got all of this rolling because Andre published your novel?"

"*Negativo, compadre.* There's no money in writing. You know that." He flicked his cigarette away. It fell, a wobbling red point in the night, to the street below. Its coal splashed on the pavement. "I write because I want to. It's all that matters in the end."

Was he putting me on? I said, "You mean you're still writing?"

"Sure."

"With all . . . I mean . . . this?" I pointed back into the castle or whatever it was he had. And he said, pointing out at New York, "And all that, too. I own the whole fucking town."

"But why? All this? If writing is enough?"

"Security, Jack. Like you, I need lots of security. It brings me peace of mind."

POP

POP

POP

I'd pushed the dream too far. I stood face to face with myself.

The night was cold, and everything was dissolving.

I stared down at the cars in the parking lot thinking: the eleven o'clock news should be on.

December 8th—

When I rang the bell of Gail's apartment, there was no answer. I didn't know what to do. She'd said she'd be home by six o'clock. She could be right behind me, coming up on the elevator. I leaned against the corridor wall. I walked from her door to the elevator a couple of times. The couple who lived across the hall came home and nodded, having seen me around, but they didn't know who I was or where I belonged. At six-thirty I decided to go downstairs; I didn't want to look like someone loitering in the corridor.

My impulse to leave was rational. But she'd never stood me up before. I couldn't figure it out. I picked an oversized chair near the door, where I could see everyone coming in. The doorman glanced at me once, long enough to place me, then resumed his evening meditations. By seven-thirty I was hungry. The doorman said if I went out to the highway, turned left and walked about a quarter of a mile, I'd come to a store that sold groceries and cold cuts.

It was getting dark and a wind had come up. Walking along, I thought I was probably being silly—getting something to eat when she'd be home any minute. But I felt grim and I think I knew it was going to be a long wait. I meant to wait. I bought two corned beef on rye with slaw and two beers. Off in another area were shelves of wine. I picked out a Montrachet, and headed back.

We'd said we'd meet; nothing had been said about what

we'd do. I planned to take her to dinner at the Clam Broth House in Hoboken, but if she got back late that was out. We could eat something at her place and drink the wine. What about the beer and the two corned beef? Should I save them or eat one? The idea of the wine was a crazy impulse. I thought of throwing the wine away—but that was foolish.

Upset, I went back to the lobby hugging my packages. The doorman said she hadn't come home. I sat down, put the packages by my feet and took out a sandwich and a beer. She'd had an appointment that afternoon with a young producer who was, she said, lining up a cast for a new show. That was all I knew. I ate a sandwich and drank a beer.

It was at least an hour later—I'd finished the other sandwich and beer—when I realized Janice was standing on the other side of the glass entrance door staring at me. She seemed to materialize gradually. That image, that woman behind the glass, that figure who stood there so quietly like someone frozen in a block of ice, was my wife. Under her arched thin eyebrows, her eyes stared in at me with an expression I had never seen on her face before. There was no rage, no resentment. She seemed emotionally smashed, drunk, but there was also a touch of fear in her eyes. Whatever she was feeling had made her stop outside that door until she could recover; and even when she knew I saw her, she did not move. I think she didn't know what to do.

I nodded at her.

She came inside and stood in front of me, both hands on her purse. "I thought you might be here," she said. With sorrow. Sorrow for me and for her—for both of us, I guess.

In anguish I laughed. "I've been waiting for you."

"You're not waiting for me."

"What are you doing," I said, "scouting for your lawyer?"

"No."

"What made you think I was here?"

She didn't answer.

I gathered my trash and the bottle of wine and stood up. We walked out to the car.

"How did you get here?"

"I took a taxi."

We got in and I drove toward the bridge. So far neither of us had given anything away.

She said quietly, "Who is she? One of your students?"

And then I wondered whether Gail had tried to get a message to me and if she and Janice had just had a long talk. "How did you know where I was?"

But Janice was quiet about what she knew—these were only the preliminaries, the slow continuation of something building that would go on building for weeks and months, maybe forever.

I could have started lying. Perhaps she wanted me to. A couple of excuses ran through my head, worth trying. I couldn't. I was sick. Even with Janice sitting beside me, I wanted to know where Gail was and what had happened to her. Why pretend? I'd been caught, that was all. Not in bed. Worse. Caught in humiliation. The picture story of the rejected lover for Janice to take home. And she knew it too.

When we got upstairs, I put the wine in the refrigerator. I went into my study and sat in the wing chair and stared out at the tops of the cars in the parking lot and at the street and at the windows of the city housing apartments. Janice stayed in the living room.

I called Gail at eleven-thirty. No answer. I called her again at midnight. No answer. She did not answer until one-thirty. I shut the door of the study and said, "Jesus Christ, Gail, where have you been?"

Her voice was soft, hushed, mollifying. "I couldn't call you. Mr. Jacobs wanted me to come along to a party and meet some people and we all had dinner. I couldn't call you and this was very important, Jack."

"Okay," I said. "Good night. I was just worried. Good night."

"Is she better in bed than I am?"

"No."

"Then what is it?"

How could I explain? It was all so complicated.

"It's not the quality, it's the quantity."

"I suppose you think that's funny."

"I mean some men need more than one woman day after day, all their lives. It's not a matter of preferring one woman, finding the best and sticking with her."

"Variety is the spice of life, is that it?"

"Janice, I'm trying to tell you that I like you and the home we have, but I look around me and think, this isn't enough. There's got to be more."

"That's all very well for you to say . . ."

"I know there's got to be more."

"More sex?"

"Yes . . . yes . . . sex, yes, sure . . ."

"And what about me?"

"What about you?"

"Don't I count too? What about my sex needs? Maybe I'd like some variety. I suppose that would be all right with you?"

I thought about it. "No, it wouldn't. I wouldn't like it."

"What could you do to stop me?"

I shrugged. "I'd divorce you. I don't know what I'd do."

She looked startled. "Is that what you want? Another divorce? Because if it is, I want to know right now."

I shook my head.

"Well . . . I'll have you know in no uncertain terms I am

not about to have you divorce me on the grounds of adultery. Just because you sneak around, because you think you're so smart . . . Listen. You know what you are? You know what you are? You're a male chauvinist pig." She whipped her face from me, heavy with the bitterness of her thoughts. It was the first time I'd known her to take a women's lib stand on anything.

"Anyway," I said, "don't tell me you haven't had variety."

"What?"

"Variety," I said, sucking wind to help my throat work. "What the hell, you've had it."

"How would you know? If you weren't so selfish . . ." Now she had her rage out on all sides. "You don't take enough of an interest in me or in anything I do to know, to know anything."

"What I want to know is . . . is Perse my child?"

"What? Oh, that's dirty."

"It's dirt you put . . . in my goddamn head, Janice."

"When?"

"You know when. I'll tell you when. About the time you were burning everything I had, my clothes, my manuscripts. You burned all my manuscripts, including a book I might have published."

"Listen, that was something I said when you were trying to come between me and Perse . . . and you know it. I could have killed you . . . that was when I said—'How do you know, what makes you so sure she's your child?' "

"I'm *not* sure. I *don't* know. Never did. You shacked up with that guy, that colonel, that night in Lexington."

"That's a lie."

"You came down the stairs from up where his room was. I know. I was sitting in the lobby where I could see the door to the street."

"I don't care what you say you saw. I've never hurt you the way you've hurt me."

"You burned all my notes, my journals. And what about that old boyfriend you were dating while I was in the Army? And that time we were splitting up and my closest friend goes to see you to see if he can patch things up and you let him stay the night? Good god, Janice, knock it off."

"You don't know how you've hurt me." She started to cry.

"Janice, listen to me. You and I both, we've both fucked around. What does it matter? Do I ask you what doctors or ward boys you're screwing in the hospital linen room? Leave me alone. I don't want to rasp away like this, as if I'm gagging to death on chicken bones."

"You don't even know what matters. You don't know, do you?"

"Janice, look out the window. Look around you on the street. Read the papers. The world is coming to an end. That's what matters."

"You don't know. You've never known."

December 9th—

My daughter, who's now heard all, has chosen scorn. I spoke
to her briefly on the telephone and got her scorn. I don't scorn
her scorn. She's a good woman, a good mother, a good wife. So
is my wife, her mother. The world is full of good women, and
that's a fact. My mistress, my girl friend, my companion, is a
good woman too. Good, wise women are all around me.

I feel only weak and guilty and bullheaded, bullheaded as
hell. Perse wants to talk to me. I've agreed to meet her at a
motel coffee shop halfway between New York and Boston.
Alone.

The next day—

Early snow drifted around the car tires in the lot. Her brown
station wagon was parked near the door to the coffee shop. She
had a dent in the rear fender that made identification instant
and sure.

She sat in a booth alone, on the far side of the room, and I
knew at once I was in for a bad time. I love my daughter with
a fierce, proud and painful love. She can hurt me as no one can.

"Well, who is she?"
"Perse, this isn't something I can talk about. She's a
woman."

"Do you love her?"

"Yes, I guess I do."

"Then you're getting ready to walk out on us again, is that it?"

I shook my head and spoke slowly, reminding myself not to get tense or push my voice. "No, I won't do that unless your mother tells me I have to get out. I don't want to do that again."

"Then get rid of this woman."

I said nothing.

As if I'd said something, she said, "Just stop seeing her."

I nodded.

"How can you love this other woman when you say you love Mother?"

I sighed. "I guess love isn't all that exclusive. How do I know how these things happen?"

"Is it sex?" She was just not going to understand.

"No." My voice was going. It had sunk to a rattling whisper.

"Does Mother actually mean to put up with this?"

"We haven't talked it out yet."

"I suppose she thinks you're going to get over this woman if she gives you time. I suppose she thinks if it isn't this one it'll be another one. How can you do this to her?"

Perse put her face in her hands. I'd never seen her so upset. Our coffees sat between us almost untouched, gone cold. When she took her hands down, she started in on me, viciously. My split with Janice and our divorce came up once more, something I'd never been able to explain, because Janice, in the years I'd been away, had filled Perse's mind with so much garbage. I could clean it all up, and back it would fly. It was ground we'd gone over and over. Now I listened, waiting for her to wind down. Her hands clenched and unclenched.

She tossed her head, her long hair fell back in her face, tears got in her hair. I wanted to cry with her. People at the counter were watching us.

"Go to your goddamn Samarkand and take your cheap little bitch with you. You shouldn't have come back to us, don't you know that? You came back because you're weak and spineless. You were dead to us. The dead shouldn't come back."

"I don't believe you mean that."

"We were better off without you. What good are you to us?"

"Yeah, well, I'm here, Perse. Your mother took me back. Let's accept that."

She squinted off across the tables; and I said, because I felt her softening, "I tried to come back sooner. Your mother is peculiar. As forgiving as she is unforgiving, but it took me awhile to see. I'd have been back sooner if I'd known. You remember the time I turned up at the house and she wouldn't let me in? I had presents with me and she wouldn't let me in? She wouldn't unhook the screen door to let me pass them in? And there the two of you stood, staring out at me, both of you dressed up, hair fixed up, me dressed up, shoes all shined; there we all stood. She told me to leave them on the steps. I wanted to come back home then. I was there ready to come back that day, and she sent me away. I went away. You remember? I walked all the way to the end of the street and I stopped and stood looking back, waiting for any kind of sign. I stood there at least half an hour and nobody took the stuff I'd brought inside. And you know, all I'd have had to do was go back to the screen door and tell her I was sorry . . . but I didn't know that was what she wanted from me. It seemed too simple. I didn't think there was anything I could say or do that would help, nothing, not then, not later. So, Perse, I'm telling you now, too, I'm sorry. Please, give me a break?"

She started to nod her head and then changed it to a shake.

Little fast shakes. She closed her eyes. I looked at my watch. It was way past time for us to go. She left. After she left, I felt for my wallet. I couldn't find it. I'd forgotten it.

Oh, it was worse than that, worse than that, much worse. I keep going over and over it. I hear her say, "We're not at all alike . . ." I'd been trying to offer her my friendship, at least that, and she said, "You're not at all conventional and I am. I'm a very conservative girl. I belong to a church and I believe in God. I vote Republican. I do community work. I love my kids and I have a husband, thank God, who loves me. You weren't around when I needed you and I can see you can't help yourself, but I cried and cried because you weren't there and then I decided you couldn't care less about whether I was crying over you or not and I stopped. I am not going to cry over you anymore. This is the last time. Mother can if she wants to, but I'm not going to. I need the life I have, and I won't have it upset and my husband won't have you upsetting us either. I didn't even dare tell him I was going to see you this morning. He doesn't understand you and who can blame him? You don't like him. You wouldn't like our friends. You have nothing in common with us. We're all very straight young people."

"Perse, I'm basically a square. It's taken me a long time to see it, but I'm a square. I'm conservative."

She shook her head.

"Why do you think I worked so hard to get Janice to come back to me? Honey, I love you. You're my little girl. Don't act like this."

She got up quickly. "Please," she said, "I don't think there is any more for either of us to say."

I put my hands under the table because they were shaking and I didn't look up again until she'd left. I sat breathing deeply in and out. When I thought I had myself in control, I got up and left, too. On my way out, feeling for my wallet, I caught sight of myself in a mirror. I looked like hell.

Perse came all the way in from her car to pay—I'd caught up with her as she was turning to drive out of the lot.

On almost any given day and at almost any time I will hear a voice in my head saying, "Things have got to get better." There are days I know things will, because they couldn't get any worse.

And I'm not the only one. Fred was telling me today about his problems with the dean and the provost. "I feel," he said, "as if I'm living under a glass bell. I don't expect to get anything I ask for anymore, and when I don't get it, I have this exquisite feeling of fulfillment."

More on Samarkand.

This distilled from a book by Sven Hedin called *The Silk Road*—the longest and the greatest and the oldest of the world's overland roads, it ran from the Pacific Ocean across the middle of China to Samarkand, not so much a road as a trail traveled by two-wheeled carts and camels carrying bales of silk, headed for ancient Greece and Rome, that trail a long channel of dust in the summer, in some places its roadbed sunk into the ground from fifteen to twenty feet. Nobody knows how old that road is, there's no record. The silk came down such a long trail to Europe and passed through the hands of so many merchants that those who finally wore the material had only a vague idea where it came from.

One branch of the Silk Road went from Samarkand by way of Seleucia to Tyre on the Mediterranean, and from Sian to Tyre the road, following the bends, ran around 6,000 miles. It was an interplanetary journey. Marco Polo, one of the early travelers, never quite got to Samarkand, passing below it on his way east. From Seleucia, another route west ran up to Constantinople and on to Budapest, through Vienna, then branched over to the European capitals.

I saw myself starting from Europe, retracing that trail backward to its beginning on the coast of China—following my own inclinations—moving southeast out of Vienna, edging around Hungary and Bulgaria, dropping down the Dalmatian Coast—working around to Greece and Athens—and then up to and through the Bosporus to Istanbul, or old Constantinople, moving sometimes by water and sometimes by road, but traveling by car, riding in it or shipping it with me. I wouldn't take the most direct route to Samarkand, no use beelining there. I wanted to drop south to Baghdad. Samarkand didn't figure in those tales of the 1001 nights that Fletch and I read as much as Baghdad, so I had to see Baghdad. Baghdad on the Tigris. Then move across the old kingdom of Persia toward the Caspian Sea. Eastward, that huge plateau of old Persia, range after range of mountains extending into India and up into China. Samarkand to the north of those mountains, on the edge of the plain of West Turkestan.

After hanging around Samarkand awhile, head into and across China. Arrange that with the Chinese? Would they understand? My trail led north of Tibet across the Gobi—called on my map "the rainless district" and referred to by Hedin as the almost unknown land.

Hedin, speaking of someone who might make such a journey, said, "He will return with memories of picturesque, swarming China, of the oases on the edge of the Gobi, the mysterious deserts between Tun-hwang and Lou-lan, the wild camels' desolate homeland. He will have seen a glimpse of the wandering lake and the belt of vegetation which is just being born again on the banks of the river Kum-daria. He will have seen the sand dunes on the northern edge of the Takla-makan and the East Truki oases at the foot of the Celestial Mountains. The summer sun of Central Asia will have burnt him, and he will never forget the howling of the sandstorms or the hissing of the snow blizzards in the winter. He will have made the acquaintance, if a fleeting one, of travelers on foot and on horseback, and the silent procession of camel caravans at the side of the road.

"From the countries west of Terek-dawan he will preserve the memory of another world—the splendid mosques and mausoleums from Tamerlane's time in Samarkand; the theological colleges of Bokhara, with cupolas and minarets gleaming in gaily colored faience; Merve with its traditions of learning and knowledge; the mosque containing Imam Riza's tomb, to which pilgrims still throng from all over Iran; the romantic land of Persia, home of Hadji Baba, and Baghdad, the city of the caliphs and one of the principal scenes of the Arabian Nights.

"From Ankara and Istanbul he will enter the noise and hurry of Western life, and he will think with regret of the great silence and peace in the deserts of Asia . . ."

Black Friday the 12th—

I waited the usual hour or so in Dr. Baker's reception room, admiring his classy patients and furnishings. His fees ran high but no higher, I suppose, than those of a hundred other doctors of exalted reputation. My TIAA benefits through the college would be covering most of my expenses, so I could relax a little on that score and even feel like a big spender, one of an elite group. Was the blonde with the high breasts across the way a famous singer? Actress? We were all a poised and well-dressed lot, looking as if we were taking time out of busy and gratifying lives. At least, I liked to imagine I looked that way, too, and I dressed up for every trip I made to see Baker. Mostly, patients glanced at one another, eyes never meeting. Mostly we stared into magazines or books we'd brought along. Our fortunes, even our lives, might hang here in balance and you'd never guess it. Some of the young women were accompanied by children and I never knew if Baker examined the children or the mother, or perhaps all of them in a line. Not likely. The wait of an hour or two, then his two-minute examination could easily blow half a day's pay for some of these men and women. But when you got Dr. Baker to look down your throat, it was easy for a patient and his family to feel they had done all that was humanly possible for the one who was ailing.

I'd already seen a lot of highly recommended ear-nose-throat guys and they'd been having their way with me for over four years. Convinced my ailment was psychosomatic, Newman had put me in a hospital under sodium amytal for an hour while he probed my depths to locate the psychological cause for my hoarseness. A lot of people think I must hate teaching. No, I love teaching. Newman couldn't pin it on that. Newman couldn't even pin it on the voicelessness of a writer made manifest in his throat. In short, he found no psychological cause—except for the general state of anxiety I spent my days enjoying.

It was Baker, some three years after my first operation, who discovered what all the other doctors missed: a polyp *under* one of my vocal cords. He missed it on one operation himself. The polyp had been there so long, he said, there'd been this change in its cell structure. In his office now was the biopsy reading from the Mayo Clinic.

I sat in his small bright room listening for him. He was still a couple of cubicles away. Someone was going ahhhh and strangling. The gagging and ahhing kept on and on. I heard footsteps; a white gown flashed past the door: his assistant, a black man in glasses who had powerful arms and shoulders.

When Baker appeared in the doorway, his nurse behind him, I knew I was in for some disturbing news. He didn't step inside. He paused and looked straight at the wall, and I didn't get my usual cheerful greeting. His nurse knew what he knew. She was looking at me.

Baker grabbed my record folder from its rack, briskly whipped it open and studied it.

"So the slides came back?"

He nodded, frowning. Then he turned the folder toward me and lowered it so I could read what his finger pointed at. I made out a couple of lines: "*Carcinoma papilloma* . . . radical treatment not yet recommended." I sat there trying to remember what *carcinoma* meant. Was it bad?

I heard him talking about Mount Sinai Hospital, Monday, another doctor, X-ray therapy. X-ray therapy? I adjusted my

glasses, studied the Mayo Clinic report again. I had him go
over everything once more.

"I thought you said X-ray therapy would burn up my cords?"

He nodded and said, "I know. That's been my experience.
But we have to do something."

Bad news. Go buy something. On the way home I bought
a two-inch-wide leather belt with a heavy brass buckle.

Blood on the moon—

My own reaction was only one example of the curious ways people greet bad news, really bad news, about themselves or those close to them. I was still in a state of shock when I got home and I telephoned Janice at her hospital to get some of it off my back.

I told her what Baker said. She took it with the same professional calm Baker and his nurse had: grim but cool. "What will you do about teaching?" she said, thinking at once, I suppose, of my income, or—could it have been?—of its importance to me.

"I haven't thought about that yet. I haven't had time to think about anything. I'm going to have a drink now and do some thinking."

"Oh, God," she said, "now this."

"What?"

"Nothing," she said. She was losing her poise. "I'll be home for lunch. Stay there." Where did she think I was going? Straight over to Gail's?

I hadn't called Gail all week. I'd paced around wanting to but hadn't.

By the time Janice got home, she'd had time to do some thinking herself. She was in her own state of shock and in her nurse's white when she came through the door. She hadn't hung around the hospital to change. Her eyes wide, face stiff with remorse. All in all she looked worse than when she walked in on me over at Gail's. She didn't say anything for a while because she didn't know what to say . . . or do.

Her mother died of cancer and I knew she was re-experiencing that. The old lady died while Janice and I were divorced. A long, painful ordeal. The suffering and the screaming went on for months. She'd told me how the old lady in her fits of pain had torn the sheets and clawed the wallpaper beside the bed. She'd had X-ray therapy, too. It hadn't helped. Nothing helped. There was apparently no painkiller made to help her. Janice had stolen heroin for her, got it anywhere she could, and it hadn't helped. The old lady, a big-boned woman who weighed in her prime almost 180, got thinner and thinner. When they buried her, Perse could have picked her up and carried her a hundred yards—her face already a skull's. I'd heard the story a hundred times. Janice was still grieving, still snagged on the horror of it.

My mother died of cancer, too. It seemed to be as common as the cold. My father saw her through it, the X-ray therapy and the long decline. Then he died of it, his bed brought down from upstairs and set up in the living room. He spent his last days gazing out at the lawn, watching cars go by.

While we were eating in silence, she said twice, "Well, I'm just not going to worry about this." But the fork in her hand shook. She couldn't finish eating. She pushed her plate back, put her head in her hands and shook her head. She began to cry. She wailed, "I have just not come all this way, I have not gone through all we've gone through to have this happen now. I won't have it. I won't."

In a minute she took her napkin and wiped her eyes. Then she threw it down and glared at me. "Who is this man Beirne at Mount Sinai? Why is Baker sending you to a radiologist at another hospital? What's the matter with his hospital's radiologist?" She was furious now, on the attack, more like the old Janice I knew.

"Baker said he wanted to send me to the best man in New York. He said this Beirne may be the best man in the world. I think he's developed some treatment of his own."

"When do you see him?"

"Monday afternoon."

"I'm going to see him with you."

She didn't have that afternoon off, but I could think of nothing to do or say that would stop her. Her reaction had settled into rage, an emotion she was comfortable with and one I could live with, had lived with for years. At least, she was no longer furious with me. One remission anyway. We spent Saturday and Sunday in nervous peace. She even cooked my mother's recipe for spaghetti sauce.

Monday, driving over to Mount Sinai, I said to her, "You mean you still want me around, no matter what happens? I could come out of this without a set of vocal cords, you know."

"Yes."

"If I have no voice, I can't teach. And if I can't teach, I'm too old to get any other kind of job."

"I'll take you," she said, choked up, "on any terms I can have you." I had never had such an admission or confession from her in all the years I'd known her, and it knocked me reeling from a perch way back inside my mind. I operate alone, very much alone, buried and lonely under mountains of cute little tics and defenses, but she reached me.

There was no place to park near the hospital, so we pulled over to a bus stop and took a chance. Janice came with me. She sat in the waiting room while Beirne and a couple of other doctors took turns examining my throat. Beirne was a tall scholarly-looking man in his late fifties. He probed my throat as expertly as I'd ever had it done and said, yes—I was a candidate for his treatment, a very good candidate. He smiled. "I think we'll get your voice back for you, Mr. Fross." And then he left, majestically, a great man. I could see that. I had just met a great man.

The younger of the other two doctors stayed behind to take down my medical history and answer all my questions. Janice came in to join us and I said, "What is it I have?"

"Is it cancer?" she said, not mincing words.

"Yes," he said. "He has wild cells, but they're not yet invasive. Chances are, left alone, in time they will be."

He was a handsome, dark-haired man, the type I imagined Janice involved with on the nights she spent away from home. His looks, I noted, were not lost on her. She had her breasts out and her eyes were bright, but she still bore in with questions.

In sum, this young god said, you are saved. The type of wild cells now in residence along your vocal cords, multiplying at their leisure, have not yet burrowed into your bloodstream, and though they may not, it is best to rout them before they do, because they might decide to invade anytime between twenty years from now and tomorrow morning. It sounded a little like living with a lot of black widow spiders in a matchbox in my pocket. I didn't need them.

"When should he start treatments?" Janice said.

"Any time."

"I understand," I said, "X-ray treatments wipe out vocal cords."

He smiled confidence, reassurance. "Elsewhere, perhaps. But not here. In most cases, the patients with your problem get a good voice back when it's all over. Much depends, of course, on how well you're able to keep silent over a minimum of eight weeks. You'll have to conserve your voice for at least six months and we'll want to keep a check on you twice a year for five years."

When we got back to the car, there was no ticket. In luck all around.

A couple of days later: Metro's reaction, or rather Fred's reaction when told, was one of wary but genuine concern. I think he was wary because almost no one came to his office who wasn't trying to get something out of the department and Metro: a raise in pay, tenure, a promotion, a better class schedule, smaller classes. Almost everyone he saw had some angle he was working and ready to work him over for. What he gave me was his usual defensive sympathy, his helpless shrug and wilted look, all stepped up a few powers because the thought of X-ray therapy shocked him.

I'd met him in the hall and we'd walked back to my office, where we could talk. My office was in the silent, almost unoccupied wing.

When we were settled, I said, "Fred, will you find out what the fuck kind of benefits there are around this shithouse? I called Administration this morning, talked to Orkmund, and he says we don't have any TIAA disability benefits. Only really tenured professors are taken care of. I have tenure, but I don't know if that's going to cover me. I'm not real around here, never have been. All I want to know is, should I lose my voice, will I get any benefits for my long and dubious service to dear old Metro?"

He grinned. I could talk to Fred. He knew all my grievances. Anyway, I did not want his pity and I had seen it looming up.

I laid it all out then, the six weeks of treatment, five days a week, the weeks of absolute silence and the weeks after that of using my voice softly. I thought I'd be able to handle my classes, I told him, if I didn't have to teach a full schedule. I wanted to teach, I told him. I expected to teach—without a voice. I'd use notes, write them in class and let some student read them aloud. My classes were mostly students reading their own stories, then taking turns commenting on what they'd heard—my two advanced classes at least. My beginning class in poetry, fiction and drama required lecturing. That's the one I'd want to drop. Did he have any idea who might take the class over?

I'd hoped he'd say he would, but he looked off and out through the window of my office, where a pigeon was braking to land on my windowsill. "You might talk to Thorpe," he said. "But let me see if I can't get you a medical leave of absence. You're taking too much of a chance, Jack."

"I've taught with notes before, during periods I had to be silent. After all those polyp operations. I can handle it."

"And I'll find out what I can about disability benefits, but it's true we don't have any. An ad hoc committee meets. I sat on one of them when Ashburn had to quit teaching because of his lungs. The committee decided what to give him. You'd have your TIAA benefits, you know, if you had to quit."

I shook my head. "I've already checked into that. I'd get about seventy-five bucks a month."

"Seventy-five? After all your time?"

"Lecturers didn't qualify for those benefits until a few years back."

"Well, shit," Fred said with resentment, expressing my own feelings exactly. I'd spent a morning learning how little I was worth if my paycheck stopped. What locked Fred and me together was our shared frustration about Metro, a rancor shared, I suspected, by everyone on the faculty and the administration, all the way up to the embattled, weary president. Nobody is happy or popular in an institution going slowly broke.

I wanted to tell Gail, of course, but I hadn't seen her since the night she stood me up. I was still too ruffled to trust myself over there. I didn't want to turn up in a mood to make her suffer for my suffering, to borrow a tactic of Janice's.

Newman took my news hard. He took it personally. I began to think I should make a study of the reactions I got when I told people I had a slight case of cancer. But I more or less expected his reaction, so it wasn't easy to tell him our sessions had come to an end.

On Thursday morning I said, "I think I'll take the chair today."

He sat down behind his desk and said, "Well, all right." But he had that What's This? look he got when he was alerted.

I sat down in front of his desk and tried to keep looking at him when I spoke, shrunken head to head shrinker, so to speak.

When I'd had my say, all he said was, "I've heard of the goddamndest dodges people take to get out of analysis, but this one beats them all. Radiotherapy?" He was ready to explode, and I edged back in my chair. "You can at least keep coming until the treatment starts."

"No," I said firmly. "He says it's bad for the cords to use them under tension."

"Tension? You're not under tension here."

"Not as a rule," I said, "and that's one of our troubles."

"Oh . . . what do you mean?" sounding like Janice.

"I mean, if I have any problem to work on, it's the unwanted child syndrome I can't seem to shake. It's a problem I had as a child. We've talked about it enough. It's something I never worked out with my father, the feeling he never really wanted me but had to have me around, and I was trapped, we were both trapped . . . with each other . . . in a kind of endless nightmare, pitted against each other, with me hanging onto my mother because I had less strength, or thought I did, than he did . . ."

This was something I'd never thought I'd drag in at a final session, but I was into it now and I went on, wheezing and rumbling, my voice getting hoarser and hoarser, ". . . and I'm still in that goddamn bind on my job, teaching courses that are all stepchildren of my department . . . Metro stuck with me and me stuck with Metro. And how can I work that out with you when you don't remind me of my father? My father was a thin, dignified, inhibited man with sad eyes. He never blustered, he never raised his voice, he never used four-letter words. You, you're like an army buddy. You're like a friend who wants to help me. I can't connect you with anybody out of my childhood, except maybe my grandfather. I got along well with him . . . or an uncle who is like an older brother. So a lot of the time I'm here and not reliving enough to feel much tension. God, sometimes I come here and fall asleep and snore and you have to wake me up. Or I lie here thinking about all the things I have to do that day, a class I still haven't prepared for, or a letter I should write, or a book I have to get. I've been through too much analysis now with you and a lot of other shrinks to still think I'm the victim of evil people or poor-me bad luck. Besides, I still haven't published another book. That's why I came to you analysts. It's still my problem."

"Problems don't exist in isolation, you dumb shit."

"Okay, I'm the problem, but I'm going to work me out for myself."

"Good luck," he said sarcastically.

His face was shadow patterns, clouds of rage with sideburns. We parted, I'd say, on bad terms. I felt no regret. I felt relief.

My voice, however, was wrecked, and I didn't try to speak again for hours.

The following Monday morning our two-week holiday recess began. Fred, to lose no time with what he thought would be Christmas cheer, called me at home. He'd talked to the dean and the provost and a leave of absence with pay was in the works. He seemed happy to have got something done and was disappointed I didn't sound delighted. "You can spend all semester writing a novel, Jack."

"But I can't concentrate on a novel with all this going on. Let me teach."

"Don't worry. If worst comes to . . . you know . . . worst . . . with your vocal cords, we've worked out a way to keep you on the payroll."

When he hung up, I called Janice.

"I just talked to Fred."

"And?"

"Metro has no retirement compensation for disability."

"Not anything?"

"He says everything is done by committee. A bunch of senior professors agree on some suitable financial crutch. I got the impression nothing disables a teacher at Metro."

"Other colleges have disability retirement. It's part of their TIAA program."

"Not Metropolitan's. You teach anyway. We've got, Fred says, a blind teacher and a couple of teachers who are damned near totally deaf and several alcoholics. If I can only wheeze and whisper, he says I can teach."

"Did you tell him there's a chance you might not be able to make a sound?"

"Yes, Janice. Yes."

"And he really expects you to teach without a voice?"

"He said I would be carried as a non-teaching teacher."

"What's a non-teaching teacher?"

"I don't know."

"And pay you?"

"That's right. Full pay was what he said. Full pay."

—and then I called Gail. I'd waited as long as I could.

Her voice was chilly. "How have you been?" she said. "Haven't seen you around."

"I've been preoccupied."

"Anyone I know?"

"Yeah. Me."

"I thought you'd have called, or something."

"You'll understand, I think, when I see you."

She said nothing.

"Can I come over?"

"Now?"

"A little later . . . okay?"

"If you want to."

"I have to see one of the professors up at school. Then I'll be over."

"See you," she said.

The students in two of my classes had merged into separate entities. Instead of being individuals all isolated from one another around a subject, they had through weekly monologues and dialogues and diatribes and collective complaints and praise formed a complex single personality. When this happened, classes became living, perishable entities. To break up two such groups was to kill them and the thought depressed me. That's what I'd been trying to make Fred understand.

Thorpe kept to his office right through Christmas recess, because that's where he wrote his novels. I took the path around our building across what used to be a lawn toward the Quonset hut where Thorpe had his headquarters. There were still a surprising number of students in ski jackets, a few in tennis shoes, walking around. Beer cans hung in some of the taller bushes like spent shell casings. Pieces of newspaper, once carefree windblown wanderers, lay partially embedded in the wintry dirt. A banner hung from an upper floor window in the chemistry building crying INDEPENDENCE FOR PUERTO RICO.

Thorpe was sixty-five years old, too old to continue in an administrative job, not old enough for mandatory retirement. Next fall he was going to need two more classes for a full work load, and Fred wasn't sure what to give him. Thorpe was a problem to the department, another academic anomaly. He had a Ph.D., but it was—ugh—a doctorate in writing as well as literature. The subject of his dissertation: nineteenth-century fantasy and its relationship to early sightings of flying saucers. A fascinating subject, but the department seemed to take it lightly. He published more books than any of us, but they were all science fiction novels and the department found his productivity an embarrassment—even now, when science fiction had achieved a tentative literary status. The real trouble: Thorpe was another of Dorothy Dole's protégés. She'd hired him, brought him to Metro while her influence still ran strong as the Hudson River—and his enduring loyalty to Dot and her commercial ideals had helped him not in the least in his long career. Dot's last act before her forced retirement had been to push through Thorpe's promotion to associate professor, and an associate professor he still remained. In an effort after Dorothy's retirement to remove Thorpe from the department, he had been appointed Director of New Careers, his teaching load reduced to one class. Now, with his retirement from administrative duties, the department would have to revive his class in nineteenth-century fantasy. Fred said the department faced the prospect with pain. As a consequence, they resolved to throw Thorpe into the rigor, if not the humiliation, of remedial composition as well as another class in advanced fiction writing. "Ask him to take your beginning class," Fred said. "He isn't doing anything. He sits all day in that office of his writing his flying saucer novels, *Red Planet, Ho,* or whatever."

I had a hundred-yard walk in open air. I took that walk a couple of times a year, and never looked forward to it. I liked him, but every visit had a lunatic sameness that made me wonder if he'd cracked from recognition-starvation or I had. Which of us was it? I'd call his extension from my office, speak to his secretary, identify myself and then get Thorpe.

"You busy? No? Listen, I think I'll drop over, okay?"

When I reached his building, the door would always be locked and I'd have to wait for someone to come and open it. Most of the buildings on our campus were locked, for the same reason all the typewriters were bolted down. Harlem was our neighbor, a community who really seemed to believe the Black slogan "You Can't Steal from Whitey."

Thorpe was a scrawny man, narrow-jawed with watery blue eyes, his head bald and shiny. Over the years, he'd picked up a tic in his left eye. When I came in through the unlocked door his secretary held open, he grinned and held out his hand for shaking. After we'd shaken, he gestured into his inner office. Then, when we were inside, he closed his door and locked it. That was part of the ritual. Although we all locked our office doors once we were inside, when Thorpe did it the locking never seemed a recommended security measure. It seemed conspiratorial.

Each time it happened I felt as if he were waiting to hear every secret I knew about Metro. I fought the feeling down. I could even understand it. Thorpe had thought his department was out to get him for years and years, and his was a valid case of paranoia. He trusted no one, not even me, but for a few minutes at least, he seemed always to want to.

So Thorpe's door would close, he'd lock it and I'd sit down on his frayed and cracked davenport.

We'd talk, but I never felt he was listening. Once he saw I'd arrived without secrets, his were the alert eyes of a listener, but no ball went back and forth. It didn't matter what I came to talk about, the conversation would slip around to his writing and the public lecturing he was doing and how much he got for his last book or his last lecture. He was apparently in demand as a lecturer because he could deftly relate flying saucers to the assassination of Jack Kennedy and the crucifixion of Jesus Christ.

But the strangest phenomenon was the way the phone on his desk rang—every visit. Always, it was word from his agent or his publisher.

It would go like this: We're talking. I've been there maybe five minutes. The phone rings. Thorpe gets up, crosses in front of me, picks up the phone on his desk, says, "Thank you for calling. Yes, I have the book contract on my desk and your advance is certainly generous." This is followed by a few more words of pleasure and conviviality. He hangs up, comes back, sits down. "That was my publisher."

It happened whenever I went to see him. Every time. I'd wait now for the phone to ring. Who was calling him? His secretary? Did she call him and hang up at once? Did he have some trick, a button under the rug he pressed? Did he talk into a dead phone long enough to get the message to me? Why did he need to have me get the message?

Once he tried to tell me that the department and its attitude toward him didn't bother him in the least, that he had another life as Director of New Careers and still another as an author and that these other lives more than fulfilled him.

But I never believed it. That's bullshit. As one bone-gnawing yard dog to another, that's bullshit.

This time I sat down on his old davenport and he sat in the chair he'd pulled up in front of me. He leaned forward waiting for me to speak, anticipation on his face. When I told him I had X-ray therapy coming up and was looking for someone to handle one of my classes, he looked concerned, even troubled, but it was slow going getting him to say he'd take the class.

"Fred tells me there's some way to lighten your teaching load next fall if you want to take on an extra class this spring. It could get you out of the remedial English section in the fall."

Still looking troubled, he said, "It's a matter of how busy I'm going to be."

"I'd like to see you do it. I'd like to see Fred give you two sections in writing." I meant it. More of his ex-students had published novels than of any other teacher we'd had in years. I'd worked with a couple of students who had become semi-famous. He'd worked with at least half a dozen. One of his rave reviews had been written by an ex-student who achieved renown.

So he was listening to me carefully because I could influence Fred—then, after a little discussion and much head-shaking over what had happened to the writing courses at Metro, the phone rang.

It was his agent. Thorpe said, "I'd be perfectly happy to let the young man quote the entire paragraph, but don't you think he should be asked to pay something nominal? Say, five dollars. I think that's customary. Certainly. Yes, it is an honor. Yes, yes, I realize he's using it to keynote his entire novel. Well, if you think he's a little strapped for money, let him have it."

He came back and sat down and we began to talk about Dorothy Dole and the good old days at Metro.

I said, "Dot's fantastic. I think she's going to outlive us all.

When I saw her in the hospital, I didn't see how she'd live through the day. You saw her then too, didn't you?"

He nodded. "Yes, yes. I had no idea she'd snap back this fast."

"Did you know she's writing another book?"

"She is?"

"That's what she told me."

"My, my. Another book. Her what?"

"Who knows . . . twentieth, sixtieth."

The phone rang again. I couldn't believe it. I stared out the window and Thorpe was saying, an aura of joy beaming from his head, "Yes, I've seen some of those out-of-town reviews. They certainly are gratifying. Perhaps we can use one in an ad. You are? In the New York *Times?* Why, that's wonderful."

Thorpe hung up. "That was my editor."

I was suddenly inspired. "Thorpe."

"Yes."

"Go see Dot." I could see her in net stockings.

"Do you think I should?" He was in some ways a shy man.

"She talked about you all the time," I lied away, "and she's lonely now. Seeing you would mean a lot to her."

"Well, I suppose I could. Call her up, you mean?"

"Sure."

"I suppose I could. One lunch hour."

"Call her today. For a Merry Christmas. I mean it."

"All right. I will," he said with resolution.

As we parted at his open door, it occurred to me I'd done a handsome thing for old Dot.

When I cut through the trampled opening in the hedge, I could see Sonnabaker, our Sanskrit man, picking up beer cans and bottles, hoping to set a good example for the rest of us.

Driving across the bridge I decided not to say anything about the radiotherapy treatments. I wanted this to be a pleasant evening—fun and laughs, making up. I wanted to know that there was one human being in the world I could sit down and enjoy myself with, that I did not impose my troubles on. You can't share troubles anyway. And I would not say anything about Janice.

At first everything went just fine. I breezed into Gail's apartment with the same bottle of wine I'd bought for our last date. Everything was grand, smiles from Gail, smiles from me.

And then, while Gail was slicing carrots on a chopping board by the sink and I was leaning against the kitchen doorway, I found myself, to my surprise, complaining about the football on her piano. What was it I said? Something I meant to be light and witty—about life, I'm sure—and I was using the football as an example. But I knew I was in trouble.

She drew herself up. "I think you're making a fuss about nothing. As it happens, I know a great deal about football."

Then, quite suddenly, she threw the knife down on the floor at my feet and followed the knife with the chopping board and all the carrots. She screamed, "I will not have you sniping at my taste. You don't like the way I dress. You don't like my friends. You don't like the pictures I have on my walls, or my taste in wine and food. What do you like about me?"

"I like your balcony," I said. I picked up the knife and put it in the sink, then went back for the carrots and the chopping block. I put the carrots in the sink and tried to put my arm around her.

"No," she said, "don't try that."

"I'm sorry," I said. "I'm uptight tonight."

"You are? What's the matter with you?"

I told her.

She grabbed both my hands and stared at me. She put her arms around me and pressed her cheek against mine.

"You're such a bastard," she said.

"I'm going to be all right."

She was shaking and biting her lip. "It's not that. What am I going to do with you?"

A card in the mail this morning from my uncle Sam, a second note telling me of his shot dead next-door neighbor. That's how life goes in the hinterlands. There's not much news. You have to send out a really big item to your friends several times, make the most of it. Once, hunting for pheasant, I peppered the whole side of someone's farmhouse. And that must have happened to Sam's neighbor: somebody not looking beyond his target got him.

Perhaps spring will come early this year.

Another Christmas at our throats. The tree is up, our decorations are on it. It's Christmas Eve and Janice is in Boston. I was not invited. Gail is in Nebraska. There is no peace on earth, and men of ill will range the land. I'm smoking pot and watching television with the sound off. Almost everything on television is wonderful without a sound track. Tucker is in the kitchen sitting in front of the refrigerator, staring at it. To each his own.

These are shadowless days. The pavement on the street is damp. There is no sense of sun anywhere. I don't know when the rain fell, but it was recently. There are no drops of water gathered in the corners of the white grillwork around our balcony; but down below, on the ground between our building and the one to the west, water has pooled in small hollows, none of the pools big enough to have interesting reflections. Two women are walking side by side up the steps toward the building across the way, one woman in a gray coat, the other in a black coat—perhaps the same two women we've seen at the level on which we live, sitting side by side on their davenport each evening, watching television. We see only the backs of their heads, and one of the women has her hair cut so short that for a long time we thought it was a husband and wife with nothing to say to one another, with nothing to do.

The gray day moves on; time exists. A gray cat, striped, paces across a stretch of winter lawn. Our own cat sleeps on the table beside me, afloat on a plain of dreams. Off in the distance, off to the left of the window where I sit looking out, up over the slope of grass that rises toward the street, on then across the street and between a couple of six-story buildings, I can see a low white shed, a metal shed perhaps, where a single bright light burns.

III

The Great God Damn

It begins—

When the alarm went off on the morning of the fourth of January, Janice was at her hospital and I was alone in bed. A cold rain fell from a soggy sky. It was a day as gray as the underbelly of a four-footed bathtub. I did not make my breakfast with any cheer.

I put on my new belt and my raincoat with the alpaca lining and went forth to catch a bus. Rain beat at the bus windows. At Ninety-sixth Street I got off and took a cab across the park.

I thought I was going to be late, but in the downstairs depths of Mount Sinai's Guggenheim Pavilion I sat and waited. I hadn't the vaguest idea what was going to happen. I'd never known anyone anything similar ever happened to. I imagined my vocal cords cured by some sort of microwave cooking process—baked by a laser beam? Forty-five minutes went by. I sat reading magazines, *Time*, *Newsweek*, all old issues, and they made what had happened months ago seem as immediate as the cheerless morning. It was hard to fix myself in time.

Half a dozen other people sat around in silence. Were they patients? Or friends and relatives? I thought I could hear the far-off surge of sea against steel hulls—as if we were adrift and nothing was going to be the same in the world any more. Were we outward bound?

Then up came a girl in a white uniform, at least six feet tall, black and fierce. I got up and followed her. Her hair was long and thick and straight. She led me past a couple of swinging doors, picked up an orange hospital robe off a counter, handed it to me, then stopped at a series of dressing rooms and opened the door to the second. "Take your clothes off," she said, paused, "from the waist up." I did as she said.

When I came out with the robe on, I followed her toward a section of the room that stood behind glass walls. We passed two gloomy men sitting in wheelchairs. They, too, wore orange robes, and sat facing a long wall with a couple of doors. Each door led to a room behind a long glass window. Below each window were control panel desks, long desks, lots of knobs, lots of dials. It was an observation window to a grim sort of studio where I would soon, I figured, be on view.

My tall black guide opened another door and I stepped into a bright room with sinks and tables and cabinets and plaster of Paris objects—objects like arm and shoulder casts, casts of torsos and hips.

Two girls frocked in white were waiting, arms folded, as if expecting me for a long time. After I'd shed my robe, I got up on the table one of them pointed at and lay down. I crossed my ankles and crossed my wrists over my stomach and stared at the ceiling. The room seemed to pitch ever so slightly. I couldn't get the sensation out of my head that we were on a ship.

They worked quickly—and as they worked, I knew what it was like to be a privileged Mayan victim getting ready to meet a rain god. I felt a marking pen touch between my chin and lips; it moved along my jaw to a point under my ear and from there straight around to the back of my neck. The marker swept down and moved around and across the upper part of my chest to the other side, from there up under my ear and down along my jaw to the point it had begun. Then grease. The area they'd marked got coated with Vaseline. Neither of the girls said a word. I hadn't said a word or heard a word from either of them since I arrived—until the blonde with the pierced ears and the tiny gold earrings said, "Hold very still now."

I felt strips of wet cloth laid over the Vaseline, strip after strip of plaster-saturated gauze. Both girls leaned over, silently working, and I thought—My throat's going to get hot. It got warm, that's all, warmer and warmer, and I lay still while the plaster hardened.

Thoughts of mummy making, thoughts of suffocation, thoughts of George Segal binding his model in plaster. I seemed to be in another century, another galaxy. Two faces, one narrow, one oval, long eyelashes, closed lips, floated above me. Silence. A faucet running, no other sound. And then I knew who I was and where I was—and in whose power. I was Little Boy Blue and I lay at last in the underworld below the streets of New York in the realm of the Great God Damn.

Whenever I thought of Gail, I thought sentiently of soft furry things like earmuffs, lap robes and bunny-lined gloves, but when she came into the coffee shop and I looked for that softness I saw only a small girl with her hands clenched from the cold. She was wearing a gabardine trench coat and a silk scarf. She came briskly past the tables by the windows looking me over sharply, as if I might have changed.

"I have had a morning I would like to forget," she said. "I am only somebody in the second act, and I have just had every good line cut to damndydamn hell. All I do now is stand there rolling my eyes and simpering. Feel my hands. God, it's cold out. Well, how did it go?"

I shrugged. "They just made a thing for my neck so far—a plaster cast. The treatments start Monday."

The waiter came to take our orders, his promptness catching us by surprise. We stared at the glass counters of rolls beyond which bakers in white suits and caps were at work, over where the odors of bread and pastry rose.

In spite of her troubles, she seemed in a good mood, as if she'd managed to get some of her problems about me resolved. My radiotherapy troubled her. Her initial reaction to the radiotherapy had been one of guilt. I got it out of her gradually. She said she thought she was responsible for my throat getting worse. She thought she'd let me talk too much, and she thought she'd complicated my life, putting me in a constant state of tension about her and Janice. So she didn't know what to do with me . . . or with herself. But would I please understand she was not going to destroy me, or let me destroy myself? She would be only a good influence, a source of happiness.

I assured her she was. "You have had," she said, "too many in-
terfering women in your life."

When the waiter left, I rasped with much bravado, "Janice
checked with her uncle in Texas, he's a radiologist, and he says
he's never heard of this bunch at Mount Sinai."

"How could that be?"

"I don't know. I'm thinking of backing out of the whole
business."

"But you can't."

"They still don't know what I've got. They can't even say for
sure that what I got will get malignant. I could take a chance,
you know, and put this radiotherapy off indefinitely. They said
I could."

"But they didn't advise you to, did they?"

"No. But I'm always suspicious with these doctors and hospitals that I'm just fodder for their theories and machines. These
doctors put out a lot of money for their machines and they've
got to keep them working to pay for them. I'm an experiment.
I think that's what I am."

Gail stared at me silently and seriously and I thought she
was going to say something about medicine or the chanciness
of everything, but she said, "Jack, are you willing to do something for me?"

"Sure. Anything."

"I said I'd never put any kind of pressure on you in that shel-
tered nest you live in, but I have a small request."

"What request? What small request?"

"Before you take on Mount Sinai, or Mount Sinai takes you
on, I want to have you to myself for a little while."

"For how long?"

"Relax. Just a weekend. Only a weekend."

"A weekend?"

"Why do you look like that?"

"Two nights? In a row?"

"Maybe three. Friday, Saturday and Sunday."

"Look," I said, "it's just I hate scenes, that's all. If I can avoid them, I'd rather. This weekend?"

She looked away. Then she sighed. "I don't know. I don't know yet. Either this weekend or the next."

"What's the problem?"

"Oh, the show, the show. What does it matter?"

"Are you going to quit the show?"

"No. Maybe. I don't know. But I have to be sure, if we go anywhere, I have a replacement."

"I suppose I could say I'm going someplace for research. Washington. Everybody goes there for research."

"We've always met at my place . . ."

"Three nights straight. That's hard."

"You don't want to, do you? If it means any trouble?"

"Look, I will, I said I will. I will."

"I just want to go away with you. Run off. Not for a night. I want to sleep, wake up, walk around, talk, eat, love, sleep, wake up."

"Jesus, Gail, you make it sound as if I were getting drafted."

"You'll still be able to talk next weekend, won't you?"

"As far as I know. But if you want to be sure, make it this weekend."

"I figure you're going into radiotherapy anyway. So talking's not going to make your voice much worse." She smiled now, put her hand over mine and gripped me. "What do you know?" she said with wonder.

"What's the matter?" I could see I'd pleased her, even surprised her.

"Nothing. Nothing at all." Still smiling and maybe pleased with herself, she creased her paper napkin, gave a little sigh and stared out the window beside us at the cold and windy street.

There was this poet who had no luck with his verse. One day it came to his attention that each time he moved, at each new address in each new city, somebody got murdered.

There was a murder in the East Village in New York, where he lived while he studied graphic arts at NYU. There was a murder in Wyoming, where he worked for a university press; and another murder the same year in Colorado, where he spent his vacation. Each time the victim was someone he knew, someone whose acquaintance he had just made. What fabulous material in my life, he decided. I should have been a mystery story writer.

He bought a typewriter. He began to keep a notebook. He moved twice again and there were two more murders right under his long nose: one death by mysterious poisoning, the other death by hypnosis. He wrote about both the murders with care, playing the role of the murderer in one story and the role of the victim in the other. He sent the manuscripts to publishers, who rejected them, he sent them to agents, who sent them straight back saying—we've read it all before. He gave the manuscripts to his friends to read and his friends thought they were superb. So he cursed publishers and agents and moved again, and this time it was he who died, and he died under the hammer blows of a horde of tiny elves, and as he died he cried —at last, at last! Something different, something new!

The horde of tiny elves made him into a thousand pairs of tiny shoes.

It is not enough to want to be a writer.

Norman had a couple of buttons missing from his black rain-coat-topcoat.

"What's new?" he said.

"Oh, you know . . ."

"How are things going?"

"Okay."

"Judy wants all of us to do something this weekend."

"I don't know our weekend plans yet, Norman. I may have to go out of town."

"Oh?"

"On a kind of mission. But I may not go. Call us." I had an impulse to tell him all about Gail and me, but didn't feel like being a big influence. I could so easily have held out a hand and led him to light.

Francine never had buttons missing, nor had I ever seen his daughter in a coat that needed cleaning as much as Norman's. An interesting situation in that family, fraught with warning.

I said, "You folks, I hear, were out of town last week."

He shrugged, looked gloomy. He hated leaving New York and he hated cars. Whenever they drove anywhere, Judy took the wheel and Francine sat in front beside her. Norman sat in the back seat.

Norman, with his missing buttons, is working a kind of pathos into his role and appearance that wasn't there when he married Judy. He used to be, as a beau, messy and happy. Now he's messy and unhappy. He's getting a permanent long look. He's given in on everything, all the way down the line.

How much of this torture does Norman enjoy? Before Judy, it was an alcoholic wife. With Judy and Francine he stands around defending a personal piece of territory that grows smaller and smaller.

Poor bastard, he loves. That's the only answer. But he'd never flashed any indication he understood Judy. Francine, on the other hand, had given repeated demonstrations that she understood Judy all too well, that she could do what Norman could never do: manipulate her with ease. Poor Judy loves her daughter. Daily, Francine's personal territory grows larger and larger. Judy treated Norman the way Francine treated her.

Judy readily admitted, quite publicly admitted, she was hell to live with; even as she was holding Norman's hand and he was squeezing back and kissing her on the cheek, she'd tell anyone how hard she was on Norman.

Sunday evening Judy rang the bell at the door and came in with a tiny jug she said contained West Virginia moonshine. We stood in the hallway. I pulled the cork and had a swig to test its authenticity. Judy couldn't come in and sit down, she said, because she was making dinner for Norman and Francine.

"This is pretty good stuff. Has just the right edge," I said.

"I thought you'd like it. What machine are they going to use on you?"

I couldn't remember.

"The Theratron," Janice said.

"I had the betatron," Judy said. "I've got sympathy pains. I know what you're heading into."

"Oh, it won't be bad," I said.

We'd straggled our way into the living room.

"Let's all sit down," Janice said.

"I can't," Judy said. "I just wanted to give you the jug and say good luck. You're going to have a sore throat."

I shrugged. "Maybe not."

"Well," Janice said, "you're going to be on a bland diet."

"I am?" That was something I hadn't remembered being told. Did they know more than I did? Now I reflected some of their anxiety. "I know I have to be silent after next week."

Judy put her hand on my arm reassuringly. "You'll still be good company without a voice. You've had to be silent before."

"People," Janice said, "save all the notes he wrote." She seemed proud of me. I passed the jug to Janice and she took a swig and passed it to Judy, who put the jug to her lips but only pretended she was drinking.

After Judy left, Janice and I watched an old Gary Cooper film called *Morocco* . . . made in 1930. Coop was in the Foreign Legion, marching away from Marlene Dietrich, the girl he loved, marching away to war, one man in a column of men whose feet all sank into the sands of an exotic country . . . and it struck me that I *was* sort of marching off next week, that I had marched off leaving girls behind me any number of times in my life.

I hadn't had to tell Janice I was going anywhere for the weekend. Gail couldn't get time off. It was next weekend now for research; but I didn't want to tell Janice yet because I didn't know how to. Maybe I'd spring it on her at the last minute.

On Monday morning the team at the hospital was ready for me. Janice had the morning off. We both got up and dressed in the dark. She drove me to the hospital and let me out a little before eight-thirty in front of the long blue awning. It seemed as if the floors in the lobby were being mopped for the day by hordes of gnarled men. I used the stairway down. I changed into my orange robe. I sat facing the rooms with the two doors, a red bulb over each door, both bulbs now lightless, a sign under each saying, KEEP OUT WHILE LIGHT IS ON. Almost no one was around, only a stunning Chinese girl in a white smock who said softly, "Good morning." She was filling out a chart. Her nails were long and scarlet.

Then, quite abruptly, brisk activity by some four or five people. They came down a hall to my left, bunched, as if they'd left a high compression chamber, Dr. Beirne leading. There were two nurses, one a woman with white hair. She had a pleasant smile when she came up and spoke to me. "Are you ready now, Mr. Fross?" I nodded and stood. She walked ahead of me with the stride of some gym teacher I vaguely remembered and stopped at the doorway to the room with the Theratron to gesture me in.

It was a big room with a high ceiling, big enough to hold forty or fifty students at Metro. Near the farthest wall from the glass observation window stood a green machine with a round sort of head, a globe, no, an ant's head it was, bent over a table. I took off my robe. I got up and lay down under the thing. I looked up into its snout, into a gridwork of dark metal bars. Inside the mouth, above those bars, a light snapped on, beamed for my throat. And then my custom-fitted plaster cast descended, edged by manicured scarlet nails. It fit around my neck and over the bottom of my chin and lay across the front of my chest. Someone stuck a soft roll of cloth under my head and tied down the cast. All the while, Beirne was calling out centimeters of measurement. When anyone spoke it was usually Beirne. He seemed as he had the first time I saw him—relaxed, sure of himself. I licked my lips. He put his hand on my shoulder and said, "I assure you, you are not on a torture rack."

Someone signaled. Gears moved. Beirne put his hands over his face, shook his head and said quietly, "No, no, no." So whoever it was steering the Theratron rotated its head over to my throat's other side and Beirne looked relieved. A beam of light from the machine hit my neck from a forty-five-degree angle and I decided the ray was passing through one side of me and out the other. Beirne wasn't looking at the plaster cast. He was looking over where the beam, I decided, hit a plate or scale.

I lay still. He scratched away at the cast with a pencil. I was getting targeted.

Then the nurse with the white hair and an Irish brogue said, "We're going to turn the machine on now."

"How long is it on? About five minutes?"

"No. A little over a minute. You won't feel a thing. Just lie very still."

I don't think I ever saw her again. The hospital seemed full of people I saw once or twice and never again. Everyone moved briskly, very briskly, out of the room, the last one out snapped on the overhead light. I was alone.

Far above me the ceiling lights gleamed, fluorescent. The room was cold. I felt the cold. I lay waiting for some sound, for something. Nothing seemed to be happening. What were they doing at the control panel on the other side of the glass window—isolating me in space and time?

And then there was something, a sound, a puff, like a quick release of air followed by a heavy click, as if the air had shoved a shutter to one side. No other sound followed, no hum, nothing I could hear, and I lay still, rigid, staring at the overhead lights until I closed my eyes. In a little while I heard that puff of air again and another heavy click.

Then all the other lights went on and two attendants were in the room. Gears meshed. The green head swiveled. They pulled my table out by its wheels. I sat up, feeling dizzy. I put on my orange robe.

When I got into the car, not much more than half an hour had passed.

"How do you feel?" Janice said.

"Like I did when I got up this morning."

Back at the apartment the mail was being delivered. In the mail was a get well card from Perse and Bob. I looked it over for a personal message but there wasn't one. Just their names in ink, in Perse's hand that looked so like her mother's.

That was Monday.

Gail was tied up all evening. I sat home and wrote mood things. One of her brothers was in town. But she did say everything was set for us this weekend. She'd made reservations at an old inn in Lambertville, in New Jersey. She'd heard it was "really, really super."

Then on Tuesday morning over at Sinai more of the same—only this time Dr. Beirne wasn't there.

When I left the hospital, I walked back across the park, hands in my coat pockets, hunched against the cold. I called Gail from home as she'd asked me to. After I insisted there was nothing to the treatments, that they were just a kind of couch session with a metal doctor, she said, "Have you told your wife yet you'll be away for a few days?"

"I will."

"When are you going to?"

"I will."

"When?"

"You can count on this weekend."

The news about Harvey Sampers, an old friend of mine, arrived in the middle of the same afternoon. I called Janice at the hospital. Her voice was shaking when she said, "Who was it called?"

"Alice."

"What happened? How did he do it?"

"Sash cord."

I heard her gasp. It was bad enough for Harvey to be dead

and gone, sunk forever into his problems and his despair, bad enough he was gone, but it was how he'd gone.

"Who found him?"

"Alice. She went down to that room where he was staying. He hadn't been answering his phone for a couple of days. Nobody had talked to him. So Alice said she almost expected this." Harvey and Alice had been separated for nearly two years and Harvey had been out of work for six months. That meant no money, too many bills.

When I hung up, I sat staring out the window, wondering what I might have done to help him. We should have had him up more often. Did he feel abandoned? Or had he wanted to die years ago and waited this long for things to get bad enough for the pressure to shove him off—down the chute?

Harvey had a combination of wit and grimness that I associated with every good literary mind and talent I'd ever met. Harvey burned and smoldered and worried and I never saw him when he'd had enough sleep. He couldn't sleep. He lay awake a lot, I knew, staring at the ceiling and windows, crazed with his personal rage and despair. I didn't know why, but because the imagination rushes in to fill vacuums in the understanding, I blamed it all on his job, and I related his problems to my own condition at Metro: the anguish suffered by men who do not really belong. Whenever he saw me he'd ask me if I had a few seconals I could spare.

He was a tall gray-eyed man who kept lean playing handball. He drank a lot, any chance he got, but I'd never seen him drunk. And he had a lot of loyal friends who, like me, probably liked him because they enjoyed what he had to say and because he seemed to suffer without accumulating malice, turning his suffering into funny stories that made my own anxieties seem a little milder. He wasn't a prolific writer, but he was one of the few writers I knew who was productive and regularly published. He was a member of the inner circle of *The New Yorker* magazine. Maybe he'd toss a key out to me. And, truth is, he was always ready to help his friends. When my novel appeared, he read it and liked it and got it a brief and favorable review. I suspected he might have written the review himself, but he denied it.

About once a year or as often as we'd seen one another, I'd run across one of his pieces under his by-line. Seeing one of Harvey's pieces would make me feel as good, well, almost as good, as if I'd written it myself. He wrote a lot of "Talk of the Town" pieces, and wrote captions for cartoons. Like so many of *The New Yorker* staff, he sometimes wrote at home—however the mood hit him. He wrote and rewrote. I think he agonized over every word. I think it took him six months of writing and rewriting to produce a single piece. I never knew him well enough to know. He, too, wanted to get a book published and had never been able to make it. So he respected me for my one and only book, and I respected him for his salaried identity as a writer on a prestige publication.

The last time I'd seen him, his suffering had made him almost too remote to reach. He had quit *The New Yorker* finally and gone to another magazine, and that magazine would shortly go broke. Magazines were folding all over the place. There was a surplus of writer-editors on the market. He had also dropped out of his marriage and there was a surplus of marriage dropouts around. His chronic despair sank in deeper and deeper. He couldn't sleep, couldn't shake his problems enough to sleep. He couldn't work because he couldn't sleep and vice versa. Janice and I had seen him last a year ago at his apartment at the Christmas party; he'd sat in the living room with us like one of the guests, preoccupied, filling and refilling his glass at the liquor cabinet. His wife was there and his kids were there and he was there, and yet he was not there.

Bad business, suicide.

On Wednesday, the green mouth of the Theratron was rotated to my right and I got zapped from a new angle. This time when the lights went on, I closed my eyes and started to count: one thousand and one, two thousand and two, three thousand and three, and so on. I'd reached a hundred and twenty when the machine puffed off.

When I got up, the Chinese girl said, "Are you talking much during the day and evening?" Her name, I saw, was a cliché, Miss Wong.

"Some. Should I be silent?"

"No, but you can start to conserve your voice."

We were alone in the room. She helped me into the orange robe. "You should not be lecturing your classes."

"I'm not," I said. "I have this amplifier. It's a tape recorder. I can talk into it and turn the volume up."

She nodded.

Out on the street, in the car, Janice was waiting. My throat felt fine.

That evening, around dinner time, my aunt, Sam's wife, called. I'd just come in the front door and saw Janice standing at the wall phone in the kitchen. "It's Martha," she said. She stood peering at me with a frown of worry. Bad news?

I took off my coat, hung it in the closet and went down the hall to my study to pick up the extension phone. I cut in to hear Martha saying, "He's been depressed since our neighbor was shot."

"This is Jack, Martha. What's the matter?"

Martha always sounded chipper on the phone, as if life were an amusing adventure, but she wasn't cheerful now. She was speaking quietly. "I'm worried about Sam," she said.

"What's the matter?"

"The doctor told him he has emphysema."

"When?"

"Last week."

"Are they sure?"

"They're sure. He has to quit smoking."

Well, we'd all seen this coming. The last time we saw him Janice thought he was already over the edge. It was his cough. He coughed and smoked and coughed. Sparks and cigarette ash fell on his lap as he coughed.

"He's pretty depressed," Martha said.

We'd had a relative, Sam's brother-in-law, who died of emphysema.

"I'm just calling to see if I can get you folks to come for the weekend. If Jack could talk to Sam, I know it would cheer him up. He's so fond of Jack."

"I only get one night off this weekend," Janice said.

"Sure," I said, without even considering an alternative, "we'll be up. Or I'll be up anyway."

And then I thought of Gail. Oh, God. Oh, Christ almighty. She'd have to understand. If I could help Sam, I had to. I could go away another weekend with Gail and write notes to her. She'd already gone through one of my silent periods. But if I could help Sam, I had only this weekend.

"Vivian and Annie," Martha said, "are here now and they'll be here until Sunday or I'd offer to put you up." She paused. "I don't know what I'll be able to feed you. The doctor told Sam he has high blood pressure, too. And high cholesterol. I'm trying to get his weight down. He's seriously depressed, Jack. He's really depressed. But I know it would help him to see you."

"Gail, listen, I'm sorry . . . what do you mean, the world turns? . . . no, I'm not taking our weekend lightly. When I started out saying something funny happened on the way to our weekend, I didn't mean to sound flippant, or, as you put it, cavalier . . . Of course, my voice sounds rotten. I'm tense. You've got me tense . . . No, everything isn't all your fault . . . Gail, listen to me, will you? Please. I'm supposed to conserve my voice, so let me come over next week and write notes to you . . . no, no, no, seeing you after this weekend isn't going to tempt me to talk . . . What do you mean—save myself? . . . Gail? Gail? Gail?"

The misplaced weekend—

Janice folded back the counterpane and took my pajamas with the white polka dots and laid them on the bed, then she laid her nightgown out beside the pajamas so when we came back from Sam and Martha's farm, homestead, home, the light of the motel lamp beside the bed would fall on them and it would be a kind of welcoming sight—to cheer us up?

We walked to the car, parked in the parking lot, checking our steps on the snowy ice, and we drove the old road again, that narrow, winding road to Sam Fross's.

Sam was the youngest in my father's family—everyone's pride and everyone's disappointment. The one with the most promise and least accomplishment. And nothing that anyone could put a finger on explained it, not booze, or wild women, or gambling. Art did it. Art was the villain.

Sam said once, "It was all those European painters who came into New York during World War II that broke my ass, them and Peggy Guggenheim. That bitch."

He blamed the abstract expressionists. Social realism was his faith, and he had never broken faith until recently, when the tides of fashion and a couple of nervous breakdowns had rammed through his natural barriers to let in voices other than Benton, Wyeth and Hopper.

Sam was my early hero. When I was ten years old and he was twenty, I'd hang around him on the occasions my father's family gathered, hoping he'd sketch me. But it was never the drawing that intrigued me. It was the attention, even the admiration he got. He said outrageous things. My mother quoted him. Laughing. My father was devoted to him and once we drove East to visit Sam and Martha on their farm, where Sam painted half the night and slept until noon. Then he rose to feed their hundreds of chickens. Later it was turkeys and then pigs and for a time goats. He was always feeding creatures.

That was in the late thirties. I didn't get to know Sam really until he had his first crack-up in the late fifties—around the time Jackson Pollock was killed.

Sam never blamed Pollock for his troubles—only Martha did. Sam blamed the painters from Europe who, with the patronage of Peggy Guggenheim, gave momentum to the abstract expressionist movement.

I often wondered about his breakdown and asked him once what happened.

"Oh, it was the tape recorder did it."

He had a big, upright tape recorder with meters and dials and for some reason or other he'd pulled out the patch cords to his hi-fi and tape recorder and then—he'd lost his instruction booklet—couldn't figure out how they went back. He kept trying different combinations and the cords got tangled, he said, and nothing worked. He kept at it, he thought, for hours—getting more desperate and furious. "Then there I was smashing the bejesus out of it and Martha and a couple of neighbors were pinning me down."

"For smashing up the equipment?"

He grinned. "I kept doing it a long time."

"How long?"

"A couple of days . . . off and on."

Janice and I had just divorced. I was living alone in Greenwich Village, in a railroad flat on Bleecker Street. I wanted company. So Sam came down for a couple of weeks of rest and stayed four months. We wandered the Village night after night, hitting all of Sam's old haunts. His friends dropped in to see him. I met them all—among them Ben Hecht, Max Eastman and Edna St. Vincent Millay.

He went back to the Catskills full of new ideas, revived by his gallery tours and his friends. He worked steadily for the next few years on a new show. His show got panned. He sold only two small paintings. A routine medical checkup revealed high blood pressure. Sam went into a depression that lasted for months. He sat staring, Martha told us, at the drip work he'd put into his rural scenes, his skies and trees. A doctor as well as a psychiatrist told Martha it might be better not to urge Sam on with his painting for a while.

Martha, through Sam's friends in New York, got a job as a photographer's assistant and in short order she was a fashion photographer, having forgot little of what she knew about art. Sam turned to making cement figures of animal-like dwarfs he called his Zaqui Coxols. He worked now in a wool bathrobe and a felt fedora.

Their farm stood along a narrow road, halfway up the side of a mountain in a spectacular setting of rock and forest. In the thirties it had been the only house on the left between two crossroads a mile and a half apart, now it was one of many, most of the houses bungalows, summer homes, second homes for city escapees, and abodes of retired men who had escaped, as Sam put it, some pitiful life they still longed to return to like old sled dogs.

We turned into his driveway between slate (bluestone) walls, our headlights flashing across lawn figures, unnamable creatures with pointed bat ears, bulging stomachs and puffy, slanted eyes, all up on four hind legs facing every arriving visitor. I saw Janice staring at them, politely baffled as always, and speechless. I kind of liked them and I'd wanted one for our living room, but Janice said, "Definitely not." They made her uneasy.

I admired the hell out of Sam. He would not admit defeat. He was, he said, in an important new phase of development. His New York gallery had dropped him, but he had his own gallery. His front yard. He had those curious figures on exhibit —and his neighbors, not so sure he wasn't a mad genius, said nothing. "My little people of the forest," he called them. "They were turned to stone at the end of the previous period of creation. Little heathen fuckers."

He was in my mind forever cheerful, foul-mouthed, a lesson to me in perseverance.

We parked by the front porch. Vivian, their oldest daughter, came to the door to meet us. In the living room a fire was burning in the big bluestone fireplace. Their Christmas tree, dry now as a dead thistle, was still up, still in its regalia. All very merry; except Vivian and her young husband, Quinton, looked tired or at least strained, and I sensed tensions—in them and in Martha, who came in holding out her hands to both of us.

"What a surprise," she said.

We were supposed to have been out driving around on a weekend, dropping in.

"What a surprise."

I was carrying a bottle of liquor I'd bought for Sam in Woodstock, all boxed in Christmas colors. She took it from my hands.

"How's Sam?" Janice said, not hopefully.

"Well, he isn't smoking," Martha said as an attempt at a cheerful start. "There's not much for dinner, I'm afraid. I rushed back from New York this morning . . . and . . . there was no time to get any shopping done."

"We're not hungry," Janice said. "We had a sandwich."

"Oh, there's food. I can always find something."

The phone in the dining room rang. Martha answered it. Vivian's sister, Annie, was calling. The girls weren't twins but, perhaps because they were Korean and sisters and about a year apart in age, I was never sure which of the two was which for a few minutes. Martha called in, "Annie wants to say hello to Janice and Jack." Janice spoke for only a minute. It was long distance. I got on. "Things have been pretty rough there," Annie said to me. "Daddy's been in a terrible state. It was *some* Christmas . . ."

When I went back into the living room, everyone was sitting quietly, staring at the fire. In behind me, almost following, came Sam.

I turned around. There he was in the archway, old felt fedora on his head, still in his wool studio bathrobe, high-top boots on his feet.

He hadn't shaved in several days, and his cheeks and jaws had a sugary sparkle. His eyes, usually clear blue-gray, the exact color of his faded denims, were bloodshot and blurred. He stood sizing me up as if he weren't sure what I was doing in his living room, as if no one had told him we were expected.

All of us either stood or sat staring at Sam, waiting for him to react, to relieve us with a quip or a gesture, but he did not move or speak, just stared, his gaze kind of smashed with—by— something; his gaze as battered as my voice.

I picked up the boxed vodka I'd brought him. "I heard you were on a diet and the guy at the liquor store said this stuff has fewer calories than his other stuff."

Sam took the package and nodded.

"Lowest in cholesterol, that is to say." My voice might have been bad, but it was working.

Except for Sam, we were all beaming.

Sam pulled the vodka out of its box and studied the label, holding it down in the light from the floor lamp beside Quinton's chair. He studied it a long time and then said to Quinton, "What have you told them?"

"Told them?"

"Did you give him a message?"

Quinton glanced at him sideways. "When Janice called, I read Martha's note to her, that's all." Quinton seemed annoyed and tired, fed up. "There was a note beside the telephone and I read it."

"What note?"

"It said they were expected for dinner. That's all."

Sam was gazing at Quinton with the same sad-resigned look he'd had for the label on the bottle. "And what message did you take?"

"None."

My impulse was to get out of the room, get out fast. I'd never seen him like this.

A silence settled over us. Sam stared at the fire and then rocked slightly and said with resonance, "Who would have thought the fuse was so short?"

"What?" I said, partly to wipe the words out. The fire went pop. Janice cleared her throat.

"Who would have thought," he repeated slowly, as if reverently quoting Shakespeare, "the fuse was so short?"

"Fuse? What fuse?"

"Come here," he said. He, with the vodka, led me away. I followed into the dining room. We went around the long dining table once in the Fross house, his parents' house in Michigan, into the pantry, where liquor was kept.

He picked up another bottle of that same brand of vodka—a half inch left on its bottom. I knew I was supposed to find some kind of significance in the two bottles, but I didn't know what the hell it was, and I wanted to start talking cheerfully and not stop. "Ha, aha," I said, as if I understood everything now. "Let's finish the old bottle and get started on the new one."

But Sam showed me still another bottle, a bottle of brandy that looked too expensive to find on the shelves of any liquor stores I used. It was unopened. He now opened it, and poured us each at least a cup apiece in highball glasses.

"I bought this," he said, showing me the brandy, "when I got back from California. It cost forty dollars." He led me out of the pantry and back to the dining room table. We sat down. Martha, on her way to the kitchen from the living room, paused when she saw the brandy in our glasses and was about to say something, but she didn't. She went on and Sam sat glaring after her.

I sipped at the brandy uneasily. Maybe he was just on a bender, drinking off a doctor's bad news.

Sam got up and went into the pantry for the vodka and two more glasses. He poured us each half a glass of vodka, finishing one bottle and starting the other.

Talking all the while—"Coming back from California, somewhere around western Kansas, I guess, somewhere in there, I finished off a fifth of California brandy I was ferrying to Martha, gift from your cousin Mildred . . . with help from various traveling companions . . . the whole fifth. When I got home . . . did you know I went to California?"

"No."

He nodded. "To visit Mildred on her caballine bordello."

"The stud farm?"

"Yes. Martha sent me off to the stud farm. Wanted to see the return of my virility. She's also having me grow a beard." He rubbed one hand over the white stubble on each cheek.

"Well," I said agreeably, "I hear a beard will do it."

He laughed and I was relieved to hear he still could. I took hope and raised my glass again.

"So I had to buy Martha a replacement bottle, didn't I? She was furious at what I spent . . . because she makes the living now, Jack . . ." He raised his voice and turned his words toward the kitchen door. "Isn't that so?"

No response.

He set down his brandy and raised his glass of vodka toward me. "Drink up."

I raised mine. "Here's to Siberia," I said with my rattly old voice.

We both unloaded half our glasses. Oh hell, I thought, he's just on a drunk.

Martha came to the kitchen door. "Sam, do you want dinner in twelve minutes, or do you want me to postpone it?"

Sam neither answered nor looked at her.

She raised her voice. "What do you want me to do? I'm waiting."

Sam pulled out his father's gold watch, read its face, and then returned it to an inside shirt pocket under his bathrobe. "Sam?"

He snarled, "What is this shit, woman?" so suddenly I jumped.

Martha went back into the kitchen. He stared at the doorway with such rage I didn't try to say anything funny until dinner started exactly twelve minutes later.

His family gathered quietly, eyes downcast. Martha and Sam sat at the ends of the long table. Janice sat beside me, and Vivian and Quinton, across the way. There were great balancing spaces between us.

Quinton cut into his slice of melon, eyes on his work.

"Remember this table?" Sam asked me.

My father had been one of the children in a big family who

gathered at Christmas for reunions. The table, when extended, could seat thirty people. My grandmother, who had taught her grandchildren as well as her children to pray and to pray frequently, presided at this table as a widow for many years. "Remember how we used to have to bow our goddamn heads?"

He had removed his hat. His bald dome shone in the light of the chandelier.

I said, "Sure. I liked it when we prayed."

He looked astonished. "You did?"

"Sure, I only prayed with one hand. With the other hand I stole olives and shrimp."

Sam laughed.

"Sometimes if I had Evelyn beside me, I got in a good feel under the table."

Evelyn was a particularly prim little girl cousin of mine and my voice for once was perfect—a dirty old man's. Sam rocked back in his chair, he was so delighted. Nobody else did. They hadn't known Evelyn.

We'd come to bring Sam some cheer and I was trying my best. "I got in a lot of good feels while Grandma led us all in prayer."

Martha had her elbows on the table staring off across the room above Sam's head. She took a drag on her cigarette and let the smoke out slowly. I said to her: "I told Sam if I could quit smoking, anybody could. You could too, Martha."

Without lowering her gaze, her eyes widened. "Why should I?" she said sharply.

"It would be good for you," I said lamely.

"The last time I saw our family doctor he told me I had the lungs of a sixteen-year-old, and there's no reason for me to quit. None. I don't have to quit."

"Mother," said Vivian, "would you like me to send you reports on what smoking does to the lungs of non-smokers who are in the same room?"

Well, I'd done it with my cheer.

"At least you don't need to take off any weight," I said quickly. Sam with his pot could stand to lose thirty pounds. I asked him how much he weighed when he got out of high school.

"One hundred and twenty-five pounds," he said.

"What do you weigh now?"

"One hundred and eighty-five."

"You should get your weight down to a hundred and twenty-five again."

"Yes," he said, "but after I got out of high school I started to put on weight. I grew a pair of balls."

"That's only another five pounds or so."

Vivian tittered. Not Martha, she knew what was coming.

"It's my balls that make me too heavy for Martha. She wants me to cut them off."

We let what he'd said pass. Sam's son-in-law Quinton, a handsome kid with a dark mustache, was keeping his gaze on his plate as he ate, silent but alert. I'd thought all along he might be the center of reason in the house, holding everything together. He was an outsider, the husband on hand with the oldest girl, a moderating presence.

We ate silently. The house was silent. I heard our forks clicking.

Martha said, "After dessert, Sam . . . take Jack upstairs and show him the study you've made." I'd already seen it a couple of times, but nobody remembered. It didn't matter.

Sam had such a brilliant beginning—an illustrious college career, straight A's, fraternity president, debating society, track team, summa cum laude—our family supposed he would prepare to go into his uncle's law firm. But Sam, who had been putting oil on canvas since he was twelve, headed from college to New York and the Art Students' League, where it was hoped he would spend a few frivolous years and then settle down in, perhaps, advertising. And he might have—except straight out of two years at the League he won a thousand-dollar prize and headed next, a man on destiny's trail, for Woodstock, New York.

He set himself up in a studio barn with two other painters and began giving lessons. One of his students, Martha, succumbed not only to his blandishments and rowdy charm, but to his talent as well. They got married and she quit painting. They bought a farm about a half hour away in the Catskills and she devoted herself to Sam to give him lots of free time to paint. They did not live high, but with the help of a small inheritance she'd brought him, they made out. They were happy. My god, they were happy. It drained away. I watched it all.

One night in the Village, in the Cedar Tavern, he said, "You think you writers have it rough? You think it's impossible, trying to figure out what publishers, even agents want? Try sometime to imagine what a painter goes through. I believe in having principles, sticking to them: Paint what you love, keep clear of fads and hustlers. Go not for freedom of technique and gimmicks, but for freedom of the spirit. That's what I believed and what I told Pollock in 1938, when he got interested in surrealism. I thought he was slipping, giving up. I tried to save him. We argued. He wanted me to join the American Abstract Artists three years after they organized. I told him he was out of his mind.

"It's hard for an artist to know what to do. I still, goddamn it, believe in my principles. When Pollock was doing that drip painting, I used to complain to Martha—he throws paint on a canvas spread on the floor, walks around in it, then puts a frame around the whole thing and says, *I did this*, signs his name. It *was* absurd, you know, until one day out at his place on Long Island I saw a lot of his canvases at once. They overwhelmed me with their power and freedom. They shook me up, made me wonder about everything I had ever done and believed in. Who knows, maybe it was just the success he was having, but I don't believe that. Then to have him turn his back on the whole thing . . . and then get killed. Senseless. Senseless, Jack." Sam's face always got pavement gray and grim when Pollock's name came up. Pollock's death probably had brought on his first breakdown.

Martha and Sam had no children of their own, but they had adopted and raised two Korean war orphans. The girls were ready for college and money was needed. The farm brought in nothing. There was only one way to get funds. Pulling himself together and preparing for his next exhibit, Sam worked some of the concepts of the abstract expressionists into his new work. By then it was too late. They'd had their day. Pop art was in. Warhol, Lichtenstein, Johns, Rauschenberg had the art world interested in a whole new kind of painting—as realistic as the vases Sam had once, as an eighteen-year-old, painted so accurately and ardently.

He cracked up again and Martha set up a darkroom on the farm and a studio with a cot and a hot plate in New York, and in a little while they were managing again.

It's been only recently I've realized who the painter was who visited Sam the week I spent on Sam's farm as a boy. They had both studied under Thomas Hart Benton at the League—where Sam first heard that vases painted with photographic fidelity were not great art.

I remember how much company they had at the farm. Painters up from Woodstock dropped in on them all the time. I remember Pollock was very drunk and Martha didn't like him and that he came and went in a Model A Ford.

I looked out one of the dormer windows across the front yard, past the stone figures on the snow-patched lawn, past the road. The trees, evergreens among all the bare ones, descended the mountainside toward the lake at the bottom. Mountains in the distance. I couldn't see them in the night, but I knew mountains were there, felt them. The lake was white, I could make its edges out, and I thought about Gail again with guilt and regret. It would have been so much better if I'd never agreed to come to Sam's. What was I doing here? Ah, Newman —was this some of the luck with which you blessed me?

Behind me at a long table, Sam found the skin magazine he'd been looking for. He called me over to a centerfold of a girl with her slip pushed down around her waist and pulled up above her crotch. She was a blonde—everywhere. Her eyes were closed, her lips slightly parted. Her left hand disappeared behind her head and her right hand played with a string of pearls that coiled around her neck and nipples. Sam brought my attention to her thighs, where, below the blur or out-of-focus haze of her bright hair, lay a tremendous cunt line that stretched from her stomach into her ass.

"They must have put that in with an airbrush." To rest my voice I was whispering. "That can't be real. Where did you get this magazine?"

"Quinton brought it for me." We eyed it awhile and then I picked up one of his watercolors; half a dozen or so lay on an open foamboard folder or carrier. "Are you painting again?"

"No. Those are old ones. I was going to take them down to Woodstock. They'll still sell things for me."

"But you're not going to?"

He shook his head. "No. Christ. Martha is keeping me hidden from everyone. I'm in bad shape, Jack."

"Because everything's hit you at once. Take it easy. Lie low. Relax."

He nodded.

"Giving up smoking," I whispered, "is a bitch. But I think what must have rocked you most was being there when that guy next door got it."

He stared at me, seeing me and back into the past simultaneously, and then after a long pause he said, "I think I killed him."

I quit whispering. "Oh, come on . . ."

He turned away. "No. I can't figure it out." He walked over and sat down in a chair by his desk.

"What happened?"

"I was out in the yard, beside the house, and then I heard this bang. It was a hell of a loud bang. And then in a minute I saw somebody running. Running . . . over across the way. He ran over beside Frank's house, and then he came running back my way and said—Frank's been shot.

"Frank's been shot? My god. I get very cool in a crisis. I said —Go back to him. And I went into the house and called the police and then I got a blanket out of the blanket chest and I went outside and across the wall and over to Frank. He'd fallen off the roof. He'd been fixing the roof and he fell down the side and off. We wrapped him in the blanket. Then we sat there and waited. There was nothing we could do but sit and wait."

"Was he conscious?"

"I don't think so."

"Then he didn't say anything?"

"Once. Once he said—leg. I think that's what he said—leg. He'd been hit here." Sam tapped his thigh above his right knee.

"What kind of a slug hit him?"

"A thirty something or other."

"Big stuff?"

"It was big. It tore him all open. But he hit his head when he fell. That's what killed him."

"Sam, you don't have a deer rifle."

"I've got a twenty-two I keep in the woodshed." He gestured vaguely off to where the woodshed was. He shook his head and hunched his shoulders and started running his lower lip back and forth between his teeth.

"Look, a twenty-two wasn't what hit him."

"I don't keep bullets in it anymore. I've taken all the bullets out."

"Listen, Sam . . . you didn't have anything to do with that guy's getting shot."

But he shook his head, shook my reassurances away. "It didn't bother me, you know, at first. Martha thought I ought to get a rest around then and she put me on the plane to California. Where I spent a couple of weeks. Had a good time. Did I tell you about drinking a bottle of brandy on the plane?"

"Yeah."

"I did? I came back and went to the doctor for a checkup and he said I had emphysema. Wham! I came home and started to shake. The shooting, Frank, came back to me. I couldn't even remember where I was when I heard the shot. I heard it though. I heard it. Why would Martha send me out of the state like that, right after a neighbor of mine was shot? All the way across the country? Did she know I shot him, or think so?"

"Who do the police think shot him?"

"They don't know."

"A hunter, probably."

"Nobody knows. Martha heard someone in the village say his wife did it. He was a mean bastard. But I don't know. I try to figure it out. I think maybe it was someone near me, shooting across me. Maybe even shooting at me and missing."

"Who?"

He shrugged. "It might have been the CIA."

"Why?"

"Or the KGB."

"Russians?"

He spread his arms and looked down helplessly. "Martha says I'm getting paranoid."

The Soviets, whose Marxist principles he had once upheld, had come back to haunt him. I'd seen or sensed that downstairs when he stood studying the vodka labels. He was studying everything for messages. Messages were being passed all around him, and he was trying to intercept a few. He was suspicious of the vodka I'd brought. He was suspicious of me.

"That was one of my mother's blankets," he said. His eyes filled with tears. They brimmed on his lower eyelids. "The police still have it. I guess it's full of blood."

I sat down across from him on a stack of pine planks. I said, "Jesus, Sam. The world we live in. Who can figure it out?" I felt overwhelmed myself. "I say it's the goddamn emphysema."

He nodded. "Maybe. Maybe. I better check about that blanket. Get it back."

"Forget it."

"Everything happening at once. Last October we were broke. Now we have some money again."

"Sam, you didn't shoot that guy."

He nodded, but he wasn't sure. "He hit his cellar steps. Its doors were open." He clapped his palms together.

I shook my head. "In books all the dramatic events are nicely spaced out, not in life. Ask me. In life they hit you all at once, a whole mountain of shit." I started to tell him about Harvey and how he wound up, but I stopped myself in time.

"You can't let this get you down. Get a psychiatrist. Get any help you can."

"Yeah."

A writing ledge from his desk was pulled out and a board of checkered squares lay on it—stretched between us on a level with my chin. We'd played chess half a dozen places in the Village those recovery months for both of us in New York—while he was reshaping his ideas, and helping me forget Janice with chess and Mayan lore and Spanish *retablos* and folk art. It was he who got me to go to the Yucatan when I wanted to go to Samarkand.

"You been playing chess here?"

"Been giving Quinton lessons."

"He's a good boy," I said.

Sam nodded.

"If he gives you any advice, listen to it. But talk to a head doc."

"They can't help me."

"By the time the bills start coming in, you'll be surprised how fast you can get your bearings again."

"Yeah."

He began to pick at the skin on the palm of his left hand. He picked away awhile, then said, "Where did I go wrong? What did I do wrong?"

I knew what he meant, but I didn't want to. I said nothing. And then he said, answering himself, "It's marriage."

"Marriage?"

I thought of Fletch. Fletch's face flashed up and out. I closed my eyes and pinched my lips between a knuckle and a thumb. "Marriage?"

Sam said no more. And did I give Sam Janice's answer? That marriage only went bad for men who couldn't grow up? It wasn't the answer. Life, life, life. Life got to all of us in time.

"I'm at where," he said, "I feel guilty about everything, my mother's death, Aunt Helen's. I went out to Indiana to see Helen just before she died. We had lunch. She died the next day." He shook his head. "Then Frank gets shot and has that fall. I can't figure it out. Could I have something to do with all of them dying? Did I open his cellar doors? I go over and over everything. I've been going over and over everything since I came back from California."

I let him cry awhile.

"How was Mildred?"

"I stayed with her."

"How is she?"

"She's fine. Her father's with her now."

"Uncle Rudolph?"

"He's in bed most of the time."

"What's the matter?"

"Arthritis."

"That's a bad rap, a bad rap. I know at least three people in the Middle West half crippled with it. Is that a disease Middle Westerners get a lot?"

"You're thinking of goiter."

"Used to be goiter. Now they stuff salt in the iodine." I sighed. "Or iodine in the salt . . . something."

"What are you doing for your throat?" he asked. "Do you gargle, or what?"

When we went downstairs, I signaled to Janice we were ready to leave. No one urged us to stay and I had the feeling again that our turning up seemed unfortunate to everyone—even Martha. We left.

Sam stared after us with such a look of general, unfocused rage Janice was afraid of what might happen in the house after we drove away.

I reported what Sam told me. She already knew. We dipped down the road between headlighted snowbanks, between leafless ranks of trees. "He couldn't have done it," she said. "He was on the other side of his roof, away from Sam, when the bullet hit. He crawled to the peak to hold on and slid over the other side. That's what happened. Only Sam can't believe it. He can't stop talking about . . . killing him. That's why they sent him to California. And they're keeping him out of the village. Can you imagine? The worry he is? And you know, he just can't shut up."

A couple of houses stood between Sam's place and the highway, but there were no lights on in either of them. "What are they going to do?" she said.

And that's what I lay thinking when we were back at the motel and in bed. What could they do? What could any of us do? You waited now. You sat by the fallen man and you waited.

I woke up once in the night still thinking about Sam in my sleep. Janice was awake too and she threw an arm across me and said softly, "You had other plans for this weekend, didn't you?"

Or maybe she didn't know I was awake and was testing me with sly questions, hoping sleep had my guard down. I didn't answer. My period of silence had begun.

First week of silence—

Mount Sinai, Monday morning. Now that treatments had
started, we got up at six-thirty to give us time to dress, have
breakfast and drive to the other side of town for my regular
Monday through Friday eight o'clock appointment. Janice
could take until noon to check into her hospital for her twenty-
four-hour stretch of duty, so she parked to wait for me, as she
planned to do every other day for the duration. She didn't like
me walking back alone.

"I know it's a lovely time of day for a walk and I know Central Park is lovely to walk across even in the winter, but you'll
get mugged."

Driving across Ninety-sixth Street this morning she said,
"There's another story in the paper about senior citizens in
New York and how they have to live. They have a terrible
time. They have so little money. They take a bus to a senior
citizens' recreation center, sing, play bridge, and eat a fifteen-
cent lunch. They're always being mugged because they're so
old."

I was getting the word, and it was fortunate I had to be silent. She was telling me again, as she had often enough, that
we were using our double income to shield us from such a fate
and that I would be worse than a fool to kick it away for a girl
or some crazy whim. It was the first oblique reference to "that
New Jersey girl" she'd made in weeks. When she dropped me

off in front of the long blue canopy, she drove on down the street to pull in by a fireplug.

I was the first patient each day. I changed clothes and went into the X-ray chamber. I lay down on a strip of cloth that didn't quite reach the cold table's edge. I looked up at the ceiling. Above me the dome of the green machine rotated to the left. Measurements were taken. I heard the sound of rubber and leather soles on the floor, the movement of smocks around legs. The door of the room closed. Overhead the lights went on, and in a moment, *puff*, followed by a leadheavy click. I closed my eyes against the light and this time didn't bother to count. I felt the cold of the table against my elbows and I thought I heard a humming sound. The machine? No, when the lights went out overhead and the staff was in the room again, I could still hear the hum.

I dressed, went upstairs and got into the car. Janice drove because she would drop me off at school. I didn't have a class until Tuesday night, but I had a departmental meeting that morning. Janice would leave the car in our parking slot and take a bus to her hospital. I had a long busy day ahead of me— for a silent man.

At first I'd thought I wouldn't attend our Curriculum Committee meeting, but when I talked to Fred on Friday he said he'd heard Thorpe planned to retire—leaving a gap to be filled in our writing courses. It occurred to me the committee might use that gap as an excuse to wipe out all the fiction and poetry sections. They might. It had been tried before. So I would attend. Though silent.

After Janice let me out, I walked across the campus and dropped in on Thorpe. We sat on his beat-up old davenport and the light from the lamp on his desk fell on his jowls. I thought of Sam. Had he killed his whole family yet?

My pad on my knees, my felt tip pen in hand, I wrote

Thorpe a message. He bent forward to watch the words appear. Then he leaned back, shook his head and said he would not retire, no, he would teach until he was sixty-eight.

I wrote again—Had he seen Dorothy Dole?

A little grin appeared on his face. He looked years younger. "Yes, indeed I did," he said slowly. He gave me a sly look. "I found her a remarkably active woman for her age—as I'm sure you did."

We moved on, over to our building, where the department held its meetings in a basement room that had long ago lost its early council chamber glory. Under the pressure of expansion, because of the scarcity of space, storage debris had accumulated around the walls, battered desks, wheelless blackboards, cartons of books and papers, a pinball machine . . . a pinball machine? How had that got there? Some of the junior members of the department once plugged it in, but it was dead.

Nobody complained any more about the junk around the walls, but for years every committee meeting suffered from the indignation, from the outrage of it all. The pinball machine alone inspired several long tirades and at least six memos.

We got used to the crap, we accepted it as one of the conditions under which we lived, like the graffiti on the walls, and the occasional robbery or rape of a teacher or student.

Fred, our chairman, or chairperson as we now quite carefully called him when female faculty were around, reigned at the head of the table in the chair with the armrests. Kate, our poet and poetry teacher, sat on his right. The meeting was already under way when Thorpe and I sat down. Kate raised two fingers in a V sign for me. Which could have meant she'd finally got a contract to publish a book of poetry or—here's to therapy. She was smoking a long, thin, black cigar.

The dean, I saw, was visiting us. She paused until Thorpe and I were settled and then went on, a big florid woman with heavy horn-rimmed glasses that she played with, opening them, shutting them, putting them on, taking them off, cleaning them, putting them down, picking them up. Watching her glasses, as I think a lot of us did, I often lost all track of what she was saying. That could have been her purpose.

If so, she couldn't shake Fred's attention. Fred listened, his head against one hand as if he were back at a briefing during the London blitz. The dean was talking about our need for more evening classes. My mind drifted. I thought of Fred in a fighter plane, that bow-tied, tweed jacketed, middle-aged academic diving around over London, gunning down Nazi bombers.

The only other full professor at the table was Cutter L. Bryant, our seventeenth-century man. He had kept the same face, agelessly, for the many years I'd been around, a rubbery, solemn man eternally in his forties with dewlaps and deep creases at the corners of his lips. He wore corduroy suits and knit ties. When he spoke he seemed to be speaking for posterity. I think he had done some acting in his youth. His eyes stared beyond us all, scornfully. When he spoke, it was more often than not with indignation. It was he who had led the losing battle against the pinball machine. It was Bryant, more than anyone, who despised the creative writing courses and, I guess, me. But I tried hard not to take it personally.

The dean had finished. Under discussion now, among the sixteen of us at the table, was the student who turns in the same paper to two different classes for credit. Was that self-plagiarism? Nobody could decide. The arguments rolled up and down the table and then, to put an end to the drooping drone, it was voted the problem be left for the individual teacher to decide.

Voiceless, I had nothing to say, but nobody noticed.

Our English honors program came up. Arthur Werter, who

was in charge of it, said the program was often confused with graduating with honors, that is to say, with high grades. Then Thorpe brought up our annual $500 Dorothy Dole Award, a prize for creative writers. Should not this also, inquired Thorpe carefully, be considered an honor? Should not the honor then appear on the student's transcript? Which in turn generated an unexpected outburst of support for the creative writing courses from long, lean, bearded Werter. Directing a friendly eye at me, he said, "Why is literary criticism being entered in that contest? It's for poetry and fiction."

He well knew the answer. My nemesis, Cutter L. Bryant, had fought to see that it was included—and now Bryant bellowed out, "Because literary criticism is also creative. It's as creative as fiction."

"And where," said Thorpe carefully, "is the category for playwriting? That, too, is as creative as fiction."

Fred frowned, thought, and then for some reason pointed a finger at me and said, "Playwriting is fiction."

Hints of academic disaster were always in the air. The dean began to hint of it again. We were holding too many classes during the day. What had happened to our old tradition of serving the community, the dropouts, the men caught in jobs they wanted to escape . . . all those people who could only attend college courses at night? If we no longer served them with night classes, had we not lost our purpose? Were we to become just another undergraduate college? And if we did, did we then have a right to exist?

Nobody answered.

She continued. The quality of our students was going down. Our tuition would rise another $200 next fall. And then Cutter L. Bryant spoke up with primed scorn. The language departments, he said, were now teaching their literature courses using

English translations—just to keep their faculty members in jobs —and the practice was cutting into the enrollment in the English Department's literature courses. His voice rose, "In the German Department there are twelve full professors and only eight majors. And the administration, you, want us to teach a course in Urban Literature."

When the dean left a few minutes later, there were expressions of dismay and futility on most of the faculty faces. Bryant had his supporters. He was as powerful as Fred. "Who wants to teach a gimmick course?" he said.

When the meeting broke up, I took the elevator to our floor with Fred beside me. I followed him out and into our men's room. A lot of faculty conferences are held informally in the men's room.

"Are you all set for those treatments?" Fred said over his shoulder.

While he was stepping up to the urinal, I wrote a message for him: "All set. By the time our midyear break is over, I'll have only a few more weeks of silence." I handed it to him while he was zipping up.

Werter had come in and gone into a stall.

"You still want to teach next semester?" Fred said with consternation. "You don't have to." Fred called into the stall where Werter sat, "Jack doesn't want his leave of absence with pay. He wants to teach."

"No, no, we can't let him," I heard Werter say. "It would ruin his voice."

"Take the leave," Fred said. "Get a lot of writing done." As if we had never discussed the matter.

I wrote, "These classes are good for my morale." I knocked on Werter's stall. When he opened the door, he took the note, slammed the door, then in a moment passed it out under the stall with two long fingers. I handed it to Fred and he studied it, shaking his head.

I think they understood, but I've never been sure.

The parking lot for guests who visited Gail's building was a cement area that ran along the highway. When I'd pulled in and parked, it occurred to me that someone Janice knew might have spotted our car there and asked, casually, the name of our friends in that building. There weren't all that many white Volvo sports cars around New Jersey with New York plates. I still didn't know how she'd found out about Gail.

I got out, locked the car and walked up to the entrance of the building, wondering whether someone was looking down and watching me. Someone had to have tipped her off.

The Christmas decorations in the lobby were gone. The doorman nodded to me. I took the elevator in her wing up to her floor and walked to her apartment and rang the bell. I'd already written across my note pad: "I can explain." I also had several typewritten pages explaining all about my uncle Sam.

But there was no answer. I rang a few more times, then slid my note under her door. When I got downstairs, I stuck another "I can explain" in her mailbox for good measure.

At ten o'clock that evening I drove back again, but she still wasn't in. Outside her door I wondered what to do. She was furious with me, I could be sure of that. What could I do except go away? Even if she were inside, ignoring me, there wasn't anything I could do. But it wasn't like Gail to stay mad for long, and I was worried. Harvey Sampers' death was still on my mind.

I went downstairs and checked her mailbox. I could see my note, so she hadn't returned. What the hell, I'd come back at six o'clock tomorrow morning, before she'd had a chance to get up. If I couldn't call her any more, my pursuit would have to be in silence.

Back home, because I couldn't sleep, I read a batch of stories and attached written comments to them. Then I selected two for classroom reading and discussion. My first voiceless class.

I ran a sheet of paper into the typewriter and typed an opening statement someone could read, whoever sat to my right or left. I kept it brief. Then I wrote a series of queries, keeping these brief too, each question intended to develop discussion a little farther, such queries as: Why is the mother so agitated by her daughter's good news?

Reading two stories should absorb nearly an hour. The rest of the time would have to be taken up by discussion. If it weren't, everything would fall apart. I couldn't tell tall stories now, my little fantasies about men sinking under the quicksand of pavement clutching Road Closed signs. I could send no more coal-burning trains across canyon-spanning trestles where the figurative reader stood without escape. Nor fall back on early recollections, epiphanies, misadventures, longings. Everything of my own was locked in me now. The subway with the air-conditioned lounge and bar reserved for one mysterious man. The camera with the human eye. The doll that kept the house awake all night with its crying. The house that floated off into the ocean and down a whirlpool. The man who threw the world out of orbit. Even Samarkand. All the stories I'd been telling instead of writing.

I'd always believed a teacher, any teacher, no matter what his subject, teaches himself. And so I'd taught myself, opened myself wide, my dreams, failures, shames, the whole works—the stuff of fiction, honestly, fearlessly, all by way of conveying that I wanted as much from the students, telling stories only to show that I wanted them to give me themselves through their imaginations and imaginings. It had worked as had no other endeavor in my life; nothing, not even my own writing, had given me such a heady sense of satisfaction and achievement. That whole way of teaching locked up now? The teacher as actor, character, leader, wordgiver, locked up? My god, now I had to be what I'd always told myself I was, a teacher—and just a teacher.

And if my voice never returned? I would be kept on the payroll as a non-teaching teacher. I had entered the Land of Paradox.

At six o'clock the next morning I was back at her door. I knew then something was really wrong, because she still wasn't in. If I had to, I'd get the management to come with me and we'd open her door. But they wouldn't be in until eight or nine, so I headed back to New York and the green machine.

They took me at once. There was the machine waiting in the dim room. They wheeled me under the head. The table growled as gears meshed and the table lifted me toward the four crossed shadow bars. Everything and everyone moved methodically.

My throat felt sore, down low, just about where I'd been told to expect it, right on schedule. I'd felt its rawness when I had my coffee last night. I'd rolled the coffee around in my mouth before I swallowed.

When I sat up and looked at the clock on the wall, five minutes had passed.

Miss Wong held my robe. I got off the table. "How is voice?" she asked.

"Is there," I said softly.

"You are not talking?"

I shook my head.

When I got upstairs and out on the street, I had a parking ticket stuck in my windshield. I shoved it in the glove compartment and headed for New Jersey. Driving over the bridge, I threw the ticket out the window. I knew it was going to be impossible to explain to Janice why I'd taken the car this once when I never took it on other days unless she was along. Okay, added to my long list of heinous crimes was scofflaw. Well, God would understand.

A woman at a desk in the management office looked uneasily at my unshaven jowls and then at the note I'd written on my pad.

"Who are you?" she said. She was a buxom woman of perhaps fifty with dyed blonde hair swept up and knotted behind her head. She looked as if she knew how to handle almost anything, especially fools.

When I'd written my name, she said, "It won't be necessary to go into the apartment, because she is not there. She left a message for you, Mr. Fross."

I opened the envelope and read, *Have gone out of town and may not be back. Please don't try to find me. You do not need me to help you destroy yourself. I don't want to see you again. I have more guilts of my own than I can accommodate.—Gail*

When Janice got home, she took one look at me and said, "It's starting to hurt, isn't it?"

I nodded and stroked my throat.

"If I were you, I'd start using your electric razor. Did you shave with it this morning?"

I shook my head.

"Ask them about that. I think you should start using the electric razor I got you for Christmas. I don't know why you don't use it. I asked the doctors at my hospital and most of them use one. I think everyone I asked said he used an electric razor. Besides, I'm tired of the old blades you leave lying around in the bathroom cabinet. They lie in there and get rusty. They pile up. I don't see what satisfaction you get shaving with those old-fashioned razors anyway. What is this—you don't have lunch ready? What have you been doing all morning?"

I shrugged.

"Sometimes I think you just sit around here and stare at the four walls."

There were a number of things I thought I might do. The theater she'd worked at might be able to tell me where she'd gone. The lady in the management office had flatly refused to on grounds of confidentiality, but there were other places I might get a lead. Several times friends of Gail's had dropped in when I was at her apartment, theater people, but I hadn't particularly liked them so I didn't know where to look them up except at the theater.

I supposed I'd look silly, asking questions with a pad and pen, but I'd have to. There was nothing else I could do. I did not even know her home town, although I could dig that up in our school records.

The next morning, a doctor at the hospital took a look at my throat. It wasn't Beirne. It was the bearded man who, the day my plaster cast was made, took the X-rays of my throat. He was totally bald, but his mustache and beard were so vigorous they nearly concealed his mouth. When he said, "Good morning," I saw only hair move.

He took a tongue depressor and lifted my upper lips. He worked his way around my teeth, looking at the gums. Then he asked how I felt. I said, "Not bad." He listened to my voice. It was understood I could speak at the hospital. Then he warmed a mirror at the end of a thin silver prong. "Stick out your tongue," he said—and he wrapped it in gauze, got a grip, and down he dropped for a look, his eye floating brightly into my throat. I tried to relax and breathe.

"Say E."

I tried.

He pulled the mirror up and let go. "Very good," he said. He must have noticed how unhappy I looked. "Some people tune in on pain. Others don't. If you don't tune in on pain, you may not feel much more than a mild discomfort. But you'll feel something, beginning today, something more than rawness."

"For how long?"

"The discomfort?"

"Pain."

"Until a couple of weeks after treatments stop. Gradually, it will go away."

"How long before I can speak?"

"You'll be the judge. And when you begin, the important thing is—never project. Keep your voice soft, tiny. Even when your cords get strength back, don't push them. If your voice feels tired at the end of a day, you've used it too much. Cut back."

"At least another five weeks of silence?"

He shrugged. "Sometimes people are told to be silent as long as three months, but I don't think you are going to find that necessary."

When Janice and I got back to the apartment and opened the door, the odor of cigarette smoke from last night's class met us. It was the final session of the semester. Everything had gone smoothly. My notes lay on the cocktail table: block printing on oblong slips of pad paper.

Trail of notes:

My opening remark is a question: would you like to continue to meet in my apartment next semester? Once I begin to use my voice again we can shift back to school. How do you vote? Please discuss.

*   *   *

All right. We'll meet here.

*   *   *

I asked last week what the assertions were in The Life of Dylan Thomas. *Please give me your papers and I'll have them read aloud. If I raise my hand at the end of any assertion, please discuss its development and illustration.*

*   *   *

Thank you all and good-by until next term.

I went down to the theater that afternoon and talked to the director and a couple of people who knew Gail, but they seemed as mystified as I was. That is, I showed them notes that asked my question and explained my silence as laryngitis.

The director was a thin young man who seemed high on something. His eyes were bloodshot and he kept staring at my tie. My notes amused him. He called the other two people, both women, over.

"I know she was upset about some fellow she was going with," the younger woman said.

As I was leaving, the other said, "It's him. He's the one. He's the son of a bitch." Someone backstage started hammering and I went out of the dusky theater into the bright light of Mac-Dougal Street.

My silence was too much of a handicap for me at the theater and at Gail's apartment house. If she didn't come back, I was going to have to wait. I'd have to wait to find her until I could speak. Unless I heard from her.

On the other hand, my silence in the classroom was curiously effective. The students, without my voice to lead them along, studied my face during readings and discussions, seeking in my silence clues to my reaction. When my notes to them were read aloud, they listened to whoever read them with a kind of rapt attention I'd never had.

Saturday night in the Village at the Corner Bistro with Janice and Alice Sampers, I wrote our orders: *two bowls of chili with onions, one cheeseburger with onion, two draft beers, one scotch and soda.* I signaled the waiter, handed him the slip, he nodded. Neither of the women noticed. The food and drinks came as if by magic.

Harvey is buried and Alice seems to have recovered.

Later, at the movie theater, waiting in line, I left them for a minute and came back with a Baby Ruth bar, peeled it and gave each of them a bite. Alice said, "You know how to take care of your women, don't you?" I ate my share painfully.

On Sunday an elderly fellow with a Spanish accent stopped me in front of our building: "Is that 501 over there?"

I have been living where I live for years, but I don't know what any of the numbers on the buildings are except our own. I was tired and I had an armful of groceries. I looked at him silently and walked past him shaking my head because I couldn't think of anything else to do. He said as I passed, "Don't you speak any language?"

By Sunday the throat was hurting all right, all right. Janice looked at me with sympathetic concern and asked how I felt. I told her by hand sign I felt great. She didn't believe me. "I want to know how you are."

I wrote on my pad: *"My throat is beginning to feel as if it were full of lice crawling around biting."*

She recoiled and said, "Do you have to put it that way?"

By that evening the crawling sensation got worse and I

calmed down with aspirin. I bought a lot of orange aspergum. I chewed it when we went to bed. I kept a wad of it between my teeth all night. The gum helped. Two days of relief from the green machine helped too.

The Monday of my third week of treatment did not start out at all well, but I discovered how Janice learned about Gail. On Monday our battery went dead. Our car in the parking lot gradually chugged its way to silence.

When Janice came out, there was nothing to do but walk her back inside the building out of the cold. I wrote her a couple of notes and caught a cab by myself to the hospital. There was a beginning-of-the-day stir in the corridors.

I took the stairway down into the hospital's depths. How far down did those steps go below Radiology? Once more I stretched out under the Great God Damn. I lay there wondering if Gail had moved in with someone. Where did that producer live?

When I walked across the park going home, I held one gloved hand over my face. The air was cold. On the other side of the park, I tried to go into a branch public library, but it was closed, and would be until ten o'clock. So, coming back on the bus, without help from *Consumer Reports*, I got off at our closest auto store. I showed the clerk my pad: *Have laryngitis; can't talk. Do you sell 12-volt batteries? Volvo P1800, 1967.* They had one: forty bucks.

Next, I'd get Janice to call AAA. If they could help me out with a booster charge, I could get the car to the auto store. Meanwhile, our upstairs friend, Judy, subscribed to *Consumer Reports* and we could see how they evaluated the battery I was getting.

But Janice was gone; either left early or beeped away. What now? Down to the car. The battery four years old. Lift the

hood. Remove battery caps and check water level. Water level
okay. Try starting again. Nope, just a weak heaving, then silence.

Back in the apartment I typed out a note to carry to Norman: *Car won't start. Battery dead. Would you dial AAA for
me? 695-8311. The car is downstairs. License 1149Y. Member-
ship number is 33133875. I hope they don't have to see my registration. I can't find it.*

I rang the doorbell and waited, then heard what I thought
was Francine's voice asking, "Who is it?" I said nothing. I
couldn't. I planted my face in front of their eye slot and rang
again.

"Who is it?"

Then I realized she wasn't tall enough to see through the
peephole. So I rang once more.

Again the challenge, this time more frantic. I had her scared.

I put my finger against the goddamn bell and left it there. It
trilled and trilled.

"Who is it? Who's there? I'm going to call the police." That
wasn't Francine. It was Judy.

I rang again. On and on we went—until I leaned close to the
door and said as loudly as I dared—which wasn't very loud,
"It's Jack."

"Who?"

"Jack Fross."

She opened the door, a look of terror and exhaustion on her
face. All kinds of apologies followed. She looked shaken. The
peephole, she said, didn't work and she couldn't understand
why she hadn't been able to get an answer.

She read my note and called AAA at once.

AAA was busy. Natch. She poured me a cup of coffee and
kept dialing. I sat in the tiny alcove off the kitchen and she
stood beside the stove, using the wall phone. Nobody else was

home, she'd said, and that's what had so frightened her. She hung up again and leaned against the wall, still recovering.

"I'm terrified when I'm alone, always have been. I'm alone here and I hear sounds and I jump. I jump. I'm not kidding."

I wrote: "What are you afraid of?"

"I don't know, that's the trouble."

I wrote and she watched my words appear: *All your years in analysis, and you never learned what you're afraid of?*

She laughed unhappily. "I got attacked once. I was a kid. That didn't help."

What did she mean? She saw my expression and said, "Nothing happened, but it could have, you know. One of those things. He, a grown man, a workman, paperhanger, got scared when I yelled. I never told anyone for years."

It occurred to me she was nervous now because the two of us were alone, but she still hadn't reached AAA and I sat tight, trying to look as unaggressive as possible, but all I could think about was how sexy a girl seems when you're alone with her, and nothing but sex was running through her frightened mind. Judy had on an old blue housecoat over, I suppose, a slip. Her long blond hair was only loosely combed. She stood between calls looking over my head and out at the balcony and beyond, too uneasy to sit down at the table. She kept rubbing her arms and from time to time I'd get quick side glances.

"I have to be in control," she said. "I have to be in control of a situation or I'm unnerved. That makes me rough on Norman. I can be a real bitch if I think I'm not in charge."

Me too, I wrote, *only worse.*

"What do you mean?"

I wasn't any good at team sports, I wrote.

"You had to be quarterback?"

No good at quarterback either. I can't seem to take command or be commanded. Can't dance. Can't drill troops. I used to march them through hedges and into the sides of bar-racks. She followed each word as it appeared.

"I'm all right if I'm running the show," she said. "When I put dinner on, I want everyone seated around the table. I don't want Francine yelling down the hall, 'I'll be there in a minute.' If I think we should all go to the Museum of Natural History, I don't want any arguments. I even have to pick the television shows we watch. I wish I weren't like that."

She tried the number again and this time she got AAA. While she was reading my instructions, I glanced out into the living room at what I thought looked like a long brass telescope on a tripod. I walked in and looked at it. When I walked back, she said, "That's Francine's."

It was one of the most beautiful telescopes I'd ever seen. It could have cost $1,000. "Her grandfather," she said, "gave it to her. Norman gets very upset when she's given expensive things."

I shrugged.

AAA would be down at the lot in about an hour.

I studied her carefully to see if my discovery of the telescope had upset her. The light from the window hit the side of her face quite softly, no shadows. She'd had her own siege with cancer, and had been through radiotherapy ahead of me. She only seemed upset by my appearance at the door.

The first thing she'd asked after she'd let me in and recovered from her fright was how many treatments I'd had so far. I flashed the fingers of my right hand twice for ten. Wasn't I bothered by it? She'd been sick. I held up a little space between my thumb and first finger, and she looked skeptical.

When I left she was pleased she'd been able to help me and thought we'd had a good visit. "It shows," she said, "you can have a philosophical discussion with someone who can't talk."

Proving what? Well, something with human and social significance.

But her eyes flicked to the telescope and I knew then who had spotted me on Gail's terrace in New Jersey. It was little Francine.

Trail of notes—

Never on Monday nights.

* * *

If you find the restaurant listed in Cue, *Beware.*

* * *

When you talk, Marvin, you use your hands very expressively, like an Italian.

* * *

Theratron.

* * *

I'm in agony, but I'm not showing it.

* * *

I lost my pen.

* * *

Four glasses of white wine.

* * *

The soup here is good.

* * *

I hate the truth.

* * *

Laura, you're another screwed up moviegoer.

* * *

We both should be barred from every movie house in New York.

* * *

Has a peculiar behavior.

* * *

If you can't run you're dead.

Fourth week—

My throat hurt, but it wasn't unbearable. I went up to school for registration on Friday morning from ten to twelve. Kate and I handled the students registering for fiction and poetry. She came in once, gave me her V sign and a punch on the arm. She'd pasted a sign on the door of her office: *Unladylike Poet.*

Fred came by during a period I wasn't busy.

Over my desk I had thumbtacked half a dozen file cards with written answers to most of the questions I was asked. He examined them solemnly, then eyed me even more soberly. "How do you feel?"

With my thumb and forefinger I cast before him the eternal symbol of perfection—the Ballantine beer sign. I smiled. I leaned back in my chair. I got up. I stood on tiptoe and held my hands high in the air. I spoke very softly—as I did at the hospital, "I feel fine."

"For god's sake, don't."

I wrote on my pad that I said as much once a week for my doctors. He was still shocked. "The voice sounds good," he said. It did. I knew it was already better than anything he'd heard come out of me in years.

Like a private eye, I spent one entire day parked in a rented car in the parking lot beside Gail's apartment building. No sign of her, or her car.

These rays produce their own kind of burn. At first the flesh on my throat turned red, a sunburned red. The blush was faint, took a week or more to be noticeable, then turned from a berry red to a beefy hue. Along about the fourth week I had a glowing burn, not yet raw, only vaguely tender, not sore. I was still wearing turtleneck pullovers. They were made of Acrilan, not quite as soft as wool but comfortable even against the burn. When I took off a pullover, the rosiness of my neck could have been left there by the sweater, the turtleneck fit so perfectly over the area exposed to the cobalt.

With a sunburn when you touch it, there's a sensation of tingling against your fingers. With this burn, the sensation sank away from the fingertips, deadened out. The skin had the feel of silk. It was slippery, smooth and dry.

Where is Gail? Where was she?

The doctor said, "Your cords are getting red. From now on they're going to be sore. You'll feel a lump in your throat and eventually you may have a little trouble swallowing." He was actually smiling, looking pleased.

Sometimes I thought I could feel the spider cells popping,

tiny little things. They popped with a sound like the cat getting his claws into cardboard. I felt the cells writhing.

I lie on the table under the Theratron and my pulse beats against the plaster cast, my plaster of Paris torture mask. I lie still, lights on overhead, wondering whether to close my eyes, whether to swallow. I imagine a moonbeam slicking through me, cleanly, painlessly, and for all its invisibility very matter-of-fact, very real.

The machine, the ray, is a presence. I'm being skewered. The green machine . . . it's a kind of being . . . if not the Great God Damn himself, then one of our local New York deities attended by these technicians, these neo-Mayan temple maidens, priestesses. They move my altar under the green god's head until his eye is above my throat. The god is awakened. He is awake. I am pierced by a fiery eye, magical, arcane, out-and-out mysterious. My flesh is fluttering like leaves in a forest.

It's not that he cares about me . . . I don't think. The girls, Miss Wong, know only my name. But here I am.

What is this, the fifth week?

The throat doesn't let me get much sleep. Last night I took a couple of huge rose and gray capsules that were packed with painkiller, but they wore off in the middle of the night. I lay awake and tried not to swallow or cough. When I did, my throat felt as if it had been scrubbed with lye.

About daybreak I dozed and had one of those realistic dreams, too real a dream to tell myself I was dreaming. I was in the hospital, in the therapy room, alone as if entombed there, and I knew with absolute certainty that an error had been made. A fatal mistake. Something had gone wrong with their calculations and they had beamed me an overdose. I found myself thinking, If you lie here one more second, there will be no reversal, no recovery. Get up. Quick. Get out.

I woke, gazed across Janice's shoulder at the light on the hallway wall outside the bedroom and thought—it's true. Was that why there were so many attendants in the room with me? Was that why the faces of the technicians, so unfamiliar, kept changing? Did the treatment of whatever I had call for extreme precaution? Was this the bed I died in?

Later, in the therapy room and afterward with the doctor, I said nothing about the dream.

The hospital seemed to think I was coming along fine.

The bearded doctor had two observers with him, a young man and a young woman. They, too, wanted a look down my throat, but every time he got his mirror beyond my tongue, I gagged. My throat didn't want to open. So he gave my throat a deep and thorough spraying and then we waited for the freeze to take.

He picked up the magazine I'd left on the washstand. It was the latest issue of *Time*.

"This must be yours."

I shook my head.

He looked at the other two. "This week's issue of *Time*? Incredible."

He scowled at my neck. "Are you still washing with soap and water?"

I nodded.

"Don't. And shave only with an electric razor. Have you got one?"

I nodded.

"And you're not wearing those turtlenecks any more?"

I shook my head.

Afterward, he felt for lumps in my throat. Then he patted me and said something about only five more treatments. "This is as bad," he said, "as your throat should get."

The two observers smiled.

I said I hoped so.

I went home and went to bed and, inoperative, doped up, exhausted, slept all day.

That night I took a Seconal and chewed a couple of pieces of aspergum. I held the gum between my teeth all night. Occasionally, I'd awake enough to feel the gum dissolving and flaking, but none of it was going down my windpipe.

Another day, another turn of the screw.

I was chewing so much aspergum now, so steadily, the sides of my tongue and the sides of my cheeks around my teeth were numb.

Classes have started.

A young male technician joined our group in the therapy room. He wore a long white smock that almost scraped the floor. His pockets were so low he had to bend to get his hands into them. A pudgy fellow, not much more than a kid; he had a double chin. He didn't smile. Nobody ever smiled in that room.

When I got off the table, he asked, "How is your throat feeling?"

I made a face to approximate what it felt like and he said, "You're peaking."

What's that? Like Macy's at Christmas?

"Wear a silk scarf around your throat."

At last—a letter from Gail. I sat at my desk at school to read
it, my collar open, a silk scarf under it.

*Clinton Darling . . . Things are still hectic, as you might
imagine, what with finding somewhere to live, rehearsals starting the day after I got here, parties practically every other
night, and the strangest people wandering in and out of my
bedroom at all hours.*

*Would you send my music case? Send it along with my mail.
I have a place with a piano in an old adobe house with fire-
places. There's even a fireplace in my bedroom. I have it burning every night—piñon wood, wonderfully fragrant. The house
is small and utterly, absolutely, beautifully white—with gray
branches between the beams, or vigas, laid in patterns all over
the ceilings.*

*The town itself is more foreign-looking and feeling than any-
place I've run into in the United States—a regular hodgepodge
of cultures, Spanish, Indian, American, post-hippie, gay, retired
couples, Mexican wetbacks, writers, painters, poets, remittance
men and gals—and a lot of non-local characters like myself
passing through. All in thin-bright-mountain air, 7,000 feet.
Imagine. I won't go into it all now, just enough to let you
know I'm spellbound. You were right—it may even be my salvation.*

*I have written Al to tell him where I am so if he does dis-
cover, as I feared, who is handling my mail, you need not be so
secretive. Let him follow me here, but let him do it of his own
accord.*

Clinton? Who was Clinton Darling?

Who was Al?

I folded the letter and shoved it into my pocket.

There was more: about the theater activity in town and a job
she had in a coffeehouse. I read the rest of it walking home.

The theater group she'd joined wasn't even paying her anything. Who the hell was Al?

When I got home, I used my voice, weak as it was. I called the airline and got a schedule of flights to Albuquerque, the nearest airport. The hell with saving my voice. But what would I do when I got there? Pencil in one hand, scratch pad in the other? I got her letter out again.

The place sounded like Samarkand, milling with Huns and Persians and Chinamen and Greeks and Turks and Romans and Manicheans and Nestorians.

I decided to wait. I had to think this out. Was the letter a deliberate cross-up? They usually are.

I itched all the time. My nose, my forehead, my chin, my chest, under my arms. There were little hairs all over me. A reaction to the aspergum? I couldn't sleep. If I managed to sleep, the drugs wore off and the soreness of my throat woke me, a dry soreness, all mucus gone.

Fingers shaking.

Cold sweats.

I made class the next night in my open shirt with a silk scarf. All night I held aspergum between my teeth.

The doctor read my note. He was a new doctor, a slim dark-haired man. He had a slight accent I couldn't identify.

"What drug," he said, "does you the most good?"

"Aspergum."

He nodded.

"The Xylocaine hydrochloride?"

I shook my head.

He seemed surprised. He would give me, he said, some codeine pills. And then he peered into my throat and informed me that things down there looked raw and beefy.

I went home. I chewed aspergum two at a time. I lay in bed. I couldn't sleep. Just lay there. Tried to read. Couldn't. The radio babbled.

For lunch I had some ice cream and after lunch decided to lay off the aspergum.

I'd bitten my tongue so much I couldn't find any comfortable place in my mouth to rest it. I lay in bed trying not to swallow, holding the sides of my painful tongue away from my teeth. I dozed, woke up, dozed. The cat came in, prowled around over the bed and left.

At four o'clock, while Janice was somewhere shopping, I got up and dressed and went out. I chewed a couple of aspergum as I walked over to Riverside Drive.

Starting up on aspergum again was a painful process. The sugar coating broke and melted and slid down the raw lining of my throat and everything in its way glowed a little redder, like charcoal in a breeze.

I sat down on a bench on Riverside and stared at Gail's apartment house. Just stared. I found her balcony and her windows—as far away and tiny as dust motes. A couple of joggers ran by. In about twenty minutes the aspergum had the throat nicely localized. Aspergum is great. Not even the canker sores on my tongue hurt any more.

The next day was another groggy day, but I met my class and got my throat off my mind for a while. That night was a groggy night. Three more treatments to go. I decided my dream was accurate: they'd gone too far.

The worst part of Wednesday was the long hours in the bathroom, sick enough to my stomach to vomit, my bowels clogged tight. I pulled the hamper over in front of the toilet, spread open a book to read. Full of cement and rock, I felt as if a mountain were in me. I thought of praying and using the hamper as an altar. I was ready to fall down on my knees. Light a candle. When I checked my weight on the scales, I was gaining. I couldn't get the shit out.

Janice came home in the afternoon and gave me a classic enema. It did no good. I thought she looked like an angel of mercy, Janice, standing there with that red rubber bag in one hand gazing down at my sweating head with such compassion. I forgave her everything. She thought I might have to be hospitalized. She seemed scared.

I can't eat.

The shit's backed up for miles and miles, for days and days, hard as the rubble of a bombed fort. All the milk of magnesia and prune juice have done for me is give me a gutache.

But I made class and after I got home, the mountain moved. I was feeling better by midnight.

At least I had an address for Gail. The next morning I dressed to go to the hospital and then to school, where I could write her. But when I looked for her letter, it was gone. I'd put it under some papers on my desk in the study. Janice never looked through my papers. It was gone. I tried to believe I'd put it someplace else, but I couldn't believe it. Janice had it.

Still, I looked everywhere. I even looked through Janice's bureau drawers and under the shelf paper in her closet. I looked everywhere. Then I had to rush out.

I was late that morning at the hospital, one of the few times I'd been late. I sat in a chair outside the therapy room. Somebody had gone ahead of me, a woman. Through the window above the control console, I could see her boots as she lay on the table under the Theratron.

The bearded doctor looked down my throat but he said nothing. He had nothing cheerful to say. The nurse beside him looked bored.

"Tomorrow," he said, "will be your last treatment."

I felt good about finishing the therapy. I walked back through the park. I walked down Amsterdam Avenue all the way home. The air, the temperature of it, was as refreshing as cool water.

When I got home, I looked around for Gail's letter. I went through all my pockets and papers.

I was manufacturing mucus by the gallon. I lay coiled all night, a paper napkin pressed against the lower corner of my lips, one knuckle of a finger clamping my mouth shut, thinking one great, all-consuming thought—Don't swallow.

I've bought some more note pads.

I'm all prepared for class.

Life is tolerable.

I saw Beirne the final morning but not to speak to. I saw him sitting at the console panel in front of the room with the betatron. He was busy, peering through his glasses at a batch of papers, working hard, as if he'd been up and alert for hours. I realized only then his eye was on me all the time. He hadn't needed to see me again.

I got up on the table for the last time. Only Miss Wong was in the room. I handed her a note. It said, *Thank you. You have all been great, absolutely great. If you now told me I had to have another thirty treatments, only the knowledge that you would be handling it could get me to rally.*

She gave me a small shy smile and said, "That's a very nice thing for you to say."

Trail of notes—

Good evening. I completed my last therapy treatment this morning. I'm liberated. However—I still have two weeks of silence ahead of me, which should be no problem for any of us. Apparently it's possible to teach without a voice, perhaps preferable. I got to liking the sound of my thoughts coming from the lips of someone else. Sometimes the voice was deep and then I sounded authoritative, or sometimes I sounded shy and decent—in other words, I found a way to pick up all kinds of character qualities I've always wanted, or thought I'd like to borrow like a jacket or tie. I'll miss that part.

Silence simply cannot be fought and I, the one she fought, was silent. I listened.

I just listened. And so all her words came back to her the way my words always came back to me in the classroom, surrounding me, sinking through me from every side . . . and after a while she slowed down, grew silent, met my silence with silence. And started up again. She thought at first she had me at her mercy, I suppose. She got everything out, and there I was, listening, never interrupting her. I had not listened to her without interruption in years.

And now she was waiting, waiting for me to scribble any kind of note. The pen and the pad were on the table. I did not get up to touch them.

I had never listened so closely before to what she said. When we argued, I listened in a different way. Now my listening possessed her, the way the listener possesses the one he listens to, the analyst the patient, the audience the lecturer, the congregation their minister.

What she had so desperately to say all got said, laid off. Is that why savages build wooden and stone idols? To lay their troubles off on? Why people have pets, and pray to crosses, worshiping in some degree anything they can lay the pain off on? And what they lay it off on possesses them.

If I just got up and walked to the table and wrote one short sentence, no matter what, I'd be an oracle. Never in our lives had I had her attention so completely. Then she started up again.

But it was all a part of running down, emptying out, her body getting rid of the poison.

I felt detached and frustrated.

How did I lay off what she'd laid on me? The analyst goes to his own analyst to lay it off. Me, I have this typewriter. In the end every author's reader possesses him.

Silence does too, his own silence, his own eternal, everlasting silence, out of which he came and into which he will return, the listening silence, the crackling silence. From whence comes the voice, the word.

"Just tell me one thing. Nod or shake your head. Do you love me?"

I knew at once the comfort of parables. No simple answer seemed complete or true, not even one nod. I wanted to write, *Do muskrats ramble?* Instead, I lost my detachment, and I found myself answering with tears.

They, too, could have been open to many interpretations, but she came over, knelt and put her arms around me. I put my arms around her, my head against her head. Words are not the language of love. It's all gesture. Inarticulate.

Yet what I felt was not love. It was grief.

Things of dismay: a pan of hot soup spilled on the kitchen floor; clenching your teeth until they crack; old suitcases in trash cans; dead light bulbs; the overdrawn bank balance; a closetful of worn-out shoes.

I've let my hair grow long. It touches my collar and curls down over part of my ears. Let the gray show.

I hate getting old, hate it.

Life is like standing in front of a pier glass making judo chops in the air while looking fiercely at your own reflection.

February 2nd—

The grip on my throat seems to be loosening. When I woke up this morning, my throat—in that area around what must be the opening of my windpipe—was raw, but not with that dry tightness that spasms. In other words, it's back to the place where the throat doesn't bother me so long as I don't swallow.

March 7th—

Today is the first day in a long time I haven't had to chew aspergum. My jaw feels rested.

Addendum

Because I hate the end of anything, this is essentially the conclusion of these aides-mémoire. My voice gradually returned and it came back deeper and more resonant than it had been before I began to lose it. I'd been warned it would be weaker, but it wasn't. Its range on the chromatic scale was almost as wide as ever, as wide as I'd ever need. It was as if the X-rays had melted off all the old scar tissue; and my vocal cords, to any inspection, were perfectly normal. No doctor on earth would have suspected I'd had radiotherapy. Baker's own reaction was: it proves radiotherapy is as good as the radiotherapist. I thought of calling Newman after my voice was back and telling him Christian Science had done it, but I couldn't.

Late that spring I left for Samarkand.

The following entries in the journal are appended because they have a bearing on that departure. It was not an easy one to make.

Early April—

I went up to school to check my mail and there was a dittoed memorandum in my box asking me to check over the galleys for the bulletin. All corrections were due by Friday. What was this? How come such incredibly short notice?

I went down the long hall to Fred's office and found the galleys on his desk, a lined yellow pad beside them. A poet with a famous name, I noted, was being hired to take over Kate's class. Our writing classes were some of the few courses around making the college any money. The department was getting interested again in our potential.

It made me sad to think Kate would be gone in the fall, though I didn't know her as well as I'd have liked. I admired her poetry, the few poems I'd seen in small press magazines, and I liked her general style. Although she had a Ph.D., she treated the academics around her in a casual good-natured manner, never more than that. I liked the way she wore sneakers, blue jeans and a suede jacket with fringe. The students in her poetry writing class brought wine every week and sat around and drank it and read each other's work. Sometimes she held classes in her apartment, though not as often any more. Once she explained, "Everybody gets to screwing." I never knew how serious she was. Another time she said, "I'm nailing my poems on trees in Central Park now. I need an audience." She was popular with her students. The department might not miss her, but I would, and her students would.

While standing at Fred's desk looking over the rest of our scheduling, in came Cutter L. Bryant. He would not be sorry to see Kate gone.

Bryant was startled to see me and, about to turn and plunge away, he paused at the edge of the great chasm that forever separated us and actually smiled across. It was more than a polite or sly smile. He had come, he explained, to meet Fred for lunch. Then he said, "You're looking well, Jack. Is the worst over?"

I let him hear my tone and timbre. "I have my voice back."

"Oh, should you be using your voice?"

"Not much in class yet, but it's back."

"That's very good news. And how are your classes?"

"I've managed pretty well."

"Indeed you have. You have indeed. I've heard a good report about you. Overheard, actually. I was in the elevator and a couple of students were talking about how you ran your class with notes, without saying a word. What they had to say was quite complimentary."

It was the first time in recent memory anyone in the department had implied or said I ran a class well.

"Thanks."

He was still smiling.

"Maybe," I said, "I've stumbled across a new way of teaching. Maybe teachers talk too much."

"It's all too easy to do the work for your students."

I was so surprised to have this alien, hostile figure listening to me that I pushed on. "It's the Socratic method, nothing more. It works beautifully with notes. I was amazed when my students started to talk—how interesting, even brilliant they were. All I have to do is be their control."

"I want to hear more," he said, touching my elbow with one

fingertip, "but don't strain your voice. You should do a paper about this. Do a paper."

He wrote a message on the pad on Fred's desk and off he went. I waited another ten minutes before a young man came in to tell me Fred was at a meeting and wouldn't get out until one o'clock. The young man was in charge of our freshman English classes, but I hadn't met him yet. We introduced ourselves. He'd heard about my classes too.

"Your students are very enthusiastic," he said, and shook my hand again. Two compliments from the department in one day. A memorable day.

I went back down the hall to my end of the building. Kate was in, leaning at the edge of her cluttered desk. When she saw me walk by, she followed me into my office. "You're looking so goddamn well," she said, "we've decided not to waste any more time worrying about you." She pretended, I suspected, to be a lot tougher than she was.

I took off my glasses, wiped them and put them on again. Tattooed or inked across her knuckles in colorful, elaborate lettering were (right hand) FUCK (left hand) YOU!

"Impressive," I said. "Tattoo artistry?"

"In time. I'm picking my script. *Littera antiqua*, fifteenth century."

"It's going to get you in a lot of fights at checkout counters." She flexed her fingers. "People are reading me these days."

"Good response?"

"Oh, yeah. Hey, your voice sounds great."

I was still staring at her knuckles. "I wish I were a poet."

"They've turned you into a butterfly," she said cheerfully, "with their X-rays. I was afraid you might come back a moth. I just wanted to tell you I got a fellowship for next year. I'm going to Iran."

"Iran?"

"You won't believe it, nobody does. But I'm going to the University of Isfahan to study Persian. I get ten thousand rials a month and room and board and my travel expenses. Iran foots the bill."

"How much is ten thousand rials?"

"It figures to around $170 a month. Why did you have to ask? Everybody has to ask."

"What's Isfahan like?" I started to get excited. But it was no use. I had no Ph.D.

"A very ancient town. That's really what I'm going for. Isfahan. Beautiful old place."

After Kate went back to her desk, I straightened mine, read my mail, filled my wastebasket with it. At one o'clock, when I went to look for Fred, he and Cutter were getting into the elevator; they had their jackets on. I rode down with them and then walked over to Thorpe's office. He was in but he was heading out for lunch too, so I stayed only a minute, about long enough for him to show me the cover for his latest book.

He put on his coat and we walked out.

"How's old Dot?" I asked.

"Just fine. She and Fred are now quite friendly, you know."

"No. I didn't."

"Yes. Yes. When you couldn't use your voice any more, Fred had to go see her himself about the scholarship matter. I'd say they're quite friendly now." He added almost grimly, "Fred, you know, can be quite the charmer when he wants to." He glanced at me, as if he might have said too much.

"Say no more," I said.

He said good-by hastily and we parted.

Late April—

I was beginning to feel reborn.

In our parking place as I closed the trunk of the car, I saw the little guy who lives at the end of our hall stepping off the curb and coming toward me with his right hand outstretched.

I almost recoiled. I couldn't believe my eyes.

He's under five feet, portly, double-chinned; he wears hats with narrow brims that would give him a comic cast if he hadn't such a fierce nose and eyes. He is a Jewish leprechaun, a Talmudic scholar, a young patriarch of a small family tribe.

"I'm going to Israel for a year," he said. "We are just now leaving."

I took his hand, still incredulous. "I hope you have a good trip."

These were the first words we had exchanged in the ten years we had lived on the same floor. For the first nine, we hadn't even nodded to one another when we passed. I had started out with a neighborly nod, but, getting no response, gave it up. We would pass one another wordlessly, without a glance, or he would look me over with his small fierce eyes as if he were taking a readout and puzzling why I could wander around at large.

Sometimes I would wonder: What does he know about me? What has he heard? Sometimes I was sure he had infallible intuition. He saw me for what I was—self-centered, erotic, blocked writer, henpecked husband, rejected father, incorrigible cheat, pennypincher, dreamer, loser, girlwatcher, moviedrugged nosepicker, and what else? There was more, much more to the depthless, endless chamber of horrors I carried around, and he saw it all, saw I was a menace, someone to keep an eye on, to avoid, a contaminated goy. He could see it. We passed and passed and never spoke and rarely nodded.

If we met in the hall by the elevator, which we did occasionally, we'd stand silently side by side staring intently at the numerals rolling on the elevator's tiny twin windows that told us where the elevator was, whether rising or descending and how rapidly. We'd watch those tiny windows, he with his fierce eyes, me with my myopic ones, without a word to one another, hands clasped behind our backs; and when the elevator door sprang open, we'd enter and stand side by side staring up at the lights that ran the numerical field above the elevator's doors. We'd land and exit side by side toward the glass expanse at the edge of the plaza, and out the door we'd go between the borders of plants and shrubs, or maybe we'd take only a step toward the door before he'd peel away and dart for our multilateral-horizontal mailboxes so that we wouldn't have to reach the door at the same time. This was not my imagination. Once I saw him hide in the corridor by the lobby elevators when he saw me coming. I had almost decided to look around the corridor corner and say "Hi" to him just as I got on the elevator, but thought better of it. Maybe he was a shy man.

I could never satisfactorily explain our curious relationship. In the last year a kind of grudging trust had built up between us. We now nodded as we passed. I'd even smile, but he never did.

And so when he came toward me hand outthrust, I nearly did recoil, but there was no weapon in his hand, his palm was open and clean, his stride sure, and on his heavy lips, inexplicably, a smile.

In the next moment I wanted to throw my arms around him,

clasp him in an embrace of brotherhood as if what I had always conjectured is true, that we are all one after all. Cutter L. Bryant, too. And Fred and Thorpe and my card-shuffling ex-psychiatrist. But I sensibly checked myself. We spoke a little more and made our exchange into the occasion it was.

I told him I hoped there'd be no more trouble in Israel, and as he turned he shook his head, his jowls shaking off the dingy prospect of that possibility forever. I had time to add, "If there's anything I can do for you while you're gone, just write, just let us know." His smile broadened. We nodded, waved.

He walked on down to the tan station wagon by the curb. His wife was getting in. I'd have waved to her, too, but she was preoccupied with the kids. So I locked the car trunk and went upstairs, feeling a generous regard for the world and for myself.

Everyone was setting out on a fabulous journey. What was I doing hanging around? I had a journey of my own to make, more fabulous than any.

If I ever got to Samarkand, I wouldn't, I decided, turn around and come back. I'd push on around the world. I wanted to follow the old Silk Road out of Samarkand all the way to its end. To the east of Samarkand stood mountain passes 18,000 feet high, mountains that reared up from something just above sea level to peaks so high it took caravans three days to reach and squeeze between them, the air so rarefied, knees trembled, and stars in the black sky loomed as large as glass doorknobs. Beyond those mountains: treeless land, the Great Gobi, and many strange things. There were rivers that changed course without warning, rivers that disappeared, and places haunted by invisible, evil presences. There was a beautiful blue lake surrounded by reeds where tigers live. No one drinks the waters. Forty rivers flow into it and none flows out, yet its level neither rises nor falls. Under its waters lie the ruins of a city and a palace. Lake Issyk-Kul.

Cities with intriguing names: Ferghana, Kashgar, Yarkand . . . all of them along the old Silk Road . . . Guma, Khotan, Cherchen . . . and far off at the end, Peking.

The next morning Janice was out on the balcony painting the redwood tables and benches. She'd bought them so we'd have something for Perse and her family to eat on when they came to see us, which might be never. I figured Perse was fed up with the two of us, but Janice knew better.

I said, "Is that anti-stain finish like the one we used on the cocktail table?"

She shook her head, but she wasn't sure what I was talking about and began to frown.

"Well, I saw that pan you had on the stove. We heated something in a pan when we refinished the cocktail table, didn't we? Is it the same stuff?"

"No, it's a paint I bought," she said defensively. "It's for redwood. It's a paint and sealer both and is supposed to protect against stains."

Our balcony is only usable for a few months of the year. Perhaps in the fall we could put a plastic covering over the table and benches to keep off the soot and snow. Even now a few flakes of burned trash were descending on the balcony. Soot descended constantly on our parked car in the lot below. The city housing projects burned their trash at night. We didn't see the smoke from their incinerators burning much by day any more. When did the incinerators in our own building burn, and in our brother and sister buildings? By night too?

Some rain started to fall from our generally overcast sky. We sat looking at it.

"If redwood isn't painted," Janice said, "weathering will turn it gray."

"The dirt won't be able to work its way into the wood either," I said.

"No."

Spatters of redwood paint lay on the cement flooring of the balcony, as if someone had bled there.

"It's a water-base paint," Janice said. "What does that mean?"

"You can thin it with water."

"The can," she said, "said you can paint over wet wood, it doesn't make any difference."

We sat looking out at the mild rain.

After Janice left for work, I called Santa Fe information; this time they had a number.

Her phone rang awhile and then a man answered. He had a deep, relaxed voice. It was the voice of a man completely sure of himself and at ease with the world. I fought back the impulse to hang up and save myself some embarrassment. I said, "Is Gail in?"

"No, she's not," he said.

"Do you know when she'll be back?"

"She should be back around two o'clock. Do you want to leave a message?"

"Yes. Tell her a friend of hers called to say he's leaving for Samarkand." I didn't know until that instant that I was.

A little after four o'clock, the phone rang. It was Gail.

"When?" she said. Her voice was remote, matter-of-fact.

"As soon as I finish my last class."

"Your voice is beautiful. Are you really going?"

"Yep."

"You and your wife?"

"Alone."

"I just called to say good for you, and good luck."

"Was that Al who answered your phone?"

"No. My father. He's here for a few days. I'm sorry about that mix-up in letters."

I took a deep breath to keep my voice from cracking. It was still a little weak. "Want to come along?"

There was a long pause. "I think not. But send me the address of a couple of your stops. I might send you a Care package."

When I hung up, I was trembling with rejection and regret. But I knew I was going. I'd heard myself say so.

May Day—

I think I put off calling the Russian Consulate for a long
time because I wasn't sure how I'd deal with a suspicious Russian voice. What would they think of someone who wanted to
follow the old Silk Road into and out of Samarkand? As far as
the Chinese Consulate went, my call to them was even more
difficult to imagine—hence make.

Then the day came: I sat staring at the open pages of the telephone book, quite amazed that I could find no Russian Consulate to call. I called the Russian Travel Bureau.

A male, American voice answered. "I'm planning a trip," I
said, "to Samarkand and I'd like to know what I have to do to
get a visa or permit to travel along what's left of the old Silk
Road." I told him about wanting to take a boat across the
Black Sea and then the Caspian, and then follow a road I'd
found on my map that ran from the port of Krasnovodsk
through Ashkhabad to Samarkand. This could be arranged, he
told me, but I'd have to map my route with great precision and
stick with it all the way and have prearranged exit and entrance
points. Just fine; and then I said did he know if I could get a
visa to go into China and continue along that old Silk Road as
far as Peking? No, he didn't; and he said he'd better put someone else on the phone who knew more about the kind of trip I
had in mind. This new voice was a lady, her voice as friendly
and American as the man's. "Oh," she said at once, "you

wouldn't be able to cross open sea inside Russian territory, let alone be able to land at a Russian seaport." It was out of the question. Then how could I follow a land route to Samarkand? Was there another border I could cross? No. What about by way of northern Afghanistan? No. No border crossings except by air. I'd have to fly from Baku across the Caspian Sea to Samarkand and the trip would have to be arranged through Intourist. Such arrangements must be made in the United States before I left and it would take me thirty days to get permission.

At which point she said, "Listen, I have a call on another line, a long-distance call. Would you give me your name and telephone number? I'll call you back."

I hung up and waited, wondering—will my name go into some file? Are they checking me out on a computer?

She called back in about five minutes and we picked up where we left off. But, in sum, there was no overland way for me to reach Samarkand—unless I wanted to go there from Moscow on a branch of the trans-Siberian railroad. As far as crossing China went, using any route at all, that was probably impossible. The only way it could be done, she thought, was by special invitation. Because that was the only way I was going to travel anywhere inside Russia, along any road of my own choice —by government invitation. I gathered I could forget about Brezhnev's giving me one.

I hung up. I thought: things are really serious around this world. The triggers of big guns stand cocked. Half the world sits in secret.

I called Sam to see how he was. I hadn't heard from him since our surprise visit, and he knew nothing about my therapy treatments. For the last month, from day to day, I'd been afraid to call—but I knew he couldn't be dead or they'd have told me. Wouldn't they?

I dialed. Martha answered, seemed pleased to hear my improved voice, but she asked no questions and put Sam on at once.

"Just called," I said, "to check if you were smoking."

"Sure am," he said happily. "I got a cigarette going in my hand right now. Say, you sound like a half-assed nephew of mine used to sound."

"I'm better," I said, laughing. "How are you?"

His story was high-speed and hard to follow, starting with a reference to a fall he'd taken out in his garage, and rambling on about how he'd got a big bump on his head and how Martha had driven him to a hospital, and how from that hospital he'd been admitted to another one, where, said Sam (merrily, merrily), he'd threatened or was said to have threatened to clobber a doctor with the handle of a mop. "Right away," he said, "they had me in one of them long-sleeved jackets that lace up in the back and goddamn I went out the goddamn window and took off across this big lawn, ass to the winter wind. The whole pack of them after me. Ran around to the front entrance and up the steps and inside to the receptionist. I told her, call the cops. I'm being robbed. The cops came. They let me on the phone to call Martha and when Martha got on the phone, I told her to bring me some Kleenex . . ."

"You sound in good shape now." He sounded too good.

"I have my ups and downs. I'm on medication."

"What medication?"

"To keep me from going too high and too low. I have a system with some kind of chemical imbalance, and that's what's been giving me trouble for years. Only they haven't got the balance right yet and sometimes I sit around here shivering from the stuff they give me."

"And smoking?"

"And playing tennis. I hang back and play for the corners of my opponent's court, don't have my old wind. I can still take you out on the court and give you a lesson."

He was surviving. We all survive. No matter what, we survive—in this life, maybe through all time.

He said, "What the hell have you been up to, or should I say into?"

"Why?"

"I finally found out why you two dropped in on us last Christmas. That wife of yours called Martha to get her to cook up a way to get you out of town over the weekend. She told Martha that just between the two of them, don't ask why and not to tell me, it was for your own good."

"I sort of had that figured out," I said. "And it did me loads of good."

"Are you behaving yourself?"

"On certain designated days."

He laughed. I laughed too. But why were we laughing?

Mid-May—

My last class was on a Thursday evening. On Friday morning
I walked up to school, turned in my grades and cleaned out my
desk. I hadn't said so to Fred or anyone else, but I did not expect to return.

Monday afternoon after Janice left for work, I packed two
suitcases and took a taxi to Kennedy. At Kennedy I wrote her a
postcard.

The plane landed in London about ten-thirty in the morning. Shaky from a night half slept, I gathered my luggage and
got myself through customs and on a bus that took me to Vic-
toria Station. There I got a cab and rode in style, for me, to my
hotel. In the room I'd been thoughtful enough to reserve in
New York the day I'd decided I was going, I unpacked. Then I
went downstairs, ordered my first glass of London beer, and let
myself think of what I'd done.

I had the rest of the day, all of the next and part of a third
in London before I made my way to Tilbury and boarded a
boat. Mayfair lay like a seacalm at my elbow. Shillings and six-
pence, florins and half crowns weighed my pockets. I composed
my fatigue and moved eventually out onto the street.

When I returned late in the afternoon to change for dinner,
I had a visitor: I opened the door to my room and she was sitting in a slip on one of the twin beds, her toenails painted
pearly pink. She was combing her hair. The radio was playing

"Britannia" or something martial. She had guidebooks in her lap and spread all around her.

"I'm here," she said, "to collect three days you owe me."

I was drunk anyway. I thought about crying, but I went outside in the corridor and stood with my back to the wall; and when I went in again, she was still there, preening.

We stayed one night in Rothenburg, an ancient walled fortress of a town with crooked, narrow streets. She'd found us a room in a small inn, not a place a travel agent would recommend, I suppose, no lobby, no desk. A woman came out of the kitchen into the restaurant where we stood to show us up the stairs, heavy legs and solid arms on her. Spoke only German. The upper hall sagged with age. But the room she took us to was large and attractive, unexpectedly cheerful—an immaculate room, feather comforters on the bed, a stove in one corner for its winter guests. There was a view from its windows of red tile roofs across the way, and below, cobblestones and a stone watering trough filled with water.

Later we walked the top of the fortress walls of Rothenburg, walked almost all the way around town, rain falling, not a heavy rain but the same light off-and-on-again rain we'd had all day. I kept the fingers of one hand on her like a blind man.

It was a fairy tale town we looked down at from the wall, a look at a Europe I thought no longer existed, medieval houses and buildings below us, a castle town certainly, gardens in backyards. She had led us upon a Germany out of the Grimms' fairy tales I'd read as a child, and the houses looked like the homes and apartments in those books of fantasy. It gave me hope for Samarkand.

We turned in early. I fell asleep while she was still moving around the room. She'd brought almost no baggage, just one small suitcase with a nightgown, a sweater and a change of clothes. I woke up around midnight. The town was quiet. She was in bed beside me, asleep, one hand curled on the pillow beside her mouth, almost touching her lips.

I felt a curious joy, as if her foldout bed had been whisked a vast distance to a new square, time, world. Across the street behind the cracks of a drawn curtain in an upstairs window a lamp was burning. I sat up. I tried to picture the sun: where was it? Out over the Atlantic? Back somewhere over Asia?

I sat experiencing the night.

Behind the curtains across the way: someone's love, hearth, comfort, German cookies, tankards of beer, family photographs, all the things I'd left behind.

And I'd left all that behind me now.

I had. Hadn't I?

80-789

DATE		
JUL 2 2 1980		
JUL 3 '80		

80-789

PJC LEARNING RESOURCES CENTER

© THE BAKER & TAYLOR CO.